A Secret Vengeance

Janey Clarke

First published in 2025 by Blossom Spring Publishing
A Secret Revenge (Devil's Mountain Series) Copyright © 2025 Janey Clarke
ISBN 978-1-917938-06-8
E: admin@blossomspringpublishing.com
W: www.blossomspringpublishing.com

CHAPTER ONE

"Help! Help me, please!"

A small boy stumbled through the doorway of the general store, his legs buckling beneath him as he collapsed onto the wooden floorboards. Blood had dried in streaks over his face and matted his hair into stiff clumps. His blue cotton shirt bore deep crimson stains across the chest, and his hands were caked with dirt and dried blood, creating a ghastly mess.

Eliza was the first to reach him. The small Mexican woman ran across the floor and knelt down beside him, her voice thick with concern. "Here, let me help you," she murmured, placing an arm around the boy's trembling shoulders. With gentle but firm determination, she half-lifted and half-dragged him towards a nearby chair.

Amy, the young girl who helped in the store, rushed forward, pulling the chair closer to make it easier for them. Together, they eased the boy into the seat, his body still quivering with exhaustion and fear.

"My brother," the boy choked out between gasping sobs. "He took my brother." He knuckled his eyes furiously, as though trying to wipe away not only the tears but also the terror still clinging to him.

The midday sun hung high over the main street of Nowhere, casting long shadows that stretched between the wooden buildings. Inside, the general store had been bustling just moments before, filled with locals coming for food and hardware, while a few dusty prospectors had stopped in for mining supplies.

But now, all conversation had ceased. Every eye had turned towards the boy who had burst into their midst, battered and bloodied. He looked no older than twelve, his clothes worn and patched beneath the bloodstains.

Now seated, the boy clutched the edge of the chair. Finally, his gaze locked onto Eliza. He recognised her. She and her husband, Manuel, had served him, his brother, and his father only the day before.

His eyes were still wide with terror, and he glanced round from one face to the other, before he finally looked at Eliza again. "My brother ... The bad man took my brother."

Eliza, the storekeeper's wife, left him with Amy, then returned from the kitchen carrying a glass and a bowl of water. Kneeling before him, she offered the glass. The boy grabbed the glass and drank greedily, gulping down the cool liquid. When he finished, he handed it back with a quiet, barely audible, "Thank you."

"Here, let me wash your face and hands. That'll make you feel better." Eliza took one of his hands and held it, ready to wipe it with the damp cloth she had also brought from the kitchen. Her eyes widened as she stared down at the small hand in hers. She had been expecting dirt, perhaps grit, maybe grass stains. But Eliza had not been expecting the amount of dried blood covering the palms and fingers of the boy's hands.

"Two men came." The boy gave a huge gulp, swallowed hard and, despite trembling, began speaking again. "Before we knew, they were there. *Big* they were, and they grabbed us. My brother, Micky, fought them, kicking out, even biting the man. But the big man ... " The boy gave a sniff and wiped his nose with the back of his hand. "That big man hit him so hard, Micky fell down. Then he threw Micky on top of his horse." The tears came again, and he sniffed.

Eliza's voice was gentle but steady. "How did you get away?" It was the question in everyone's mind. Those present had drawn closer to see the boy and hear what he had to say.

The boy took a shuddering breath. "I had Pa's knife, I was cutting ..." his voice dropped to a whisper. "When he came close enough to grab me, the knife went in him." His face crumpled, and his next words came out in a wail. "It just slid into him, and he fell down." The boy was struggling for breath between sobs. "The other man ... he didn't stop. He just rode off with Micky. Toward our cabin. So, I ran. I ran the other way. I ran to Nowhere."

A heavy silence filled the room. The gathered townsfolk exchanged glances, each face reflecting the same grim realisation.

Eliza was the first to find her voice. "Do you think you killed him?" she asked.

The boy took a deep breath, wiping his nose with the back of his hand before spreading his palms outward, displaying the blood that stained them. "There was so much blood," he whispered. "Look! Look how much blood."

Near the door, Manuel, the store's owner, met the gaze of Josh, who helped out in the store, and gave a small nod. Without a word, Josh slipped outside, careful not to let the door creak or the bell above it jingle. He didn't want to startle the boy. Josh knew what that nod from Manuel meant, and he set off for the sheriff.

Eliza set to work washing the boy's hands, the clear water turning a cloudy red. "You're new here, aren't you?" Eliza asked as she handed the boy a towel to dry his hands. "Didn't your family get land from Charles Roberts?"

3

The boy nodded, gripping the towel tightly. "Yes, ma'am. We got here four weeks ago. Pa said it'd be a grand new life for us out here. That man, Roberts, told Pa there'd be fine land for grazing and crops. But when we got there, it was nothing but rocks and dust. No water, just a poor excuse for a well." His voice carried the echoes of his father's anger and frustration.

Eliza muttered under her breath, "That man Charles Roberts again. He's not a good man."

Manuel was standing behind her. He folded his arms and asked the boy, "How many of you came out here?"

"Just me, Micky, and Pa," the boy answered. "Ma died last year. So did the baby. Pa said we'd start fresh out West." He paused, looking up at the gathered faces, his own face twisted with anguish. "Will they kill my brother?" His voice broke, barely above a whisper. "What will the bad man do to him?"

No one had an answer. And in the suffocating silence, the horror of the boy's fear settled over them all.

CHAPTER TWO

No one answered the boy. What could they say? They didn't know what was happening to the young men and boys that were being kidnapped. Everyone realised they were being taken away for some purpose. Otherwise, they would have been killed on the spot. The silence drew out, and it was with some relief that they all turned at the sound of the bell chime as the door was pushed open.

"What have we here?" The tall, dark figure of Sheriff Lance Grey entered the general store. There was a gasp from the boy as he gazed up at the figure looming over him. Tall and thin, but with a quick, controlled strength in his muscular figure, the sheriff—clad as usual in his black shirt, trousers, and coat—made an imposing figure.

"Why didn't you go straight home to your father?" the sheriff asked him.

"The man rode that way. I came *here*, away from the man. What are they going to do with my brother?" Again, the boy cried out, the frightened despair in his voice.

"The blood on your hands and clothes, boy. What happened?" asked the sheriff. Manuel seemed about to speak. He had told the sheriff on the way down to the store that the boy thought he'd killed a man. The sheriff gave Manuel an imperceptible shake of his head. He wanted the full story from the boy himself.

"I had my knife out. I was cutting and ... they appeared behind us. The man grabbed my brother first. Micky didn't stand a chance. The man ran up behind him. When I turned round, there was another man coming for me." There was a look of horrified remembrance on the boy's face, and he shuddered.

Eliza, Manuel's wife, put an arm round the boy's

shoulders and glared at Lance. Everyone standing around realised that she disapproved of this questioning from the sheriff.

The sheriff ignored her. "There was another man coming for you," he prompted the boy.

"Yes, he hit me." The boy pointed to his face. The bruise was already coming underneath the red mark of a heavy blow on his cheek. "Then he grabbed my shoulder. I had my knife in my hand and he just ran into it. I didn't even … He grabbed me and pulled me toward him, and the knife … it just slid into him. He fell down. The other man already had Micky on his horse and was galloping away. So, I turned and ran." The sobbing began again, and this time the sheriff nodded to Eliza when she ushered the boy away into the back room of the general store.

"I should get a posse together, but it's rained since the boy set off for Nowhere after being attacked. Doubtful that we'll pick up any tracks now. Not by the time I get a group of men together." The sheriff began pacing up and down the store.

Suddenly, he turned and thumped his fist on the counter. "Dammit, this has to stop!" He glared angrily at those standing around the store. "Where are these boys being taken to? Why are they being kidnapped? I need to get myself a tracker. Anyone know of a good tracker? Someone who can follow a trail? And I will need to have a few men ready to join me at a moment's notice. What do you think, Manuel? Will that work? Could you spread the word around for me?" He turned and looked at the storekeeper, who was standing solemn-faced, watching the sheriff pace around the store and work out his deliberations.

It was Josh who answered him, before Manuel could think of a sensible reply. "Ezra! You want Ezra. He's the best tracker around here at the moment. Sam, the Apache, would have been ideal, but he is still away. Put Ezra's and my name down on your list for a posse," said Josh.

"I'll come—and Zach would be an asset to any posse," Manuel said.

"Good, that's a few of you. No doubt Reuben would join in. Good." Sheriff Lance Grey rubbed his hands together, gave them all a nod, and turned towards the door. "That boy's father must be worried about his two lads. Best I get out there right away. Tell Eliza to have him ready for me. I've got to see what's happening at this boy's cabin and find this man he says he killed."

"Here, Sheriff—a cup of coffee to speed you on your way." Manuel had brewed fresh coffee, and the sheriff could not pass up any coffee, especially if it had been freshly brewed.

Eliza came out from the back of the store. "Clara is looking after Will—that's the boy's name—along with baby Isabel. He's having something to eat and has finally stopped crying. He is in such a state, so frightened and so anxious to get back to his father. I told him that you, Sheriff, would be going out right away to their cabin. It sounds as if they're living a very hard life out there, not at all what they expected. Will said Charles Roberts told them how wonderful it would all be, how easy it would be to plant and grow crops. But we all know that land is not only dry but mainly rock and stone. Getting anything to grow there would be tough enough if they had water. Without water, it's impossible."

The sheriff stood thinking for a moment and then began speaking: "I'll get a couple of men to go with me out to the cabin. Then I'll see what Will's father has to say about this business. I should imagine that he's in the dark about it. He won't know what's happened to his boys, so it's best I get out there before dark."

"Before you go, Sheriff, I have something to say to all of you." Dora walked forward into the centre of the general store, hands twisted one in the other, and she shuffled her feet. The black rustling fabric she always wore moved restlessly, betraying her agitation. "I hope you forgive me for concealing the truth from all of you. I'm so grateful to you, Manuel and Eliza, for giving me a home." Dora, a brisk no-nonsense woman, looked around at everyone, and they could see she had tears in her eyes.

The sheriff, Lance Grey, shuffled his feet awkwardly. This was getting emotional, and it made him very uncomfortable. He made to go towards the door.

Dora spoke again. "I have to confess to you a secret, which I have been hiding from you all for some time."

CHAPTER THREE

Dora waited for the sheriff to come back into the store properly and for everyone else to stop talking, and listen to her alone.

Amy watched the older woman and remembered what had happened when they had heard about the murder of George Binns, the hotel owner, by an unknown assailant. On hearing of the death of George Binns, Dora had become faint and fled from the front of the general store. Amy had rushed after her and found the woman sitting white-faced in the kitchen.

"Are you all right, Dora? What's wrong?" Amy stood beside the older woman, concern on her face. Reaching for the water jug, Amy poured Dora a glass.

Dora sat in the chair with the mug of water in her hand. She looked at it suspiciously. Amy tried not to smile, because she had never seen Dora drink water, ever.

"Can I get you a whiskey?" Amy suggested. At Dora's relieved nod, Amy carefully took the mug of water from her hand and went into the cupboard for the whiskey bottle. She poured the water away and replaced it with some liquor.

Now Dora showed no hesitation, almost grabbing the mug from Amy's hand. She downed it in one long swallow, wiped her mouth with her back of her hand, and gave a great sigh. "Thank you, Amy. I needed that."

Eliza had followed them into the back room. Amy lifted the whiskey bottle and mouthed the words, "Dora needed it."

"I'd like another, please," Dora said. "Do you mind, Eliza?"

Eliza gave a slight smile and nodded to Amy, who

poured Dora yet another whiskey.

This time, the whiskey was drunk in small sips. Amy could see the older woman visibly relax, and the pallor of her face was replaced by her usual sun-bronzed complexion.

"Thank you, Amy, for your kind help. Thank you, Eliza, for your whiskey." She smiled at both of them. But it wasn't the smile that Dora normally had. "I'll explain, but not now. Some other time."

Now Dora stood, determined to make herself heard. As Dora began to speak, Amy wondered if this was going to be the time that Dora would explain why she had almost fainted at the news of the murder of George Binns.

"No, Sheriff, I'd like you to stay for a moment whilst I explain ..." Dora's voice was flat, and her face set in unusually severe lines.

Into the silence, Dora began speaking. "My real name is Dora Binns. My husband was the hotel owner, George, who was murdered." She ignored their astonished cries at this unexpected news.

"We were married for some years and originally had a small guesthouse, which we built into a hotel back east. Then, George started gambling. It became a curse. He couldn't resist any bet or wager and couldn't keep away from the card tables. No matter what I said, he ignored me and just carried on losing money day after day." Dora swallowed hard, her eyes downcast, as if fearful of the expressions that would now be on the face of her friends. She had lied to them, and she had acted out the part of someone else, hiding her own identity.

"Then, he lost our house and hotel in one mad wager. The night before, he'd won in a poker game. Won this hotel in Nowhere. The following morning, he went to the lawyer and put the deeds in my name. I think he'd finally realised how bad his addiction to gambling had become. When he lost everything that night, he came and told me of his loss, and then gave me the deeds to the Nowhere property." Dora gave a deep sigh and looked up. "That's when I walked out on him, came to Nowhere, and pretended to be someone else."

Dora waited and watched for her friends' reactions to her startling revelations.

CHAPTER FOUR

The outpouring of exclamations and comments from each and every one of them was supportive. Both Amy and Eliza rushed up to Dora and put their arms around her.

"Why didn't you tell us before? We'd have understood and kept your secret identity," exclaimed Eliza.

Amy joined her, placing her arm around Dora and giving her a hug. "Of course we would. It must have been horrible for you, losing all your property and belongings like that. And then coming to Nowhere and finding that your hotel was only a wooden front and a tent building behind it. No wonder you didn't want to own it!"

"Well, Mrs Binns." The sheriff spoke loudly over all the comments and exclamations from the group. "Well, Mrs Binns—as we must now call you—if that's all you have to say, I must get on with finding a kidnapping gang." Again, he walked to the door and placed his hand in readiness to turn the doorknob.

"Sheriff, wait, please. I must also ask you a favour!" Dora called out to him.

The sheriff's eyebrows rose, a question in them. "Now you want a favour from me?"

"I have to go to Duloe town. There are papers waiting there that I must sign. I had a letter from a lawyer about the state of affairs my husband has left everything in. Whilst I'm away, I'd like you, Sheriff, to keep an eye on the hotel—especially after the murder of my husband."

The sheriff, holding his black hat in his hands, lifted it up and placed it on his head, settling it on its customary slant. "Of course I'll keep an eye on the hotel. That's no problem. And of course I'll keep an eye out for your husband's murderer. But Dora, may I ask if you are going to keep it? Will you sell it?"

His long face showed an interest, which puzzled Josh. Why was the sheriff so interested in who was going to run the hotel? Josh was surprised at this unusual questioning from the normally taciturn sheriff.

Dora took a deep breath. "Everyone has been so kind to me here, I plan on keeping it open. In fact, one of my objects in going to Duloe town is to buy a piano," Dora said, and looked around with delight at the exclamations of surprise from everyone.

"It's just that …" The sheriff's hand was on the doorknob, ready to leave, but still he loitered, staring at Dora under his dark brows. "Will you be encouraging the mining crowd and roughnecks that come into the town into your hotel? I hope not. Dora, I don't want this kind of hotel in our town," he said firmly, eager to avoid the fights and chaos the miners often brought.

Dora's head flew back as she emitted a cackling laugh. Josh hid a smile, and didn't dare look at Amy, because Amy had often commented on Dora's laugh, it being a loud cackle.

"Oh, no, Sheriff. I'm not encouraging miners into my hotel, far from it! My piano is so that I can have afternoon tea parties and evening music, whilst my guests dine in a proper dining room. I hope to encourage the ladies of Nowhere and the surrounding area to visit my establishment for afternoon tea."

Dora put her hands together and smiled round at the group. Amy was looking uncertain. She had embraced the frontier life since moving out to Broken Horseshoe Ranch with her father and brother. Memories of afternoon tea and stilted conversation whilst trying to act the young lady brought back unhappy memories for her. She loved her new lifestyle of riding through the foothills of Devil's Mountain and exploring caves for lost treasure. The prospect of afternoon tea parties with genteel piano music was something she would not welcome in Nowhere. But she liked Dora, so she smiled and nodded her head. After all, Amy thought, she needn't attend any of them.

Eliza, on the other hand, clapped her hands in delight. "That would be wonderful! I'd really enjoy it. I can't wait to see and hear the piano music."

Dora smiled at the enthusiasm shown by Eliza. "So you see, Sheriff, there will be no fighting or brawling in the hotel with my ladies!"

The assurances given by Dora didn't seem to make the sheriff look any happier, Josh thought. He and Manuel exchanged glances, both uncertain how Dora's grandiose genteel schemes would work in the frontier town of Nowhere.

Sheriff Grey opened the door of the general store, the bell chiming above it. He looked at Dora before leaving and nodded his head. But he could be heard muttering as he walked through the door and out onto the boardwalk. "Ladies in the hotel! Afternoon tea and piano music. Ha! I'd rather have the wretched miners!"

CHAPTER FIVE

"Are you going to Duloe town tomorrow?" Josh asked Dora.

"Yes, the wagon came in from town this afternoon. Slim loads up and sleeps overnight, and makes an early start tomorrow morning," Dora replied, looking puzzled at Josh's enquiry.

"Amy and I aren't working in the store tomorrow. I wondered if I could join you and go into Duloe with you tomorrow morning. What do you think, Amy?" Josh looked at Amy, seeking her agreement for his journey to Duloe. There was no need for him to explain why he wanted to go. She knew—and had even suggested it earlier that week.

A look of comprehension passed over her face, and she looked at him with a nod of approval. "Yes, Josh, I think that's a great idea. If you stay overnight in Nowhere, you can be off with Dora early in the morning. I can return to Broken Horseshoe Ranch this afternoon."

Amy, her brother Ben, and their father, Luke Tanner, had recently arrived at the Broken Horseshoe Ranch to start a new life after the death of their mother. But her father had contracted the lung disease that had killed her mother, and was unwell. Given a map and a gold coin by an old prospective friend, Luke had come to this part of the Devil's Mountains to search for the lost Jesuit gold. Uprooting his family and bringing from the comfortable life they had lived out east had been a tremendous change for Amy and Ben.

Dora looked pleased at this news. "Josh, you can stay in the hotel tonight. I would be very grateful if you could accompany me to the lawyers' office tomorrow in town.

Whilst I can do the business on my own, they much prefer a man to be present." Dora gave a snort of disapproval at this stupidity. As if she needed a man to help sort out her affairs! It was a *man*—her husband—who had got them into the mess she was in today!

"If that's settled between y'all, why doesn't Amy leave now for the ranch? It's still early in the afternoon, and she can be home well before dark," suggested Eliza.

"That's a good idea. I'd far rather Amy travelled in daylight," agreed Josh, with relief. "I'll get Bella ready, and the buggy for you," he told Amy.

Josh went out and down the back steps of the general store to the small stable yard and the stable where Bella, the ranch horse that was Amy's preferred mount, was housed with Manuel's horse.

Amy soon joined him. "I've got everything now, Josh. There are quite a few vegetables here that are all bruised. I know Tom will love making something delicious for us for dinner out of them," Amy said. She placed the bags on the floor of the buggy and settled herself on the seat before taking the reins from Josh's hands.

"Sounds good. I don't know what I'll get at the hotel or in Duloe town. But I can only hope it will be worth it," Josh said. The look of intense worry was back on his face. That look always appeared when thinking of the man who was determined to kill him. "I don't know if I'll find anything out on this visit. It's probably going to be a waste of time," he said.

Josh had been found unconscious in the desert by Amy and her dog, Meg. On recovering consciousness, Josh had found that he'd lost his memory, and it still hadn't returned. Having no memory of what he'd done before his new life at Broken Horseshoe Ranch and Nowhere, he found it inexplicable that someone should seek his death. But, for some time now, a man they called the Duke had sent assassins to kill him. Josh didn't know why. He couldn't even remember his own name, let alone what he'd done in his past life.

Amy shook her head at his dismal thoughts. "Yes, it may be a waste of time, but you can't be sure of that. Whatever the outcome, it'll be worth making the effort. Sitting still and waiting for someone to come and kill you is no good. Better you try to find this man. At least you're doing something. Remember, you're out looking for information about Charles Roberts. I'd also have a look around for information about that company he said he owns. You know, the one that handles all the sales of the land to the new homesteaders. He hides behind that company. There may well be more information about it. If you could find out who is backing him, giving him money for it, that might well be your man, Duke."

Amy sat back, reins ready in her hand. That was a long speech for her, one that she was determined to make to help Josh focus on his search in Duloe. A quiet girl, she thought hard about things, and could reason as well as Luke, her father, now.

"Well, Amy, you sure talk a lot of sense sometimes! That's such a good idea. Yes, someone at the hotel may well know Charles Roberts and his company. But I'll need to be careful. I don't want my nosing around to get back to Charles. It's far and away the best thing for him to think that we're just sitting waiting for the next assassin to arrive in Nowhere."

His hat was pushed back from his face, and he glanced down at the girl before looking up at the sky. "You'd best get going, Amy. There's still time for you to get back in daylight. Remember, ask Ezra if he'll come and help the posse track those villains that took the boy."

Josh stepped back from the buggy and watched as Amy drove out of the stable yard. With approval, he noticed she had her rifle ready beside her and her Colt at hand, ready for any danger that might threaten her.

He stood in the stable yard, thinking over Amy's words. She had been correct. Charles Roberts wouldn't lay himself open for public disapproval. He would hide behind a company. Tomorrow Josh was going to find out about that company, and about Charles Roberts himself. If, as they both thought, he was in the man's pay who was determined to kill him, the more information he could find out about Charles, the better.

"I'm a sitting duck here in Nowhere. But I'll not sit quietly. No more! I'm going to find out who is seeking my death. And I'm going to find out why he wants to kill me. Tomorrow is my first step in finding out the truth!"

CHAPTER SIX

Josh left his hotel room the following morning and made his way to the dining room. The room he had slept in had just been built, and the smell of sawdust still lingered. The bed was made of rough-hewn wood and had a basic lumpy mattress. He had thrown the pillow on the floor; it had been dirty and smelly. He didn't fancy laying his head upon it. In many ways, his bedroll out in the foothills or out in the desert around Broken Horseshoe Ranch had been preferable to his night spent in the hotel room. Josh could only hope that once Dora had taken full control of the hotel she would upgrade it. It was a poor standard.

Dora was fussing around her luggage, so Josh didn't have to lie about having a good night's sleep. "Good morning, Josh, I won't be long. I think Slim is nearly ready with the wagon. You go on out and get in it, and I'll join you in a moment."

Josh downed the cup of coffee given to him by the old guy who helped in the hotel and picked up a biscuit and some bacon before heading out to the wagon.

"Any luggage?" Slim asked as Josh came to stand beside the wagon, which had already another fellow traveller sitting in it.

"No, I've just got a small bag," Josh said. He held up the small bag that Manuel had given him for his unexpected visit to Duloe town. The general store sold various items of clothing, mainly workwear: the basic trousers in wool cloth, canvas, and heavy denim, along with flannel shirts. The ladies were catered for with simple blouses and dresses, but most women in the area carefully sewed their own dresses. They supplied all other items of clothing for their family from the fabric that Eliza carefully picked out to have readily available in the store.

Josh sat on the wooden bench inside the wagon. His canvas bag held a clean shirt and all the other essentials that Manuel had decided he needed for his trip to the town. Josh wasn't sure that he needed everything that Manuel had insisted he take. But he was grateful to his friend and accepted everything pressed upon him, getting pleasure out of the satisfied face of Manuel.

Dora joined him a few moments later. A large box and case were lifted into the wagon by the surly Slim. "How long are you staying for, Mrs Binns? You've got enough in here for over a month." His voice held a reproof, and he glared at the woman. But Dora was used to surly men like him and just ignored him, seating herself beside Josh.

Josh had known the journey would be long, dusty, and tiring. It was—but what he hadn't reckoned on was the incredible boredom that he endured as the wagon journeyed over the desert trails, the only interest being the looming Devil's Mountain, and others ranging alongside. How different it was when he had ridden along these trails, rather than being bounced up and down, with every bone being jarred in the wagon.

"Here we are! This is the beginning of Duloe town. My, how it's growing. Each time I come into the town, more buildings have gone up, and there are more carriages, and horses everywhere. I think the silver and goldmines up in the mountains are bringing folk flooding into the area," said Dora. She was sitting on the edge of the bench, and she peered out, trying to get her bearings. "Here we are. Slim promised me he'd stop here for us."

Much to Josh's astonishment, the wagon stopped just

20

as Dora had asked. The surly man got down and put her baggage out onto the sidewalk. Slim gave Dora a brusque nod before climbing up again and weaving the wagon along the busy street and on to the livery stables.

"This is a boarding house I'm staying at, Josh. Mrs Maguire is a good woman, she keeps a clean house and she'll find you a space to stay." Wearily, they both walked along the sidewalk to the wooden house with the sign in the window: *Boarding House. Clean Beds Available*.

Dora approached the door and gave a loud knocking tattoo. Josh smiled to himself. No one inside could fail to hear that knock.

A big, round woman with red cheeks and a wide grin opened the door—though it would have been nicer if she had more teeth. "Dora! Good to see you, my girl. Come on in, and we'll have a dish of tea. And who is the fine handsome man you've got with you?"

Dora was folded into the arms of the woman in a bearlike hug. She turned to Josh. "This, Josh, is my good friend—Molly Maguire. She'll make you welcome here, even if it's only in the back kitchen." Dora looked enquiringly at her friend Molly, then pushed Josh forward.

"Sure, any friend of Dora's is welcome here. Come here, young man!" Before Josh knew what was happening, he too was enveloped in a bearlike hug. The surprising strength of the woman had brooked no refusal from him, and he found himself clasped in her bosom. All he was conscious of was a smell of baking—and of clean laundry as he was finally released.

"You're welcome for now, Dora, but only for a couple of nights, my dear," Molly said as she opened the door wide, gesturing for them to come in.

"Why? Why only for a couple of nights? Not that I'll be wanting to stay longer, but what's the problem, Molly?" Dora said. She placed a hand on the other woman's shoulder as they walked through and stood in the centre of a large kitchen.

On one side of the kitchen, Josh could see a couple of large carpet bags standing next to an ancient dresser. He put Dora's baggage down beside them. Josh saw Dora's quick eyes rest upon them immediately, and she turned to face her friend, a look of enquiry on her face.

"What's this, Molly? You're packing your bags?" Dora asked the other woman.

"That man! He's got me fired. Said as how I'm not doing it properly. I'm too generous with the food and spend too much money on cleaning materials. That's how you run an excellent boarding house. That's why people keep coming back." The rosy cheeks of the woman were now wet with tears, and she gave great, hiccupping sobs.

"What man? Who's done this to you?"

"Flashy young whippersnapper, he is. Goes by the name of Charles Roberts."

CHAPTER SEVEN

"Charles Roberts? I thought this boarding house was owned by a woman. What's happened? What has Charles Roberts got to do with it?" Dora, astonished at this news, turned and asked Molly.

Then Dora looked across at Josh, who was standing open mouthed. She had been informed about the situation with Josh, and the possibility that Charles Roberts was in league with the yound man's stalker. Josh's visit to Duloe town was explained to her by Amy, and Dora fully intended to help him in any way she could. To find that the moment they arrived in Duloe town, the name Charles Roberts was brought into the conversation had left both of them stunned.

"Sit down, here. Let me get you both a coffee. After your long journey, you must be parched. Then I'll tell you all about it," Molly said, opening the kitchen door wider and ushering them both further into the cosy room. Old-fashioned, with a stove giving off a tremendous heat, they saw the coffee pot sitting beside a cast-iron pot of simmering stew. A wonderful aroma made Josh's mouth water, and he realised how hungry he was. A plate of fresh biscuits sat on a table.

Both Dora and Josh saw Molly would not be content until they had drunk the coffee and sat down at the table with her. Josh's nose had been twitching the moment he entered the kitchen. The smell of freshly brewed coffee overpowered that of the stew.

"Thank you—I really needed this after that dry dusty trip here." Josh looked into his empty mug with sadness and glanced up hopefully at Molly.

Distraught as the woman was, she couldn't resist that

pleading glance from the handsome young man seated opposite her. With a wry smile at him, she refilled the cup. "I have a stew simmering and will have bread ready shortly from the oven. I'll dish it up for you both in a little while."

Impatiently, Dora said to her friend. "Yes, we can wait, Molly. But first, tell us how Charles Roberts got involved with your boarding house?"

Molly paused for a moment before she answered. "This house was owned by Mr and Mrs Simpson. He was shot a few months ago, leaving her the sole owner of the boarding house, and a large emporium up the road. She is a plain woman who had previously inherited the properties from her father. It was obvious to everyone that her husband, Mr Simpson, married her for her money. Now he's dead, and Charles Roberts has courted her and is planning to marry her shortly. It's a disgrace. The town is in an uproar. Far too soon to get married again after the death of one husband—and to such a man as Charles Roberts!"

Molly drank the last of her coffee, putting the cup down with a decided click. "He's already taking charge of the properties, managing all the finances, and this boarding house is not required any more by Charles Roberts. He says that it is running at a loss, which it isn't."

"I can vouch for that. You are always busy. I've seen you turning folk away. Why did he say it's running at a loss?" Dora asked Molly.

"Charles plans on turning the house into a saloon, or a private gaming club, with card games and roulette tables. As you can imagine, Molly Maguire would not fit in an establishment like that! Wouldn't be seen dead in it anyway, not a God-fearing woman like me." Here, Molly folded her arms and glared defiantly at the two of them, as if making certain they got her point of view.

Swallowing a laugh at the woman's fury, whilst sympathising with her predicament, Josh asked her a question. "Where will you go? What will you do?"

Molly pointed to the two carpet bags sitting in the corner of the kitchen. "All my possessions are packed and ready to go. Where I'll go to, I don't know."

Dora jumped up, her chair hurtling back across the floor. She ran over to Molly and flung her arms around the woman. "With me! You're coming to Nowhere with me. I need you to organise the hotel that my fool of a husband won in a poker game. It's in a terrible state. Do say that you will come, Molly. It will be such fun for both of us, living together in the hotel."

"Me? Come with you? To Nowhere and help you in the hotel? I'd love to, Dora! I thought I'd end up on the street." Again, tears ran down the red cheeks, but this time they were of joy and hope. Soon, Dora was crying too.

At this emotional outpouring of the two women, Josh got up and went over to the stove and refilled his coffee cup, turning his back on them. When he thought they had quite finished, he turned round to them both. "What can you tell me about Charles Roberts? You must know quite a bit about him, Molly. Please, tell me all you know about him."

CHAPTER EIGHT

"You haven't told me why you want to find out more about Charles Roberts. What's this man to you, Josh? I don't like him and think Mrs Simpson is silly to get involved with him. If you don't want to tell me your business, fair enough. But if Dora vouches for you. I'll definitely help you." Molly said.

Dora took it upon herself to answer Molly. She could see that Josh was looking for the right words to answer Molly, and was struggling to find them. "Best you don't know what it's about, Molly. But it's important we find out what we can about the man. Let's just say, he's up to no good, and we want to find out every little detail about him. It has to be a secret, Molly. Charles can't find out that Josh is in Duloe looking for information about him. Are you willing to keep Josh's secret, Molly? It's important. His very life depends upon it. Do you think you can keep it a secret, Molly?"

It was agreed between them. Molly would keep Josh's secret and try to find out what she could about Charles and his business dealings.

Molly wiped her face and jumped to her feet. She went to the stove and began dishing out the stew. The smell of the stew had not been a lie. It was delicious. The fresh bread mopped up the gravy, and Josh sat back in his chair, his stomach filled and with a feeling of contentment.

Josh was on the trail of the man who sought his death. Arriving in Duloe town was the first act in his resolution to find out who was sending assassins to Nowhere to kill him. The chatter between the two women seemed to pass over his head as he sat lost in his thoughts.

After the meal, Molly took them upstairs to their bedrooms. Each had a single room, and Josh was impressed. This sparsely furnished, simple room sparkled with cleanliness. The spotless linen on the bed was inviting, and he looked forward to resting his weary bones on it. He was still aching after the jolting wagon journey, and wondered if he could face it again the next day, or whether he should stay for one more night in Duloe.

Josh put his bag on the single wooden chair beside the window. He gave another glance towards the bed, promising himself that he would soon be in it, resting his tired body.

There was a crash of the front door being flung back, wide open. A man's voice boomed down the hall. "Hello, Mrs Maguire! Charles Robert here! I want a word with you."

Dora acted first. In a moment, she dashed into Josh's room. Grabbing Josh's arm, she pulled him from the chair he had been sitting on and pushed him towards the window. "I'll throw your bag down out of the window after you. Best you get back to Nowhere," she whispered. Josh flung the window open and looked out. Below him was a bare earth yard, a washing line hung with damp sheets stretched across part of it. A sloping roof over the kitchen provided him with an easy descent to that yard below. Before he could think of anything else, he put his legs out of the window and slid down the roof, hoping that the noise he made would not be heard inside by Charles. He landed on his feet and turned to look up at the window.

"Here, Josh, thank goodness you didn't unpack anything," Dora said. His bag was hurled from the window and he caught it, moving silently as he did so.

"Thanks, Dora," Josh said.

Dora whispered down to him, leaning out of the window. "Go to the livery stable, straight up the road, and it's on your left. Slim will have a bed for you. He always has some for overnight travellers that can't find—or can't afford—hotels, and they stay in the stables. Best you stay there until the wagon leaves at noon."

Josh gave Dora a wave and gingerly backed away from the wall of the lean-to kitchen, the light streaming out on the small yard from the kitchen window. As he glanced around, the subdued light from the window showed a small yard full of boxes and clutter, and the line of washing. He pushed the damp sheets aside. But before he walked further away, he stared into the kitchen at Charles.

The first thing Josh noticed was that Molly was also a quick thinker, just like Dora. His telltale plate and cutlery were whisked away in a trice and put in a bowl, along with the other two plates. Nothing was left behind on the table to give the impression that a third person had been eating a meal.

Conscious of the need to be quiet, he looked around. It wouldn't do for him to stumble over something and make a huge clattering noise. As his breathing calmed down and his ears became attuned to the night noises of the bustling town around him, he picked out the words spoken in the kitchen.

A man's voice was the first he heard. That must be Charles, he thought.

"Mrs Maguire, I've called at this late hour with your wages. Tomorrow, I have men who are about to start work in the house. I paid you in full, including today. I'd like you to vacate this boarding house first thing in the morning." Molly was shocked into silence by the harsh words of Charles. She stood in the kitchen, then walked over and sank down in a chair, unable to move or speak.

Charles walked into the kitchen and placed some coins on the kitchen table. As he did so, his eyes lit upon Dora, who had followed him into the kitchen. "Dora! What are you doing here?" The astonishment on his face at the sight of the woman, whom he usually saw working in the general stores in Nowhere, made Josh smile.

"I came in today on the wagon. There is business I must attend to in Duloe." Dora said, her voice giving nothing away and a slightly pleasant look on her face at his arrival. Josh was surprised at how well she was hiding her true feelings from the man.

"Well, I'm afraid you'll have to leave tomorrow morning, Mrs Maguire—and you too, Dora," Charles said to Dora, before turning again to Molly.

"I'm going to stay here tonight, Mrs Maguire. I know you had a spare room. It's still available, isn't it?" Charles said. "Have you any food left? I had a long ride into town this morning and have been busy with business affairs all afternoon. I haven't eaten all day." The words on the surface were pleasantly uttered, and polite. But Josh was aware of the arrogant manner in which he had couched his demands. It made his blood boil to see the pleasant Molly only give a nod and turn back to her pans on the stove.

A long moment passed as Josh stared through the window at the man who was in league with the stalker. How he would love to walk in that door and punch Charles again and again, until he told the truth. An unbidden thought crossed his mind. Would he have done that before the blow on his head? What sort of man was he before he had lost his memory? It always came down to that. There was no getting away from it. Who had he been before he had been left in the desert to die? What had he done to be given that death sentence? And an especially cruel, lingering death sentence in the Arizona desert!

CHAPTER NINE

Josh shrugged his shoulders, picked up his bag and made his way as quietly as possible out of the yard behind the boarding house. The wooden boardwalk stretched out through the heart of the Western frontier town. Josh moved with deliberate steps, the creaking boards beneath his feet echoing in the night's stillness. Dim lanterns flickered in front of saloons and general stores, their feeble light barely penetrating the darkness. Here the air was thick with the scent of dust and the drifting wood smoke from stoves and distant campfires. He could hear, in the distance, a coyote howling.

Some of the wooden structures on either side of the boardwalk stood silent. The harsh sun and unforgiving winds had weathered them. A few horses were still tethered to hitching posts, and shifted uneasily as he walked past, their eyes reflecting the lantern lights from the windows.

A swinging door creaked open and closed in front of him. It was a saloon, and he could hear the murmur of a poker game, and the aroma of beer and stale sweat from the men inside drifted out as he walked past.

When Josh had arrived in Duloe town it had been late afternoon and, although the light had been fading, there were still people moving around, finishing the day's business. Now, it was predominantly men he saw. The women that were around were not the respectable ladies of Duloe. The women he saw made him think of the titles they were given: ladies of the night and soiled doves. He walked past them, thankful he'd had a meal and grateful for the information Dora had given him about where he could sleep that night.

When he reached his destination, Slim was seated in a chair at the front of the livery stables, a jug beside him. "You were on the stage this morning. Ready to go back to Nowhere tomorrow?" he asked Josh.

Josh agreed he was ready to go back to Nowhere tomorrow and asked if a spare seat in the wagon was available.

"Usually plenty of seats going to Nowhere. Only gets full with the people wanting to get out of that dump!" Slim took a swig from the jug, gave a sigh of appreciation, and wiped his mouth with the back of his hand. "Yes, plenty of seats tomorrow. You're the only one so far."

"Dora told me you have beds for overnight travellers," Josh asked the man.

Slim laughed uproariously at that. He needed to take a swig from the jug to help with his laughter. "I like that! Beds for overnight travellers—must remember that." Without moving from his chair, he pointed behind him: "Down there—old Abe will show you where to go. No fancy beds, though; a straw mattress is what you'll get. You can pay me tomorrow morning with the fare to Nowhere."

"Thanks," Josh said, and left the man, who was now cradling the jug in his arms, his eyes slowly closing.

The heavy wooden doors of the stable were open, revealing the cavernous space within. The combined smell of hay, straw, saddle leather, and a hint of manure gave each livery stable its own distinct aroma. He could hear hooves thudding on straw-covered ground as a horse moved. Occasionally, there came the snort or whinny from a restless steed.

In the corner, the wagon that had brought him into

Duloe town stood silent. Having borne the brunt of the day's travel, its wheels and body were coated with a film of dust. Wooden benches, scarred by years of use, offered a place to sit, awaiting either the arrival or departure of the stagecoach or wagon.

The horses were placed along one side of the large building. At the far end were smaller spaces, with partitions between them. Canvas bags, plainly stuffed with straw, lay in each space. With a sigh, Josh walked towards them. He thought longingly of the bed he'd left behind in the boarding house. That villain Charles would sleep in those fresh sheets in that pleasant-looking bedroom.

"Hey, mister—over here! You can sleep on this one," said a grizzled man, bent over with age. He pointed to the far end of the barn and led the way.

Josh followed him and threw his bag down on the lumpy straw mattress. "Thanks," he said to the small man, who had lit an oil lamp on the table against a wall.

"That light is there for other folks coming in. My job is to put it out later." The man seemed proud of this task and fiddled about with the lamp before turning round to face Josh. Then, he lifted the lamp up from the table and came forward, holding it up, better to see Josh's face.

Josh backed away as the wick flared up at the sudden movement, illuminating old Abe's face and his own. He saw the man's eyes widen and the jaw drop as he clearly recognised Josh.

"It *is* you! Didn't sound like your voice, though. Losing that English accent, ain't you? What are you doing here, Duke? Last time I saw, you said you were going back to England. What's keeping you here?"

CHAPTER TEN

Open-mouthed, Josh could only stare at the man. What was he talking about? *Who* was he talking about? He must get more information from him. But how? The old boy was not too bright. He could tell that not only from the man himself, but from the way Slim had spoken of his double. I must be careful not to alarm him, thought Josh.

"Where was it I last saw you, Abe?" Josh asked the old man, hoping for a helpful reply.

"Here! In this very stable. You brought in that fine horse of yours for me to look after for the night. But you were staying, then, in the best hotel—not dossing down on the straw." Abe had come closer to Josh. With his watery grey eyes, he peered up at the young man in front of him.

"No, it's *not* you! You're not Duke." Josh would have liked to move away from the old boy. He reeked of drink and the stable itself. But he didn't dare: he might halt the flow of words. Old Abe continued speaking. "No, you're not him. Duke wouldn't dress in ordinary clothes. Nor would he ride in a dusty wagon. Got a fine horse, he has. Mind, you look like him, right enough."

Josh stared at the man, wondering how much more information he could glean from him. "What's that Duke doing around here? If he's English, why isn't he back in England?" He finally spoke, hoping his words would not halt the flow of information from the old man.

"Come all the way from England, the Duke said. Unfinished business to attend to. He had a nasty look on his face when he said that, mind you. Don't think he lives around here, anyway. Duke lives east somewhere." With that, the old man moved away, and Josh had to be content with the information he had garnered from him.

Josh had a disturbed night. The hay poked through the cotton covering of the mattress, irritating him as he tossed and turned. Was this visit to Duloe town a mistake? There had been one disaster after another. Perhaps not, he mused. Old Abe's remarks about Duke, and the resemblance between them, brought to his mind the information given to him by a previous assassin.

Memories returned as he thought back to the conversation he'd had with a man who had been sent to kill him. The words that the man had told him came back to him vividly: "You look like Duke, the man who wants you killed. As alike as two peas in a pod, that's what you are. He acts like a lord, but you are just ordinary." After Josh had captured him, these words were added to the little knowledge he had of the man Duke. Both Josh and Amy had agreed to let the man go, after getting as much information as possible from him.

All night long, Josh had worried about these words from the former assassin—and now he had old Abe's words to throw into the mix. What did it mean? In the middle of all these thoughts and worries, he had fallen into a light doze and had woken both exhausted and itchy.

Josh awoke to the smell of coffee. He stretched as he stood looking around the livery stable. Slim stood at the front of the open doors, the early morning sunshine flooding into the large building. The horses were restless, knowing their day was beginning.

"Coffee. It's hot, so come and get it," Abe called to Josh when he saw him moving about.

"Biscuits and bacon, to have with your coffee. And I'll have the money from you for the night's lodging and the fare to Nowhere," Slim said, walking towards Josh. "I'm waiting for Miss Dora. She said she had a parcel for me to take back to Nowhere. Said I needed to store it on the wagon. I'm clearing out the wagon now, ready for it. But I've got the post here for Nowhere."

Slim held a bundle of packages and letters in his hand and reached into the wagon for a canvas bag. "I sort out the post into bundles. The twine pieces go round each separate bundle: one for the general store, another for the hotel, and saloon. The rest go in one mixed lot. Josh, can you sort that out for me whilst I get on with this wagon business for Miss Dora?"

of packages and letters, were placed into Josh's hand. The canvas bag with the twine pieces was placed into his other hand.

CHAPTER ELEVEN

Josh couldn't believe it. Here he was, thinking his trip to Duloe town had been a big mistake. The journey, he felt, had been a fruitless waste of time. Now Slim had given him the post to Nowhere: all the post, packages, and letters!

"Sure, Slim, I'll gladly sort it out for you. Got nothing else to do, have I?" Josh said, as he went over to sit at the bench and sort out the bundle of mail. At first, he stared down at it, piled high on the bench beside him. Both Amy and he had gone over the many ways in which he could try to see the letters coming into Nowhere. They both had been at a loss, and could only hope he might look at it in the wagon on the journey back to Nowhere. But now, as luck would have it, Slim had handed all the mail going into Nowhere to him. A smile hovered on his lips and he felt, for the first time since he had arrived in Duloe, that things were finally going his way.

The new homesteaders received a handful of letters. He wondered how they'd feel, getting letters from the homes they had left behind. Then he found a collection of wanted posters and a couple of official-looking letters, all addressed to the sheriff's office. Idly, Josh wondered what they contained. The general store had leaflets from the growing catalogue industry—smart men advertised their goods in leaflets and catalogues that were sent to general stores like Manuel's. Customers could browse these and order whatever they wanted.

Then, at the bottom of the stack of mail, he found a couple of letters for Broken Horseshoe Ranch. Both were addressed to Ben. Josh, his curiosity aroused, held them both up to the light, hoping to find out what was in them.

No, that gesture was futile. He'd have to wait till Ben opened them at the ranch.

Josh finally came to the letters he was looking for. Several letters were addressed to Charles Roberts. Some had clearly been forwarded from a newspaper office. Josh put these to one side. They were, he thought, from prospective homesteaders, hoping to come to Nowhere. For a fleeting moment, Josh wondered if he should tear them up, so saving the future homesteaders a lot of grief. Shaking his head at the thought, he tied them up in a bundle.

Then he found it. There was no doubt in his mind. This *had* to be from Duke: the paper was a rich cream colour, of a quality and thickness that Josh had never seen before. Well, not since his blow to the head. Perhaps he'd written on, and used, this quality paper in his past life. A confident and bold black writing was scrawled across the envelope, addressed to Charles Roberts.

"This must be from Duke. Quality paper, and written in a flowing hand. I wonder what's inside it?" Josh muttered to himself.

Josh held the envelope up to the sunlight. Before he did so, he made certain that Abe and Slim were busy elsewhere, and not watching him. He could see, even through the thickness of the envelope, the bold black writing. But he couldn't read it. Disappointed, he placed it down on the bench beside him.

"I'll just tie this lot up and place them in the bag," Josh murmured, and carefully did so. That letter, addressed in the bold black handwriting to Charles Roberts, lay beside him on the bench. After he tied each bundle up, he glanced down at the letter.

"Some of these letters have been damaged," Josh

muttered, as he fingered a couple of the letters that had been knocked about on their hazardous and lengthy journey, almost coming adrift from their original seal or envelope.

Should I say that the letter to Charles got damaged on its way to Nowhere? Josh thought, holding it in his hands. Should he open it and pretend it got damaged in transit? Would it be believed that it had arrived in Duloe in such a state? He turned it over and over again, wondering if answers to the evil that had been stalking him for so long lay in his hands. Josh put the letter back down on the bench as he placed the newly tied bundles of post into the bag.

"What the hell?" The shout came from outside the livery stable. Slim's voice was raised in outrage and could be heard all over that part of town. "Woman! You told me you'd be getting a package for me to take to Nowhere. You told me to clear out the wagon to give it space. And now, ... and now you bring this! You expect me to transport it all the way over the rough ground, through the canyons and over the foothills of the Devil's Mountain, all the way to Nowhere! You're mad, woman! And you must think *I'm* bonkers, just like you!"

CHAPTER TWELVE

Josh jumped to his feet. The voices had startled him. He closed the bag up, ready to put it on the wagon for Slim. Then he realised the letter addressed to Charles Roberts still lay on the bench beside him. Josh picked it up and was about to open the bag again to slip it inside when, on an impulse, he thrust the letter deep into his trouser pocket.

Slim's exasperated voice rose to a new high, outraged level. His shouts at Dora, Josh thought, could now have been heard all over Duloe. "It's a piano! You want me to transport a *piano* all the way to Nowhere? Woman, don't you realise that it's a track most of the way? It's over rough terrain and even goes up part of Devil's Mountains' foothills. My wagon isn't built for transporting pianos. My wagon is for people and packages!"

Josh walked out of the darkness of the barn and into the sunlight. He raised a hand to shield his eyes against the sudden harsh glare. His lips twitched in amusement as he watched the two figures standing opposite each other. For all the world, he thought, just like two fighting cocks facing each other, preparing to do battle. Dora had her hands on her hips and was standing in front of the piano. The two men standing beside it had pushed the large instrument on a trolley. Facing her, Slim's weather-beaten face had become a fiery red with anger. Josh could see his hands clenched into tight fists, the anger and frustration at Dora and her piano building up within the man.

"How do you expect to grow your business if you can't even transport a piano? I thought you had big ideas to make your name in transporting goods between Duloe and Nowhere. Abe told me that there is only myself and

Josh going to be travelling back to Nowhere today. So, just for today, I can ride up front with you, and Josh can ride alongside us, ready to help when necessary. That means the whole wagon can be given over to my piano." A satisfied smile crept over Dora's face as she explained to the infuriated man opposite her exactly what he had to do.

Josh admired Dora's pluck in standing up to Slim. He shifted his gaze to Slim, eager to hear the man's reply.

"If—and I say *if*—I transport your wretched piano all the way to Nowhere, you have to be prepared to pay for any damage to my wagon. That is a tremendous weight for my wagon to carry over the road to Nowhere," Slim began saying when Dora tried to interrupt him. He raised a hand to halt the flow of words that he knew would erupt from the woman. "And I will not be responsible for any damage to your wretched piano! Do you understand? If my wagon breaks down, you can pay for its repairs. If your piano breaks, that's up to you." Slim folded his arms and glared at Dora. He had said his piece to her, and he expected her to agree to his terms.

Josh watched this byplay between the two of them and grinned. Grudgingly, Dora nodded at Slim and turned to gesture to the two men who had brought her piano down to the livery stables. They pushed it nearer to the wagon. Josh put in a lot of effort to help the men, and Slim, move the massive piano onto the wagon. It was hard suppressing his amusement at the language used by Slim and the two men. He also kept a close eye on the wagon's axles—both he and Slim were worried they might not hold the heavy weight of Dora's piano. He was astonished to find that Dora stood by without giving the men instructions, without commenting on the bad language, but just watching closely to ensure that it was done with due care towards her piano. Josh's respect for her increased when, at the conclusion of a massive effort by the four of them, she stepped forward and reached into a large bag that lay beside her.

"Thank you. I appreciate all your hard work," Dora said to the two men, and passed over some coins. Their appreciative thanks at this unexpected reward sent both men off with grins. As Josh watched, they headed straight to the nearest saloon.

Slim was double-checking that the piano was tightly tied down to ensure it wouldn't shift during the journey. Dora walked over and stood behind him. He stepped off the wagon and turned to face her. Josh watched Slim's face darkening as he expected more rude comments from Dora.

"Thank you, Slim—there's a bottle of whiskey waiting for your arrival in Nowhere at the hotel," Dora said. "I'll be back in a moment. Just got to get a last package from the store. Oh, and on your next trip to Nowhere, you'll be bringing my friend: Molly."

"What a woman! Annoying, but at least she appreciates the work we put in," Slim said, watching as Dora walked up the street, her black skirts rustling as she strode out with the determined walk she'd always had. "Still, she's a mighty fine woman in her own way," was the grudging compliment from the livery stable owner, his eyes still upon her figure as Dora walked into a store.

CHAPTER THIRTEEN

Josh had been watching Slim, and he gave a wry smile to himself as the older man turned away and began preparing for the journey ahead. Most of the work had been done earlier by Slim, Abe, and himself. Josh followed Abe back into the stable. They found a horse and saddled him up for Josh. It was a toss-up, Josh thought, between the jolting hardness of the wagon and the plodding ride on the horseback to Nowhere. On balance, he thought the horse might give him a more comfortable ride. The wagon's jolting and tossing had caused him discomfort and a feeling of helplessness. Whilst riding the horse on the long journey could be tiring, Josh felt it was preferable to the bumpy wagon ride.

Trotting alongside the wagon, Josh shifted restlessly on the horse. He had got used to riding Star from the Broken Horseshoe Ranch and found this horse to be a plodding slug. During one of his restless movements, he heard a rustle coming from his trouser pocket. It was the letter! He'd forgotten all about it. He remembered picking it up, and then Dora had arrived with the piano and he'd dropped it into his pocket. The bag containing all the post and packages for the people of Nowhere now lay beneath Slim's seat on the wagon. There was no way Josh could present him with the letter that was now shoved into his pocket. How would he explain it to Slim? Why had he taken that letter, especially out from the rest of the post? It would look very suspicious, and there was no way that Josh wanted to arouse questions in Slim's mind about him.

"I've got the letter now. I didn't intend to have it in my

pocket, but it's there," Josh muttered to himself as he rode along, deep in thought.

Later that afternoon, at almost dusk, the wagon containing the piano arrived in Nowhere. Surprisingly enough, the journey had not been too difficult, and the trail and tracks to Nowhere had been travelled surprisingly quickly. As Slim explained to Josh, there had been no rain to bog the wagon down with its heavy load, and having only the piano itself had made the weight less than if they had a full wagonload of passengers and their luggage. Horses had been changed at isolated ranches on the way. Josh had been given a fresh horse, but each time, it seemed to be worse than the one before.

As soon as the wagon arrived in front of the hotel, it had been met by an interested crowd. Hours past its usual time of arrival, it had been anxiously awaited. The wagon carried all sorts of equipment, post, and sometimes money and valuables. It could be a tempting target for bandits. Sheriff Grey had been the first to welcome the wagon as it came to rest outside the hotel. "What happened, Slim? Why are you so late?" The sheriff walked over to the dusty occupants of the seat and looked them over.

Josh hitched his horse to the rail and gave it a pat of thanks. But the truth was, he was glad to get off the beast; he disliked its jogging, plodding motion, and the long hours in the saddle had made him sore.

Dora explained to the sheriff and then went to the boardwalk, standing with hands on hips, directing the removal of her piano into the hotel. A considerable crowd drew round, staring in disbelief. Josh moved to the back of the crowd with speed. He'd done his bit of getting the piano onto the wagon. And he'd helped Slim on the journey. No way was he helping to get it off and into the hotel. There were others hanging about in the crowd that could do that, he thought. He set off to the general store.

Josh's arrival at the general store was met with surprise. Amy was just getting ready to return to Broken Horseshoe Ranch, but as Eliza and Manuel were eager to hear what had happened to Josh in Duloe, she removed her jacket and sat back down.

"Why are you back so early, Josh?" Amy asked, as she settled on the chair.

"I wanted to find out what I could about Charles Roberts, as you all know. I'd hoped to wander around and ask questions without Charles knowing I was there. We all said that there was a need for secrecy. He wasn't to know that I was investigating him, and trying to find out the identity of my stalker," Josh replied.

"Surely you didn't find everything out so quickly? In just one day?" Manuel's voice held disbelief as he stared at the dusty, dishevelled young man in front of him. "Let me get you a drink, and you can tell us what happened."

Josh took a deep breath and gratefully accepted the glass of whiskey that Manuel had poured out for him. He began his story.

CHAPTER FOURTEEN

Josh took a large drink from the whiskey and began speaking. "I had just arrived at the boarding house, which was managed by Molly Maguire, a friend of Dora's. We had eaten a meal, and I was getting ready to go to bed up in my room." Amy still sat on her chair, and now Manuel and Eliza had drawn closer to listen to his story. The general store had emptied. Not only was it getting near closing time, but the excitement of the piano's arrival outside the hotel had emptied the store in a flash.

"There was a loud knocking at the front door of the boarding house. It was thrown open and crashed back against the wall, and a man's voice shouted out." Josh paused, taking another sip from his glass, and looked round at his audience, who were waiting with bated breath for his resumption of the tale. He appreciated their interest.

"The voice shouted out, and it was Charles Roberts. He demanded a bed for the night—*my* bed, in *my* room! Then he told Molly Maguire that she had to leave. He was turning the property into a gaming club type of saloon."

"What did you do?" Amy asked breathlessly.

"Dora rushed into my room and flung open the window. I climbed out of the window and slid down the roof of the kitchen lean-to, and Dora threw my bag after me." Josh waited for the appreciative murmurs that he expected from his audience.

Instead, they all burst out laughing.

"To think that you were trying to avoid Charles Roberts. Not only did he arrive where you were staying, he even took your bed!" Manuel roared with laughter and slapped his thigh.

A sniff was all that Josh could manage in reply to this. Then he began telling them about his search for a bed that night. "Last night, I slept on a straw mattress in the livery stables," he told them, and took pleasure in the horrified gasps that greeted this remark. Somehow, Josh didn't want to tell them all about the conversation he'd had with old Abe about the 'duke' who looked like him. Not now, not then. He felt he'd rather discuss it with Amy at a later date. "I slept on the mattress and was woken up by Slim and the arrival of Dora. They were arguing about bringing the piano back to Nowhere."

Josh explained to Amy, Manuel, and Eliza how the journey from Duloe to Nowhere had been accompanied by a piano. He found it difficult. Because it had been a dreadful experience—not helped by Slim's cursing and swearing, and Dora's increasingly angry remarks at Slim. Worst of all had been the constant stopping and starting on the journey, to ease its passage over the rough terrain.

"There would be a loud pinging noise from the piano. Dora would shriek that the piano was being broken. So, Slim would stop the wagon. We'd all climb into the wagon and check all the ropes and blankets surrounding the piano. That took a time, because we had put bales of hay around the piano against the canvas walls." Josh ignored the giggles from Amy, Manuel, and Eliza.

He continued speaking, but gave a grateful nod to Eliza, who refilled his glass with yet more whiskey. "I was already suffering from that dreadful hay mattress. The added scratching from moving stuff from around the piano and its hay bedding made it worse." To prove his point, Josh scratched at some of the irritated red marks on his face, hands, and arms. He took a large drink of whiskey before continuing his story.

"It was coming up the inclines that were the worst. In the end, Dora drove the wagon and Slim and I helped push it up and over the worst of the hills. Then it needed all of Slim's skill to stop it running away down the hill."

By this time, his three listeners were laughing openly. Josh threw them a nasty look and carried on speaking. "We left early in the morning. Slim said it would take extra time and that he would not hang around to leave at mid-morning as he usually did. Old Abe was to tell anyone that wanted the wagon to come back the next morning, when he would definitely be on time."

"So, you left earlier than usual? But you were still late getting into Nowhere." Eliza sympathised with him. "What a horrid, long journey."

Josh threw her a grateful glance. There was somebody who sympathised with him, he thought. "Yes, we left as soon as we'd packed up. It was barely daybreak. We were grateful to Dora, as she had the forethought to bring along some food and water for us. Slim and I had the usual amount, but we hadn't reckoned on it being so long a journey."

Eliza went off to the kitchen. Moving Amy's pens and notebooks to one side, she placed a large plate of Mexican goodness on the desk: "Come on, Josh, sit down and eat. You'll feel better with some food inside you."

Josh moved stiffly over to the chair. His limbs were complaining after the night spent in the livery stables, and the day's riding, and the added exercise of shifting the piano. As he took a seat on the chair, he moved slightly to find a comfortable position, and suddenly heard the faint sound of paper rustling from his trouser pocket.

CHAPTER FIFTEEN

After a moment's hesitation, Josh ignored the rustling of the letter. Instead, he reached for his fork and began eating the tasty dish that Eliza had set before him. He was consumed with curiosity to know what was in that letter. Somehow, he didn't want to bring it out and discuss it in front of Manuel and Eliza. They were aware of his stalker, and had even assisted him in the past. This letter, and his discussion with old Abe about Duke, felt personal in some way. Later, he would open the letter and discuss it with Amy, along with Abe's thoughts on Duke and the resemblance between them.

Josh finished his meal and found Manuel and Amy had the buggy ready for the journey back to Broken Horseshoe Ranch.

As they drove out of Nowhere, Josh began speaking: "I feel as if I have been away from Nowhere for days and days, but it's only been a short time. I can't believe how much has happened."

Swallowing a grin, Amy looked at her companion. "Yes, you seemed to be very busy during that short time. Sliding down roofs and helping bring pianos to Nowhere was certainly more than you bargained for when you set off the other morning," agreed Amy.

The sun was dropping down behind Devil's Mountain, its last rays stretching over the track ahead of them. Familiar as it was to both of them, Josh, after the trip away to Duloe, felt anew his love for this land. "It's good to be back," he murmured.

His voice only just reached Amy's ears. She smiled to herself. Yes, it was good to have Josh back. He was right: he'd only been away a short time—but Amy had realised the depth of her involvement with Josh during that brief absence. She didn't realise how much he made her feel at ease, whether they were travelling or on the ranch. His presence made life simpler and safer.

"Much as I appreciate Eliza and Manuel's help in this stalking business, there are things I didn't tell them today. I'd far rather talk them over with you first, and then with the others at the ranch," said Josh.

Amy turned to look at him once more. She noted the deep lines that had appeared in his frown, and could see by the light of the setting sun the worry that had appeared on his face. Whatever he had to tell her, it was of some importance. "Well? What are these things?" It seemed to Amy that Josh was wondering how to tell her, and she could feel him trying to gather his thoughts.

"Old Abe told me about the man they call Duke. He'd met with him and talked to him a few times. Old Abe had been unwilling to give me much information. For some reason, Abe didn't want to talk too much about Duke. I could see that he was frightened of the man and kept looking around in case somebody heard him talking about Duke. The man has power and money to frighten people, even an old stable hand like Abe." Josh sat back, happier now that he could talk this over with Amy.

"Interesting—but it doesn't give you any more information. Now you know Duke was in Duloe, and now you know that someone else—apart from that assassin guy we spoke with some time ago—thought you looked alike. Strange: why should someone who looks like you, and is possibly a family member, wish to see you dead?" Amy said, a finger at her lips as she began to chew the nail thoughtfully.

Reaching into his trouser pocket, Josh produced a

letter. He explained how he had got it and sat with it in his hands, turning it over and over. "I don't know what to do. Should I just slip into the mail tomorrow when we get back to the general store? I think I could easily do that, if you distracted Eliza."

"No! We open it and see what is in it. You think this is likely to be from Duke to Charles Roberts, don't you?" Amy asked him, looking down at that letter, which Josh was still turning over and over in his hands.

"What if it ..." Josh's voice drifted away. He desperately wanted to know what was in the letter, but was frightened. Somehow, the unknown memories he had lived through and carried with him were perhaps better not known at all.

The buggy stopped. Amy jumped down from the buggy, and looked up at Josh. "Come on, get down and we'll light a small fire. We'll have a look at the letter, just the two of us. If you don't like what's in it, we needn't tell anyone else about it. You can even burn it. It will only be between the two of us. What you think, Josh?"

CHAPTER SIXTEEN

The darkness was creeping over the land. Storm clouds hid the moon from sight, and the atmosphere seemed charged with electricity. The last farewell from the sun lit up the approaching clouds with eerie lights around them. The storm clouds charged down from the foothills of the Devil's Mountain towards Josh and Amy.

Casting an apprehensive look at the approaching storm, Amy began gathering kindling and a small fire was lit, and they hunkered down beside it. Josh took the letter from his pocket and slit it open in one swift, determined movement. Amy was right: he had to know what was in it. He held it between them both, and close to the tiny fire so that the flickering light illuminated the sprawling black script. Anxious as he was to read the words, Josh couldn't help but appreciate the beautiful quality of paper that the letter was written on.

"There are only a couple of sentences," Josh said. He held the letter further down and still closer to the firelight, the better to see it. "Harry Martin will arrive and stay at the hotel. A well-known vicious killer who will dispatch Josh Barnes. Duke." Josh gave a sigh of horror as he read it out.

Amy took the letter from him and read it herself. She murmured, but with a deadly intent that was surprising in the normally placid girl: "Harry Martin, we will wait for your arrival. Shame we can't give this to the sheriff, but it would take some explaining as to how you got it. Josh, I wonder if he is on a wanted poster? I'm going to look at the sheriff's office. If Harry Martin is on one, we can get him arrested. If not, we are ready and waiting for his arrival and we can be prepared." Amy's voice held an assurance she was far from feeling.

"What do I do? Hide from the wretched man? Avoid Main Street? Yes, Amy, we know what it is we are waiting for, and who it is we are waiting for. But I don't see how we can prepare for it. How can we?"

The despondent tones in Josh's voice made Amy angry. She stood up and kicked over the fire, stamping out the ashes until they had all gone. "I think your visit to Duloe was a success. You found out more about this so-called Duke. You've intercepted a letter from him to Charles. Now Charles won't know *who* is coming to kill you. So, he can't give Harry Martin any help. So that's good for us. Come on, Josh, let's get back to the ranch."

They had journeyed for some time in silence, each deep in their own thoughts. Then Josh broke the silence: "Talking it over with you, Amy, makes the way ahead seem clearer. Everything happened so fast in Duloe, that I was uncertain which way forward I should go." Josh's voice tailed away into the growing darkness of the night.

Amy knew it took a lot for the normally reticent Josh to speak out about his innermost thoughts. "I'm not surprised, Josh. Sliding down a roof, sleeping in among the horses, and coping with Dora, Slim, and that piano must have turned your head into a whirl." Amy laughed, her chuckle in the gloom beside him making Josh smile. "It must've been quite an experience on that journey with them."

Josh gave a snort of laughter at her remark. "It certainly was some experience! Each homestead or isolated ranch we stopped at for a change of horse caused even more trouble. First, Dora said the horses weren't strong enough, and second, she insisted that the piano had to be securely tied up even more. And, to make things worse, I always got another plodding horse for the journey," said Josh.

Amy knew Josh was smiling as he said this and felt pleased that he felt so much better that he could laugh about his experiences. She opened her mouth to comment on the letter from Charles. Before she could speak, the gunshots began.

The silence of the night was shattered by gunshots and shouting. Josh and Amy were nearing the ranch and the disturbance they heard was in front of them and close to the ranch itself. Urging the horse forward at a much faster pace, Amy leaned forward as the buggy raced towards the gunfight.

CHAPTER SEVENTEEN

Further shouts could be heard, then another gunshot. The shouts echoed over the desert land towards them.

"It's Ben! That's Ben, my brother!" Amy cried out as the buggy hurtled and jolted even faster over the uneven ground.

Thrown about on the seat, Josh found it difficult to hold on and grab his gun at the same time. He reached for his rifle and fired a shot into the air. Then he shouted Ben's name as loud as he possibly could, hoping to drive off the attackers.

Between the storm clouds, there had been shafts of intermittent moonlight. One such eerie light illuminated the scene ahead of them: two horses stood sentinel beside the fallen figures on the ground.

"Ben! Ben, are you hurt?" Amy threw herself off the buggy as it came to a halt beside the fallen figures of the two boys. Crouching down beside them, she feared the worst—neither of them seemed to move.

"I'm all right Amy. It's Chan. He's dead." Ben's voice broke as he crouched over the fallen figure of his friend.

"Out of the way, Ben—let me look." Amy pushed her brother aside gently. Josh knelt down beside her and they both huddled over the fallen boy. The faint moonlight showed him lying almost motionless on the ground.

Then the young man stirred as Josh's hands ran over his limbs gently to see if there were any wounds or breaks. Josh sat back and looked at Amy, shaking his head.

"Can't see any damage. Chan seems unhurt. Did he fall off his horse, Ben? Because that could have done it. He may have hurt his head when he fell," Josh said. Then he turned to look at Ben and put an arm on his shoulder. "What happened? How many men attacked you?"

"There were two of them," began Ben. He was still a young boy in many ways, and his voice betrayed the shock and fear that he had endured. A hand went up to rub away the betraying tears as he continued the story. "I thought we were being followed for some time, but every time I looked round, there was nothing to be seen. Then they raced up to us, firing their guns—not *at* us but *over* us, and telling us we had to go with them. Otherwise, they would kill us. They were big men and seemed eager to capture us. I heard one tell the other to make sure we didn't get hurt. That we would be no good to them if we were injured," Ben said.

Whilst Ben was talking, Amy had an arm round Chan and was helping the boy sit up as his head cleared. "What happened? Those men they shot at us. My horse reared up, and I fell," Chan murmured.

"Don't talk. You banged your head when you fell. Do you think you can stand up, Chan?" Amy said, and both she and Josh helped the boy stand. The horses were still standing there, both well trained by the boys. "I think you two should ride on the buggy back to the ranch. Josh and I will ride your horses."

The lights spilling out of the windows and door of the Broken Horseshoe Ranch showed the occupants had been alerted to the sound of the gunfire. The glint of the moonlight on guns could be seen as they approached.

Josh called out as he drew nearer to the cabin: "Josh and Amy here! Ben and Chan are coming along behind us with the buggy. They were ambushed but are fine." With relief, Josh saw the guns being lowered and placed back in holsters or pockets. The inhabitants of Broken

Horseshoe had turned out in force at the sound of the gunshots and were ready for any marauders.

There was an immediate hubbub as the two boys drove up in the buggy.

"Inside, Ben—take Chan in with you. Amy, help them inside whilst Ezra and I see to the horses!" Josh shouted at Amy, the wind hurling his words away. He saw her nod, as she understood what he was asking to do. Grabbing an arm of each boy, Amy pulled them towards the open door of the cabin.

Nancy was holding it against the force of the wind as she helped both boys inside. It was Nancy who took charge, ushering both boys into chairs, checking them over for wounds and all the time issuing orders to everyone.

CHAPTER EIGHTEEN

The storm broke after they reached the safety of Broken Horseshoe Ranch. Thunder rolled around them, reverberating as if amplified by Devil's Mountain close by. The lightning revealed Josh and Ezra's worried expressions as they hurriedly took the horses to the barn amidst a torrential downpour, with raindrops feeling like sharp lances on their faces and limbs. In minutes, the ground was awash, and they were struggling against the wind that threatened to blow them over with its extreme force.

"Where has this storm come from? There was no sign of a storm earlier." Ezra came into the cabin, stamping his feet, fresh from the barn after removing the saddles from the horses and bedding them down for the night. "Nuisance! It's happened again. Each time we have a chance to track these men to their hideout, it rains. Seems like the devil himself is looking after them," the old man said.

The warmth of the stove was welcome, but the overpowering smell of wet woollen trousers and jackets drying in its heat was almost suffocating in the confined space. The attack was discussed again and again, both boys being thankful that they had been rescued by Josh and Amy's late arrival.

"That rifle shot of yours, and the shouts from you, Josh, made both men turn and run away. They didn't want to take on anybody else. I think they thought we were easy enough to capture on our own, but not with others arriving," Ben said, as he looked gratefully at his sister and Josh. The ambush, the purpose for it, and the men who had attacked Ben and Chan had been discussed in minute detail.

"Josh has some news from his trip to Duloe," Amy began, her gaze intent on Josh. Because of this, she missed the look that passed between Luke and Nancy, which was followed by Nancy's shake of the head.

Josh couldn't have asked for a better audience. There was silence when he told of his journey and arrival at Duloe town. They listened with rapt attention as he explained how he had to climb out of the bedroom window, sleep on a prickly, smelly hay mattress for the night in the livery stable. No one laughed. Amy, keeping a close watch, saw a few lips quiver—but their attention was unwavering as Josh continued with his story.

"Here is the letter. It mentions a man called Harry Martin. It means that Charles doesn't know about his arrival, so perhaps we can get to the killer first. I don't know what I'll do, though. We cornered one assassin, and he fled when we threatened him with the sheriff."

Luke stared at the letter, which he was holding in his frail blue-veined hand: "I agree with you, Josh. This is no ordinary paper. Whoever wrote this letter has money to spend on excellent stationery. The writing is confident and sprawls across the page arrogantly. It's a puzzling situation, Josh, but I think you're doing the right thing." The older man smiled at Josh, whom he had come to know, and cared for deeply. "Now, at least you have the benefit of knowing who the next assassin is when he arrives. That gives you a breathing space, Josh. Once you get rid of him, your stalker will still wait for news. It will take time for him to contact Charles and ask what has happened, and then Charles has to reply to him. No, Josh—this gives you some time, during which you can investigate Charles and his business dealings even more."

"What d'you mean, Pa?" Amy asked, looking at her father, puzzled at his last remark.

"I think Charles Roberts is not a very honourable man," Luke began. He paused to let the snorts of laughter and mutters of agreement from the others in the cabin die down. "If you can look into his business dealings, I think you may find hidden illegal practices. These could well be used against the man by the sheriff."

Nancy slapped her hand down on the table. Everyone jumped. "That's good! Luke, that is a good idea. Both of you working in the general store should be able to find out more about him and his business. Luke's right, that may be the way to get rid of the arrogant Charles Roberts. And Josh, without him in Nowhere your stalker would lose his chief ally."

"Luke, thank you for thinking of this. Amy and I will get onto it right away," Josh said, and he looked at Luke with hope in his voice and a new determination on his face.

CHAPTER NINETEEN

"Flora has been staying with us for a short time now," Nancy said, and smiled at the girl who was sitting on the floor and leaning against the older woman's knees. In her hand she held some material, which she was sewing with minute stitches, and when Nancy spoke of her, Flora put the sewing down in her lap and looked up at the older woman with a shy smile.

The work-roughened hand of Nancy stroked the dark hair of the Indian girl seated at her knee and smiled down at her. "Luke and I have been talking. But we feel that this is a decision that has to be made with all of you present, and we wished to know your views on it. Flora has settled in well with us. We hope to find her family, but we may not—and this is something Flora, despite her young age, understands."

Amy glanced over at Josh. He raised an eyebrow at her, wondering what was coming and if she knew about it. A shake of Amy's head told Josh that she was completely unaware of this recent development at the ranch.

Luke had placed the letter from Duke down on the table, smoothed it, then folded it up, and placed it back in the envelope. He began to speak: "Flora enjoys living here—she likes the company of Ben and Chan, and sharing a room with Amy." Here Luke smiled at his daughter wryly, wondering how Amy felt about the newcomer settling into her tiny bedroom. Amy said nothing, but waited. Her father continued speaking.

"Flora is worried about her future. She has been asking us what will happen to her if her family doesn't come back." Luke continued and gave the young girl a smile. "Nancy and I feel Flora fits in so well with our family here that we would like her to stay with us. If her family is found, and they are willing, we will be glad to have them move onto the ranch. How does everybody else feel about that?"

Luke's sharp eyes glanced round the room, and all he could see were smiles of agreement. "Now, if anybody doesn't want Flora to stay with us, now is your chance to get rid of her," he said with a chuckle, and a smile at the young girl.

Flora looked horrified at this and stared at each person in turn, waiting for that one person to refuse her presence in the ranch family. There was laughter at this expression on her face, and Amy held her arms out wide: "Of course we want you to stay, Flora. We love having you here." The little girl jumped to her feet and flung herself into Amy's arms.

"I'm helping Nancy with the sewing. And I help look after the baby, and I can do anything else you want me to. Can I really stay here? For ever and ever?" Flora clung to Amy, but then she lifted her head and looked over Amy's shoulder. Her wide eyes again looked from person to person, so desperate to be assured that she was welcome.

"Of course we want you to stay. No one else can keep up with that wretched baby now he's crawling. If you continue to look after him, I'm delighted you're staying, Flora," said Tom. Knowing that Tom produced the most wonderful food, baby David—who had an amazing appetite for such a young child—was constantly getting under Tom's feet hoping for tidbits from him. Only Flora kept David out of mischief when Amy was absent.

The night passed with the storm still raging outside. A tremendous gust of wind seemed to shake the ranch house to its foundations, and then all was still. To those who were still lying awake, it seemed that the storm had blown itself out, and only the gentle patter of rain could be heard as the thunder and lightning moved away across the desert.

Next morning, they were all awakened by brilliant sunshine. The heaviness of yesterday, and the storm itself, seemed but a distant memory. Amy, woken early by David, had wandered out onto the porch, the baby in her arms, sleepy after his breakfast.

Flora joined her, her tiny hand creeping into Amy's free one. "I like it when you're back at the ranch. Do you have to go into Nowhere to the general store?" Flora asked Amy. "Everything is better when you are here."

Amy was startled that the child expressed her own thoughts. She was finding it more difficult by the day to leave the ranch. Amy could see that Luke and Nancy were struggling to cope with the young David and the demands of the ranch itself. Her father's health had improved and the Indian medicine he was using had halted the disease that was bad for his lungs. But she could see that it was only temporary. The coughing was so much better, but she could see his body becoming frailer each day. Amy felt that the general store no longer needed her as much as the people on the ranch did. Now Flora had put it into words. The young girl also needed her, as did her father.

"For the moment, I do, Flora, but perhaps I can stay at home more often now that I do the account books for the businesses in town," Amy said and patted the girl's head as she did so, giving her a warm smile.

"That would be good. Everyone wants you here now at the ranch," Flora told her, before skipping back into the cabin.

Ben and Ezra had gone to see to the horses first thing. They were also checking around with Josh to see what damage the storm had wrought on the ranch. Amy watched as they inspected the outside of the cabin, the barn, and the vegetable garden. She called out to them.

"Is everything all right? Has there been much damage?"

CHAPTER TWENTY

It was Josh who turned round to her and replied in answer to her question: "No, surprisingly enough, the only damage is in the vegetable garden. Most of the plants have been flattened, but their stems aren't broken badly, so they may survive."

It was Ben who shouted, alerting them to the aftermath of the storm behind the cabin. "Look! Over there, beside the spring. The old tree has been hit by lightning, and the whole of its trunk is split in two," called Ben. He, Josh, and Chan raced towards it. Their progress was hindered by the many puddles they had to avoid, or else splash through, to reach it.

Broken Horseshoe Ranch was fortunate in that part of its land abutted a tributary of the Avon river. There were also a couple of springs. One only appeared after heavy rains, but the other was constant, even if it dwindled to a trickle during dry spells.

Even from the porch, Amy could see the gnarled old tree now split, one half uprooted and lying on its side. The spring that was at its foot could be seen bubbling into a sizeable stream. It was a strange, unusually shaped mound of rock that rose from the surrounding flat land. The spring was at the bottom of it, and shrubs and trees had grown up around it. Ezra told them that the first settler to the area had found the spring when he was near death and completely out of water. As his hands scooped up the water to drink, they caught on a broken horseshoe, and that's what he called his ranch after.

David was now sleepy, and Amy placed him in the large wooden drawer, which he was now rapidly growing out of. Flora had already rushed to join those gathered around the spring, and Amy and her father walked up to join them.

They were all looking at the fallen tree and the bubbling spring. Chan planned new irrigation channels to his vegetable garden, from its flowing bounty. Josh and Ezra, however, were looking at the tree and wondering whether to chop it down.

But it was Luke who wandered over to the foot of the rock formation. The tree's roots had spread far and wide, and when it had been struck by lightning it had been uprooted and the ground disturbed. A hollow at the bottom of the rock's formation could be seen, and Luke stooped to look at it.

Amy heard her father's indrawn breath and turned to see him on his knees, scrabbling with both his hands at the dirt. She ran over to join him and dropped to her knees beside him. "What is it, Pa? What have you found?"

Luke, his hands grimy from the dirt, scrabbled around a bit more before one hand emerged from the dirt. He held it up so that he could see the object more closely, and Amy, who had joined him, looked over his shoulder.

"It's a gold piece! And here's a piece of leather—and look Amy, wrapped inside the leather I found a tarnished silver crucifix as well." The smile that spread across Luke's face at the satisfaction of his significant find made Amy hug her father.

"You did it, Pa! You were right. There *is* Jesuit gold on Broken Horseshoe Ranch itself. Maybe the broken horseshoe that the first settler found was from one of the Jesuit horses," Amy said, and took the silver crucifix from its wrapping of leather. Though blackened with tarnish, Amy recognised it as silver.

"Gold is always the same when you find it. No matter how long it has been buried, no matter if it's newly mined, it's always a bright shiny gold," Luke said. "But this is just as good. To think that the last person who touched this crucifix was probably a Jesuit. I wonder where he was riding to? Perhaps he was from one of the few mission buildings further down toward Mexico. I know they explored all this region. He dropped it, or maybe he hid it away here. Whatever happened, I am now holding it." Luke's hand, gnarled and frail, held the crucifix reverently, and his eyes watered slightly as he gazed down at it.

By this time, the others had gathered round and were all searching frantically in the dirt.

Luke held out a hand to stop them: "No! Not like that. We must take care and search properly. The ground is unstable here and remember those booby traps. Just because it's on our doorstep, doesn't mean it's any the less dangerous. Josh and Ezra, take charge of this. I'm suddenly exhausted and must go back to the ranch." Luke tried to rise, but his knees refused to hold him. Josh stepped forward and gave the old man his arm and steadied him up onto his feet.

"Come on, Pa, let's get back to the ranch. Wait till Nancy sees this. She and Tom have been busy whilst we've been finding treasure. And I must go back to help with David." Amy coaxed her father back to the ranch, and helped the trembling old man as he clutched the treasure in his hand, a broad smile of satisfaction on his face.

CHAPTER TWENTY-ONE

Next morning Broken Horseshoe Ranch was a hive of activity. Usually, Ezra would come from the small cabin that he shared with Leah at the back of the ranch house to join Ben in the stable. They always got the buggy and horse ready for Josh and Amy to travel into Nowhere. Both Nancy and Luke were usually late sleepers. Tom, sorting out the provisions for the day, would be joined in the kitchen by Amy, Flora, and baby David. By the time David had been fed and changed by Amy, Nancy would have risen to take over the daily babysitting duties. Not today. Everything was different this morning.

"You're up early, Pa. And you, Nancy—I'm surprised to see you up and dressed at this hour," said Amy, looking up in surprise from the bowl that she was spoon-feeding David from.

Luke, her father, walked over to the table and, pulling a chair out, sat down on it. He smiled at her, his face eager with anticipation: "I want to get plans in place for organising the dig at the spring. Must be done properly and carefully. We need to get the dirt out of the hollow, but must make certain that there are no booby traps." Luke began eating his breakfast absent-mindedly. He thanked Tom, who had placed it in front of him, all the while fingering the few artefacts they had discovered the day before. His enthusiasm for his new discovery had made it impossible for him to sleep late that morning. Last evening had been spent comparing these discoveries found on the ranch with those Amy and Josh had found on their travels.

Josh had joined the others and stood beside Tom at the stove, plate in hand, eating the fresh corn bread and crispy bacon. Tom grinned as he passed Josh a large mug of piping hot coffee. Josh nodded his thanks, and took an appreciative sip despite the scalding liquid almost burning his tongue. He turned to the others and spoke: "The first thing I'll do when we get to Nowhere is to speak to Sheriff Grey. He needs to be told about this latest attack on the boys. I'm worried that these bandits are getting closer to properties now. The villains seem to get bolder each time they attack," Josh said, as he stood drinking his coffee. "You must all take care and be seen together. Carry your guns with you at all times. They must've been watching the ranch for some time, and knew when to swoop down to capture the boys."

Tom stood at the stove. He had grown in the last few months since his arrival at Broken Horseshoe Ranch. The thin, emaciated Chinese boy had filled out and grown both in stature and confidence. Taking control of the kitchen, and proving most successful at it, had given him a place in which he felt confident and happy. He folded his arms and turned to face the group sitting or standing around the cabin. "I've made sure that today's meals will be simple. I'm going to come out with the rifle and help stand guard. There's no way I'm going to have my young brother and Ben attacked again. I'll be ready for them if they dare to come back a second time."

Josh nodded his head at this remark from Tom. He drank his cup of coffee and agreed to a second cup from Tom. "Good idea, Tom—the more of you they see standing about fully armed should deter them."

Ezra, who had also come in to join the group and enjoy a cup of coffee with them, spoke up: "My wife, Leah, is also coming to stand guard when we work on the spring diggings. That's what she says, but I think she's as keen as anyone to see what we find today," Ezra said, looking down at the exciting finds from yesterday.

The buggy was halfway to Nowhere before Amy gave a chuckle: "They are all going to be standing around with rifles, all ready to ward off any intruders."

Josh gave a guffaw at this. "Rubbish, Amy! They are standing around hoping to find more gold. The guarding of the boys is their excuse. Not one of them wants to miss out on the latest discovery at the spring." Josh glanced across at his companion. She had been quiet on the way out from the ranch. He himself had been lost in thought. Luke's discovery had been exciting, but the ever-present fear of his stalker preyed on Josh's mind. To frighten the man Harry Martin away was the obvious thing to do, and he appreciated the advice they'd all given him. But how he was to do it before the man drew his gun and killed him was a complete puzzle to Josh.

CHAPTER TWENTY-TWO

The silence lengthened between them, both absorbed in their thoughts. Then Amy blurted out her worries: "Sheriff Grey really has to do something now. He can't just sit back and have everyone frightened, wondering where those bandits will come next. What are they doing with the boys they capture? What do they need them for?" Amy's hands clenched, revealing white knuckles in the morning sunlight.

The fears she had felt at the sound of Ben's voice when he was being attacked seemed to sweep over her again. He was so precious to her. Both of them together had coped with the illness of their father. Neither she nor Ben could envisage a life without each other. Both of them realised the severity of their father's illness. Losing their mother had left a huge gap that still had not been filled, and Amy was sensible enough to realise that it never would be. Her father, Luke, had been flirting with death for many months, and his ever-declining health made her aware of his mortality as nothing else could have done. Her brother had been a bright spark in an increasingly tough world. The thought of losing Ben had become too overwhelming to face last night.

Now, on this journey to Nowhere, she wondered if she could ever think about losing her brother—but knew she could not, and again that thought was shelved. Amy felt this was the time that she must act to keep her brother safe with his friend Chan. If Luke didn't galvanise Sheriff Grey into action, she, Amy Tanner, certainly would!

Josh jumped off the buggy as Amy drove it into the main street of Nowhere: "I'll go straight away to Sheriff Grey," he said. Amy watched his tall figure as he strode up Main Street. The physical work he did on the ranch and at the general store had given Josh a more muscular physique than when she had found him unconscious in the desert. His shoulders had broadened, and his stride, with the constant activity, was much more purposeful. His gun hung in its holster, always easy to reach—if necessary—in an instant. She smiled as he raised his hat to the two old ladies who had recently arrived with their brother to Nowhere. They had lost their money and property when their brother had plunged into speculative investments. On reading one of Charles Roberts's exciting and so-called lucrative land deals, they had been persuaded by their brother to make the exhausting journey out to Nowhere.

Amy relied on Josh. She didn't want to. Amy felt it was dangerous for her, her family, and Broken Horseshoe Ranch to depend on the young man. Her feelings for him had to be ignored. There was no way she could rely utterly on him. He didn't know where he'd come from; he didn't know what he'd done in the past. For all anyone knew, Josh could be married and have a wife and children wondering where he was and what had happened to him. How could she give her heart to a man who didn't know who he was, or even what sort of man he was? The Josh that she knew now was a kind, caring, dependable man. He was a man that any woman would be proud to know and love. And Amy knew, deep down within her heart, that she loved Josh—but there was always that barrier. Never knowing about his past life drove a wedge between them.

Bella settled into the stable. Amy picked up the fresh vegetables Chan had cut that morning for Eliza, and she ran up the steps into the general store.

The storm had hit Nowhere that night just as badly as it had out at the ranch. Main Street was awash with puddles, and in some areas the mud stretched from boardwalk to boardwalk, making it impassable for those with clean footwear.

"Did you have any damage here?" Amy asked as she entered the store through the back door, taking off her coat and gloves.

"No, thankfully, only the stable yard got flooded, as you no doubt saw when you arrived," Eliza said, rushing up to kiss her friend good morning. "What about you out there at the ranch? I was worried, because the storm clouds seemed far worse over toward the mountains."

Amy put the basket down on the counter for Eliza to look through. "No, just like you, we had puddles like floods, but nothing was damaged. We picked the best of the vegetables that were untouched, but some of them got blown over and are a little bruised." She looked up as Clara walked through from the hardware area. "Hello, Clara, how are you today?" Amy said.

In fact, Amy felt there was no need to ask the other woman how she felt. It was obvious from just one quick look at her. That timid lady who had arrived with her husband, the preacher Jeremiah, had vanished, to be replaced by a more cheerful, alert woman who returned Amy's comment with a beaming smile.

"Amy, how good it is to see you! I feel I have much to thank you for, you and Josh. Life is so much easier for me now. Manuel and Eliza have asked me to take over Dora's place in the store." She had come up close to Amy, and now she leant forward and gave her an awkward hug. "I shall enjoy working with Manuel and Eliza, and, of course, you. Remember, Amy, if ever I can help you as you helped me, don't hesitate." The words tumbled out of the woman's mouth, heartfelt and sincere. Amy, who was not a hugger by nature, could only return the woman's embrace with a gentle squeeze and a smile.

"Where's Josh?" Manuel had entered the store from the hardware area carrying a couple of boxes piled high, one on top of the other. "I need him to help me out with this heavy lot," he said.

"Josh came in with me. Don't worry, Manuel, he'll be here to help you soon. He had to go up to see Sheriff Grey."

CHAPTER TWENTY-THREE

At their questioning looks, Amy told them about the attack on Ben and Chan. Shaking his head, his long, straggly grey locks moving in an agitated manner as he did so, Manuel said in an exasperated voice: "Something has *got* to be done. Life in Nowhere will not be calm and settled until these bandits have been discovered and shot. I hear those homesteaders, the new ones on Charles's land, are frightened to death and walk around everywhere with their guns. Especially the couple of families that have young boys. They're truly frightened. Sheriff Grey has to do something about it. We can't go on living like this. I've even heard that there are a couple of gangs hiding out in the mountains. They rob banks, and even trains, and then come and hide up in Devil's Mountain, knowing that it is impossible to find them."

The door of the general store had opened whilst Manuel was walking up and down on the floorboards, waving his arms around in exasperation.

Josh walked in and heard the last of Manuel's agitated speech. He was in full agreement with him and began telling them about his meeting with Sheriff Grey.

"The sheriff *is* doing something. Tomorrow, he wants everyone to search for these guys. There have been many sightings up at the old crossroads, where the trails lead up to the mountains and over the hills to Duloe and further south into the Mexican villages. He wants me to ask Ezra to come out with us tomorrow, Amy. There's another old boy who thinks he can track a bit as well. Let's hope we can pick something up, but it's doubtful after the storm."

There was silence as everybody thought about what Sheriff Grey had said. Amy murmured, "He has to do something. He can't just sit back and wait for the next attack. Maybe if they see the posse, and that the sheriff is out looking for them, they'll move on."

The wagon from Duloe was only a twice-weekly occurrence, and an event much anticipated and celebrated with noisy excitement. The livery stable was at the top of the township on Main Street, and the forge faced outward towards the road from Duloe town. So, it was Reuben the blacksmith who always saw all the vehicles that came into Nowhere, and the carriages and horse riders that proceeded outwards. He was, like others, eager to welcome the new occupants of the wagon. The interest aroused by every new passenger and every unusual package that was delivered from the wagon made the day of the inhabitants of Nowhere. To announce the incoming wagon, Reuben made a loud noise on the metal triangle he had hung at the entrance of the livery stable forge.

The loud clanging noise alerted those in the general store as usual, but this time Amy, and Josh rushed to the door and raced out onto Main Street. Amy was conscious of not having her coat, but—despite the rainy weather— she had felt it necessary to see who had arrived on the wagon. Josh, who had been out on the delivery run with Manuel, had just returned. He was first through the general store doorway, and looked up Main Street to where the blacksmith was standing at the entrance of the forge door, his brawny arms with the bulging biceps hanging motionless at his side, a heavy hammer in one hand as he stared up the hillside at the incoming wagon.

"Expecting someone, Josh?" Reuben asked the young man who had joined him, then he turned to look behind Josh at the sight of Amy, who was now running to join them.

"I … er … it was …" Josh stammered, floundering for a reply to the blacksmith. Not eager to give away the fact he was looking for a man arriving to kill him, he was at a loss for words.

It was with a great relief he heard Amy clear her throat. She began talking: "It's a parcel, Reuben. My father is expecting a parcel and, as it's fragile, we both wanted to make sure it had arrived safely." Amy glanced at Josh and smiled at his grateful nod at her quick reply.

They both waited anxiously; the wagon seemed to take forever, coming down that last incline into Nowhere. Josh, who remembered the being on that self-same wagon the other day, now realised the skill that Slim possessed—and was using to the utmost—to stop the wagon running away by itself at breakneck speed down the steep incline.

"Finally! It took forever to reach here," muttered Josh.

Amy cast him a sympathetic look. The wagon *had* seemed to take a long time coming down the hill, but then, as it drew to a halt in the livery stable yard, Amy stood up on her tiptoes to see into the wagon itself. Reuben put forward a large box, his gesture to the passengers who wished to descend.

"If only we knew what he looked like," muttered Josh, beside Amy.

"At least we know his name. We can always ask Dora, or sneak a look at her guest book to see if he has arrived," said Amy.

"If we find out who he is, what do we do then?" Josh was puzzled over this fresh problem he had to face.

CHAPTER TWENTY-FOUR

A tall woman, encased in a large, voluminous duster coat to protect her clothes from the wind-blown dust and sand that had stirred up around her on the journey, climbed down from the wagon.

Reuben stepped forward and held a hand out to guide the woman down the box and onto the ground. "Here you go, ma'am. Step down on that there box. Welcome to Nowhere, ma'am."

The tall lady carried a capacious bag, bulging at the seams. Several parcels hung from her fingers. They were lumpy and misshapen and tied up in a variety of string-like baskets. She stepped onto the box and gratefully received Reuben's hand, and then down onto the dust and dirt of the livery stable. She looked down Main Street and her eyes widened. "Is this it? Is this Nowhere? I thought it was going to be a town," she said to the burly blacksmith standing beside her.

"Yes, ma'am, this is Nowhere. Sure is a pretty little place, isn't it?" Reuben replied, smiling down at her, his pride in his small township obvious. The woman gave the view she had of Nowhere a mighty sniff of disapproval, and then said to him: "Where's the hotel?"

"Down there, ma'am, where you see the sign swinging in the breeze. The finest hotel in Nowhere, ma'am. Have you booked a room?" Reuben asked her and then took her bag. "I'll bring this for you, ma'am. What name shall I tell them in the hotel?"

The woman was flustered and began dropping her belongings. Both Amy and Josh went to her aid. Her many parcels had fallen onto the dusty ground and they began helping pick them up. Reuben, by this time, had her large box and carpet bag and was helping her walk along towards the sidewalk in front of the hotel.

Glancing into the wagon, Amy saw only another woman seated there. There was no man. Her heart sank as she realised Harry Martin could not be coming to Nowhere today.

The young woman was smiling and shaking her head at the other woman, whose exit from the wagon had caused such a fuss. As she saw Amy looking in at her, she rose to her feet and walked towards Amy, ready to get off the wagon. One hand lifted her skirt, and the other carried a small reticule and a larger carpet bag.

"Can I help you?" Amy asked, reaching her one hand that was free of the tall lady's packages up to take the carpet bag from the young woman. "I have one hand free," she said, smiling at her.

"Yes, please, take my carpet bag. It's not too heavy, and I can climb out myself. That lady seems to monopolise everything and everybody around her—and thank you," she said as she jumped down onto the dust. She grimaced as a dust cloud arose around her pretty boots, but then stuck a hand out towards Amy. "Let me take the bag now, and thank you." Amy, after relinquishing the bag to her, shook the other's hand, noting the soft leather gloves that encased the delicate hand and fingers.

"I'm Lily, Lily Truelove. I've come to Nowhere to look up my brother." She added: "No doubt I'll be going to stay in the same hotel as that woman. The journey was made so much longer than it needed to be with her constant complaints and fussing."

"I'm Amy, Amy Tanner. Come on, let's get you to the hotel and you can freshen up after that journey," Amy said, smiling at the other young woman. Amy enjoyed living out West. She had embraced the lifestyle with alacrity, loving the freedom to dress as she pleased. Her small men's boots were sturdy and strong, her heavy-duty cotton skirts swung from side to side, their unusually short length weighed down by the shot she had placed inside the hem. This stopped them blowing about in the heavy winds that swept across the desert lands. It also helped disguise the pockets in the skirt, which always contained her knife, in its homemade fabric sheath, and her Colt pistol. Her suede jacket—or sometimes a leather one with fringes—had capacious pockets as well, and softened with the continual wear, often enabling her to push up the sleeves when it grew warm. Her only concession to femininity was in the many-coloured bandanas she wore, sometimes matching her hat, of which she again she had a few, including a favourite red one.

"Is it always so hot here?" Lily asked her as they trudged through the dust down Main Street from the livery stables towards a hotel.

"Sometimes it gets hotter I'm afraid," Amy said. "But you get used to it. Coming from the east myself, it took a while."

Amy was puzzled by this young woman, but her thoughts were still on the missing Harry Martin. Where was he? Why hadn't he arrived today, as he'd said he would in his letter?

CHAPTER TWENTY-FIVE

Walking alongside Lily, Amy cast a sidelong glance at her, taking in the outfit the other woman wore. Her costume was of a serviceable wine-coloured wool, very suitable for travelling. The boots she wore were a functional black, as were her gloves and the pretty reticule that hung from her wrist. Lily's clothes were cut and styled in a fashion that Amy had never seen before, but she knew instinctively that they were of the highest and most expensive quality and style. They were, however, well worn, and Amy could see the small patches and minuscule darns. The tiny leather buttons up the side of the boots were echoed in the long cuffs of the gloves she wore. The skirt swung as it reached down to her ankles, the cut of it emphasising her neat waist and hips. Amy was certain that Lily wore a corset—something that she herself had thrown away gladly on her arrival at Broken Horseshoe Ranch. No woman had a posture or silhouette such as Lily had if she hadn't been wearing a corset.

"You booked a room at the hotel in advance?" Amy asked as they walked along the sidewalk towards the entrance of the hotel. "There are only a few rooms there suitable for a lady."

"Yes, I sent them a letter saying that I'd be here for an indefinite time. I'll have to see if I like it in Nowhere. I've also got to find out whether or not my brother will welcome my visit." Lily said this with a look at Amy, and gave a snort of laughter at Amy's puzzlement. "Let's just say my brother and I have had our differences in the past. I'm uncertain of how he will react to my visit."

"Your brother is …?" Amy didn't want to pry, but she

was eaten up with curiosity. She was busy thinking over all the men in Nowhere who could have this elegant creature as their sister. There was no one she could think of. Who could it be?

Almost as if she could hear Amy's thoughts, Lily touched her arm and whispered in her ear: "Sorry, Amy, I'm not going to tell you who he is. He may well disown me, and I may embarrass him by my arrival. So please, Amy, I shouldn't really have told you I'm coming to see my brother. Can you keep my secret?" Lily took Amy's hand and pressed it gently. Amy had turned to face the young woman and now stared into her face full on, as if seeing it for the first time. The bonnet matching her outfit had a turned-back brim with a delicate lace trim in the same wine colour. The brown curls cascaded down in ringlets, framing a plain homely face. And those bright brown eyes sparkled with amusement as they looked at Amy's puzzlement.

"Yes, of course I can keep a secret. But is it necessary? Surely your brother will be delighted to see you," Amy said, returning the squeeze of her fingers.

"I doubt it. But we never know, with men, do we? I see my travelling companion is about to book in. I shall go up and join her." She walked towards the desk at reception. Despite her femininity, Amy noticed she had a loose stride, and walked with a confidence that was unusual in a woman with her looks and obvious class.

Reuben and Josh were both standing at the hotel's reception desk, the parcels and boxes at their feet. Dora came bustling out of the back room to greet her new guests with smiles of welcome.

"Welcome to Nowhere. I hope your stay will be comfortable and that you will enjoy your visit here. Your rooms are ready, and if there's anything else you need, please let me know."

Dora pushed the large reception book, in which all the guests had to write their names— or at least their mark with a cross, whilst Dora wrote out their names. Dora said to the tall lady, "Your name, please," and handed her a pen.

The lady took the pen from Dora, dipped it again in the ink, preparatory to signing her name. She wrote it with a large flourish.

Amy stepped forward to relieve Reuben of the parcels he was holding. "I'll take these, Reuben. You get back to the forge. Slim will be waiting for you to with the horses." The huge man gladly surrendered the finicky parcels and fled the hotel. Clad in his everyday clothes, with the leather waistcoat and apron he always wore, he seemed out of place—and felt it in the hotel lobby.

Amy looked round at the hotel with pleasure. No longer dusty and unkempt, the wood panelling and the marble floor—newly installed by Dora—gleamed and sparkled with care and attention. New drapes had been placed at the window and door fronting Main Street, and gave an air of gentility previously lacking from the makeshift building. Through an open door, Amy caught a glimpse of the piano, brought on the previous wagon trip with Josh under such difficulties. Now it stood proudly in a room that was acquiring the genteel fabrics and furniture that Dora was so insistent on bringing to Nowhere.

"I'll take your box and bag, and Amy will bring your parcels," Josh said to the woman, who was turning away from the reception desk, having signed the guest book. Dora stepped out from behind the desk, the swish of the black fabric on her skirts rustling as they went across the tiled floor. Always dressed in black, her gowns were made of the finest materials and never looked drab or dusty, as black garments often do. "If you follow me, please. Your room is up the stairs. This way, Mrs Martin."

"Don't call me Mrs Martin, please dear. Harry I am, to one and all. Never took to being called Harriet—the same for Mrs Martin. Harry I was as a girl, and Harry I'll be for the whole of my life." She stomped up the stairs after Dora. Newly constructed, the second floor of the hotel was soundly built, but still shuddered a little under the footsteps of Harry Martin.

CHAPTER TWENTY-SIX

Following on behind the two women, Josh was carrying the heavy box and the carpet bag. He stopped behind them both on the stairs in order to speak to Amy. Josh lowered his voice, the surprise clear on his face as he stooped to speak to her on the lower stair.

"Harry Martin! *She's* Harry Martin?" Josh whispered to Amy. It wasn't a statement, but a surprised question. "What do I do now? I can't threaten a woman, can I? What do you think I should do?" The 'Code of the West' meant no gentleman would attack or ill-treat a woman. Josh found that this fresh development of Harry Martin being a woman had overturned all his plans. No longer could he carry out his ideas of how to deal with Harry Martin when he arrived in Nowhere. They had been suitable for a man—but now they were useless.

Amy didn't answer Josh. Whilst Dora walked on in front of them, oblivious to Josh's whispers, Harry Martin, at one step ahead, paused and threw a suspicious glance back at both of them. We have to be careful of this woman, thought Amy. She's no fool, despite all the fuss and bustle she creates. What a superb disguise for a killer. After all, who would suspect this matronly, fussy woman to be an assassin?

Nothing more was said between them. Amy hadn't dared answer Josh's whispered remarks. But she was thinking about his questions. The door opened to the room that Harry Martin would occupy for her stay. Again, Amy was impressed. The bare room had the minimum that was needed, but it was clean and fresh-looking. The linen looked fresh, and the floor was swept.

"Thank you all. I don't know what I'd have done

without you. Silly me getting in such a muddle—but as I travel about, I need all my little comforts. Thank you." Harry Martin smiled at Josh and Amy as she told them where to place the large box, the carpet bag, and the many stringy parcels that Amy had been carrying. Dora stayed behind to explain the rules of the hotel.

Josh and Amy smiled at Harry, and immediately ran down the stairs and raced out of the hotel, back to the general store.

"When you whispered to me, that woman was suspicious. I didn't like the way she looked at us and tried to listen to what you said," said Amy.

The concern in Amy's voice made Josh stand still in the middle of the boardwalk and stare at her. "You don't think she heard me, do you?"

"No, I don't think she heard you. *I* found it difficult to hear you, and you had turned away from her." Amy, by this time, had also stopped and looked at Josh, a frown knitting her brow. "But what worries me, Josh, is that she is not the silly woman she appears to be. Those eyes of hers are shrewd and calculating, and that smile of hers when we left her made my flesh cringe. I think she's very dangerous, and Josh, just like you, I don't know what to do about her either." In silence, they both walked on towards the general store. They both had plenty to think about.

On reaching the boardwalk in front of the general store, Josh took Amy's arm. "There *must* be something we can do. We've got this information, and we can act on it. Let's think about it, and if necessary, I will threaten her—just like we were going to do with the *man* Harry Martin."

Amy opened the door of the general store. Whilst her

hand was on the doorknob, she turned to look at Josh. "We'd better be armed and ready for trouble. That woman who calls herself Harry Martin won't take kindly to being told to leave town without earning her reward."

CHAPTER TWENTY-SEVEN

The dusty horses standing outside the general store looked as if they had been ridden far.

"Looking at the equipment on that horse, I reckon those belong to miners. It's good to

see Manuel's venture into selling mining equipment is paying off," said Josh as they entered the store.

There were two men standing at the counter, supervising the groceries and equipment that was being piled up around them. They both wore faded canvas trousers, their shirts were patched, and their boots were scarred and pitted with the heavy rough ground they had been working on. Around their waists there wore heavy leather belts, normally used for holding mining implements but now holding knives and guns. Both men turned towards the door as Amy and Josh entered. One man, older than the other, had grey hair, which was matched by his moustache that hung over the mean-looking mouth. His eyes narrowed in a quick survey of them both. Obviously, he was judging whether they would be a danger to him and his friend. The younger man was swarthy, with sleek black hair and dark eyes that lingered on Amy's figure.

A young boy was with them. Floppy blond hair hung over the thin face and worried blue eyes. His clothes were also faded and patched, and the boots he wore seemed too big for his slim feet and his narrow ankles. Josh noticed his hands were calloused and bruised. He was helping the men with the packages they were buying and getting them ready to load on the horses. To Josh's eyes, the boy looked frightened and nervous, and his hands shook as he carried out the instructions from the men.

Amy walked to the back of the store and sat down at the small table she used to do accounts on. Josh noticed her eyes were on the men, and she cast him a speaking look before sitting down.

So, Amy thinks they look suspicious, thought Josh. His eyes took in again the frightened face of the young boy, and the way the two men stood alert and ready for trouble. They were big men. Josh reckoned they would be vicious fighters, used to brawling all their lives and handy with their fists. He made his way over to the vegetable section of the store and began moving the fruit and potatoes around. There was no need for him to do anything to them, but it made it look as if he was busy and occupied, and so would not come under the gaze of these two men. His glance, on entering the store, had rested briefly on both Eliza and Manuel as they sought to supply the goods the men wanted. Eliza had looked frightened, her face pale, whereas Manuel hadn't looked at him, almost as if he didn't dare to—and he also looked worried.

Josh then moved some lemons about. They were very popular for many cooking and drinking recipes that the locals in Nowhere used frequently. He glanced over his shoulder towards Amy and saw that she was seated still at the table but well back from it. Josh saw her pistol was on her lap, and the sheath with the knife was placed on the table, hidden by a book.

Without making direct eye contact with him, she gave him a nod, and he realised she was watching him out of the corner of her eye.

They all agreed afterwards that it had been Eliza that had been the catalyst for the volcanic action that had erupted in the store that day.

"I was only being kind. That boy looked frightened. I just thought …" Eliza had said, throwing her hands up in the air when they discussed it afterwards.

About ten years old, thin, with several bruises and gashes on his limbs, he had been wiry enough and strong enough to help the men carry some of the stuff out to the horses. When he came back in, Eliza had given him a hard candy. The boy had taken the candy from her and stared at her, and then at it, with disbelief.

Then he threw himself down at her feet, grabbing her round the knees and wailed piteously: "Don't make me go back with them! Please, don't make me go back there!"

"It was almost as if no one had been kind to him ever," Eliza added afterwards.

Eliza was trapped. The boy had her anchored to the ground. Without kicking him away, she couldn't free herself from his grasp.

It was Manuel who shouted. "Duck everyone! Get down." He pulled his gun out and fired a warning shot between the two men.

Josh, realising the lemons and potatoes were no protection against gunfire, threw himself across the floor to Amy. He helped her upend the table in front of her as he slid to a stop on the floor beside her. The heavy oak table was some protection against the gunfire that had erupted.

The older man, standing at the counter, realised what the boy had done and how he had given the game away, and pulled his gun out and started firing at Eliza and the boy. Eliza was no fool. Her early years in a wild Mexican town, and several instances of gunfights in the general store itself, had given her a sense of what to do in a crisis.

That was to fling yourself down on the floor, fast!

Ignoring the boy who was still clutching her skirts, she threw herself down behind the counter and, as she did so, pulled the boy with her. Manuel glanced at his wife with approval. Then he tried to raise his head and shoot the man. But a bullet flew past his ear, and he realised that was a mistake. Manuel, with a defeated sigh, slid down beside his wife. Eliza had pushed the boy off her and he was now curled up into a ball, whimpering. Eliza reached under the counter and produced the shotgun that was always kept there.

CHAPTER TWENTY-EIGHT

There was a silence. Eliza gripped the shotgun but didn't move. Josh and Amy behind the heavy oak table looked at each other, but neither wanted to raise their heads. That would have been a terrible mistake.

"No need for anybody to be killed!" shouted the man. "Let me and my partner load up and ride off. You can keep that wretched, snivelling boy. Was no damn good anyway."

There was silence. Josh, from behind the table, could hear movement—and he was going to peep around the side of it. When Amy pulled Josh back, shaking her head, they heard the man speak again.

"You folks stay down for a while. Let us get clear of the town and nobody gets hurt. No need for a shootout in here."

There was movement from the two men. They could hear one go out. Jangling the bell over the door made them aware of his exit. A few more moments and then they could hear the other man still moving around the store. The bell jangled as his partner came back in. "Don't anybody move until you hear us ride away. Any false move and you'll all be dead."

Manuel's quavering voice shouted out: "Yes, that's clear enough. Leave us be and just go!"

One man laughed at the quavering note in Manuel's voice. "Snivelling shopkeepers are all alike. Cowards!"

Josh, from his vantage point, could hear rather than see the kerfuffle from behind the counter. He smiled to himself, and then looked at Amy, who was also grinning. They both knew that Eliza was having to restrain her husband from jumping up and blasting the bandits with his gun. No man likes to be called a coward, especially not a snivelling one. Josh thought Manuel was furious, but thankfully Eliza had the good sense to restrain him. As Josh peered round the table, he saw the men pick up the last of their goods.

One miner reached into his pocket and flung a small leather bag onto the counter. "Don't say I never pay my way!" he said. "I didn't need to pay for the goods. We could have left, but it's not the way I do business. Keep the boy. He's no use to us. Thanks for the help."

The bell jangled as the men went out of the store for one last time. They could hear the heavy boots stomp across the boardwalk and then the sound of horses being ridden away.

Josh jumped up from behind the table. Manuel rose from behind the counter, and he grabbed the shotgun from Eliza and ran out of the doorway. The bell jangled wildly as he did so. He stood on the boardwalk and fired a shot after the two men. The others had run out after him—all except Eliza, who was helping the small boy to his feet. Josh noticed Eliza put the small pouch left on the counter in her apron pocket.

"Doesn't he know his shotgun will never reach the men? It's a waste of his time. They're out of reach," Amy whispered to Josh as she came up beside him and the shop owner.

"Leave him be," said Josh. "Manuel is just letting off steam. He's furious." Josh gave a smile towards the plump shopkeeper who was standing glaring after the men as they rode off into the distance. "There was nothing we could do in that shop. It would have been useless fighting them. We would have only got ourselves killed. Manuel knows that, but he's just mad as hell that he couldn't do anything."

"It's not only that," said Amy, grinning at Josh. "They called him a snivelling shopkeeper. That's what's upsetting him most."

The three of them turned and went back into the store. Josh heard the bell jingle and puzzled over the fact that somehow it sounded friendly now. No longer did it have the ominous tone it had with the men walking in and out.

Eliza had got the boy to stand up, and he stood there in front of them. Before any of them could speak, the door was thrust open. The sheriff and a couple of other men rushed in to see what had happened. The gunfire had been heard all over Nowhere. Everyone talked at once, eager to have their say.

The noise had finally subsided; everyone present had spoken about the part they had played in the action. It had been talked over and over, and still they had reached no conclusion. Everyone looked at the sheriff. He stood there—a tall, dark figure clad in his usual black garb and with a frown on his face. Sheriff Grey's black brows knitted over his long, pointed nose, and to Josh he looked even more like a dark, brooding crow. A look of anger crept over his face as he gazed at the still frightened boy now sitting on a chair and eating one of Eliza's cookies. The sheriff walked over to the boy, who stopped eating to stare up at the man looming above him. The boy sank back into the chair as if expecting a blow from the man. It was obvious from his face that he had received one or two recently.

The sheriff stood over him and spoke: "Now then, boy."

CHAPTER TWENTY-NINE

Ignoring Eliza, who was signalling to him to be kinder to the boy, Sheriff Grey stood over him. "Could you help us? Can you guide us to the hideout of these men?"

The sheriff's voice was harsh, but whereas Eliza's soft words had made the boy whimper even more, the demanding tone of the sheriff made him swallow his tears and sobs, and stare up at the black-garbed man looming over him.

A large gulp, and a small, dirty, calloused hand wiped away the tears. He stared straight up at Sheriff Grey. "We came to a huge cactus. It had marks carved on it, and lots and lots of branches. Then, I heard the big man say that was an easy ride to Nowhere from the cactus. We lived beside the mine in a canyon and rode out from it through the hills." His voice trailed off, revealing the extent of his knowledge of the journey.

The sheriff nodded at his reply, then scratched his long, bony nose and looked back down at the young boy. "Good, I think that's some help. We all know where that cactus is, don't we? Broken Horseshoe Ranch is out that way, isn't it, Josh?"

"Yes, it's near to it. It's a marker for many trails branching off from it. It's almost like a crossroads," Josh replied. The sheriff paced up and down the store. All eyes were watching the man. Then, suddenly, he whirled around towards the boy. "That's good, that's helpful." The harsh tones of the man belied the kind words, and the boy gave him tentative smile.

"Now, boy, what's your name?"

"Pete," was the reply.

The sheriff nodded and gave the boy a slight smile.

"Pete, can you tell me about this canyon you were kept in? When were you captured? And who was with you?" The questions were fired at the boy, and Eliza bristled as she felt he was being bullied by Sheriff Grey. Her arm went round the child, and she gave him an encouraging hug.

Pete glanced up at her, but his eyes darted back to the sheriff, who was now looming over him again. To Josh's amazement, he didn't seem frightened of the sheriff, but wanted to help him.

"Me and my brother were out looking for water for my Pa. We just moved out here, and the land is dry. Two men came, and they rode down on us and put us on the horse to take us back to a mine." The tears began again, but he continued speaking after a large sniff. "It's a big hole in the side of a cliff. We have to dig and pull out the stones. I heard the two men speaking on the way here. There used to be lots of gold there, but not so much now. We work during the day and are then locked up at night. My brother, he's still there."

Silence. No one spoke for a moment. The silence dragged out as the boy's words were absorbed by each person present. Then the cursing began. All of them had something to say—and none of it was complimentary or pleasant—about the wicked men who had captured these boys to work in the mine.

The sheriff's words cut through the conversation: "I'm going back up to the sheriff's office. On my way, I'll gather as many men as I can for a posse. Those men's tracks are new. For once we have no rain. Thanks to the boy, we know to aim for the big cactus and then try to track them. As their tracks are fresh, we stand a chance. This time we may find that mine and free the captives."

The boy jumped away from Eliza's arms and pulled on Sheriff Grey's coat. "I want to come! Take me with you. I can show you part of the way. I want to get my brother back."

"That's a good idea," Manuel said, looking at the boy. "He may well know the way after the cactus, or at least recognise some landmarks on the way."

Sheriff Grey stood by the door and gazed down at the boy. "You'll have to keep up with us. Can you do that?" At the boy's decided nod of his head, the sheriff turned away from him with a small smile of approval. "Josh, you ride to Broken Horseshoe Ranch. Get Ezra—he's the best tracker in the area. We'll meet you at the scarred cactus. This time, I think we have a chance of finding the bandits who are kidnapping our children and young men."

The door closed behind the sheriff, then it reopened and he poked his long, narrow face back in the doorway: "Eliza, get that boy fed, and in some warm clothes, ready for the journey."

CHAPTER THIRTY

Amy had stood up earlier and was now putting her jacket on. Catching sight of Amy's movements, the sheriff pointed a long finger through the narrow aperture of the door at her. "No, Amy. No posse for you."

Josh watched Amy sit back down on the chair with the thump, a mutinous expression on her face. He knew she was as good as any man in many fraught and dangerous circumstances, but Josh also realised that having a girl along with the posse would make the men feel uncomfortable. Seated round a campfire at night, their talk would not be as free as they would like with the young girl seated beside them. Gruelling days in the saddle, and riding hard, would not be easy for Amy, tough as she was.

"Never mind, Amy," Eliza said, putting a consoling hand on Amy's shoulder. "I'll be glad of your company. Manuel will go, and I could do with your support and your gun."

Amy nodded at the older woman, placed hand on top of that one that was consoling her, and gave it a gentle squeeze. "No doubt: we'll manage here, the two of us. If the tracks are clear to follow, they should be back in no time at all," Amy said. She had been conscious of the alarm and worry in Eliza's eyes as Manuel had decided to join the posse. No longer a young man, and extremely overweight, Amy thought he may well have been a drawback to the posse, perhaps slowing them down on the journey.

The sheriff had been true to his word. In no time at all, he was back outside the general store. There was an assortment of men with him, including Reuben the blacksmith and Zach from the saloon. Eliza brought the young boy Pete out in front of the general store. A man's coat was buttoned up round the boy, with the belt tying it to his body. His mouth showed that he had eaten hurriedly and well, and he was still chewing as he climbed on the horse Reuben had brought for him. Josh had mounted up and left earlier for Broken Horseshoe Ranch. Amy was certain that he would wait at the cactus along with Ezra in plenty of time. How she wished she could go with them.

Manuel dashed past Amy onto the boardwalk to reach his horse. "Coming, Sheriff, coming," he cried out as he unhitched his horse from the rail.

Sheriff Grey took one look at Manuel. The large man was already red-faced with the exertion of getting his horse ready and rushing to leave in time with them. The tall, dark man—dressed in black, as usual—sat astride his black stallion and shook his head at the flustered, highly coloured storekeeper.

"No, Manuel—not you. I need to keep someone here I can rely on in my absence." Sheriff Grey raised himself upon his horse and looking at the assembled crowd, mainly women who had gathered round the group of horsemen, and called out to them: "I'm deputising Manuel, in my absence. Any problems you face during my absence, take them to him." Reaching into the pocket of the long black coat he always wore, Sheriff Grey pulled out a bundle of keys and threw them at Manuel. "Keys to the office and the safe."

Manuel stood open-mouthed. His disappointment at not being able to ride along with the posse was overtaken by the pride he felt on being deputised. He fingered the keys, jingling them in his hand.

"Thank goodness for that. He'd never have coped with the posse and all that riding. Even the delivery days are only possible because Josh goes with him," Eliza whispered in Amy's ear.

The crowd stood and watched as the posse turned as one to ride out of the main street of Nowhere. Sheriff Grey had promised again and again that he would ride out, capture, and bring the kidnappers to justice. Thwarted by the rains and unable to find any idea of where the men kept their hideout, he had not been able to follow through on his promise earlier. Amy watched the men go and could see the sheriff was delighted to have the opportunity to fulfil his promise at last. The crowd drifted away, and Amy, Manuel, and Eliza went back into the store.

"You stay here tonight, Amy. Josh and I thought it best you stay until you can travel back out to the ranch with someone beside you," Eliza said as they all stood in the middle of the general store. Somehow, it seemed quiet both in the store and outside in Main Street. Amy nodded her agreement. Josh had told her he would explain to her father about the posse and her lack of escort back to Broken Horseshoe Ranch. She had done it many times on her own, but things were different now. Too many men were roaming the area, armed and ready to kidnap people. Rumours swirled of bandits who plundered trains and banks, finding sanctuary in Devil's Mountain to regroup before resuming their thievery. Amy was brave, but she was not foolish.

"I'm just going up to see the sheriff's office, check it out, and see if there is anything there needing my attention," Manuel announced proudly from the doorway. Jingling keys again in his hand, he strode off up Main

Street, smiling and nodding at each person he passed.

Amy and Eliza watched him go; each smiled at the other. "Thank goodness Sheriff Grey gave him those keys. He dislikes getting older and is refusing to accept it. But a journey riding hard with the posse would have killed him!" Eliza said as she turned back to straighten the vegetables yet again.

Amy watched her friend and smiled to herself. Every time Eliza was worried about anything, she sorted the vegetables out. Moving them around and placing them in neat order somehow made the Mexican woman cope with her problems. If only I could do something like that, thought Amy. She went back to the account books. This was something she could do that would absorb her completely. It pushed the worry about the posse— especially Ezra and Josh—to the back of her mind. Now she also had Harry Martin to think about. How would they cope with her? What was the woman's plan? She must have some way to kill Josh in mind. What could it be? And how could Amy thwart that plan?

CHAPTER THIRTY-ONE

Despite the worry about the men engaged in tracking down the kidnappers, the women of Nowhere gathered that afternoon, with some excitement, in the hotel lobby. Since taking over the hotel, Dora had begun to refurbish it. The plain wooden lobby with the rickety table that did service for a desk was no more. There was a new, polished wood floor, and heavy wine-coloured velvet curtains draped the entrance door. The new staircase, winding up to the second floor, was still plain and uncarpeted.

"This way, ladies. As you can see, I have started the refurbishment in the front hall, and I have also done this room. But everything else will take time and more money to get it just as I'd like it." Dora spread her arm wide, ushering the ladies through to the room, which was carpeted and had more velvet curtains draped at its window. Standing in pride of place, in the centre of the wall facing the door, was the piano.

"Here is the piano. Somehow it survived that terrible wagon journey. It's only a small piano, and it's mostly in tune now. But we'll have to wait till someone passing through Nowhere knows how to tune it."

The ladies sat in the chairs that were ranged around the room. Small tables were placed in front of them and, to Amy's amusement, she recognised some of them from the saloon. Dora must have borrowed them for the occasion.

"This will not be a traditional afternoon tea session. Today I shall have the music playing while we sit and indulge ourselves with tea and cakes," Dora said, and clapped her hands. The smile that lit up her face as she began her first afternoon tea party in her hotel was infectious. The ladies present all smiled back at her and chatted excitedly.

"How is she going to pay for this?" Eliza whispered to Amy as they both sat bolt upright on the hard chairs they had been given.

Eliza held the cup of tea that Dora had given her in one hand, and the slice of cake on the pretty plate in her other hand, and she stared from one to the other. "Amy, how do we manage to eat and drink this in a ladylike fashion?"

A snort of laughter from Amy was quickly stifled as she saw Dora glance round quickly at her. "I've never known how to cope with it. That's why I enjoy living out West. No need to bother with this tea party nonsense."

Dora then seated herself at the piano, where she played a medley of tunes. Soon, the ladies were humming along happily in between mouthfuls of cake and sips of their tea. It was a novel experience for the ladies living on the frontier, away from the society they had enjoyed back east.

"The floor in the back of the general store needs washing. I could have had that done in the time I've spent sitting here," muttered Eliza. "I understand why you don't like this sort of thing, Amy," she added. "It's not for me. I won't be coming back again."

The young girl, employed recently, brought round another large teapot, and this time only a few more cakes. It was obvious the cakes were running out fast, and the tea was becoming watered and stewed. Amy thought back to the elegant soirées she had attended before they moved to Nowhere. This was very different. Dora brought her musical entertainment to a close with a last flourish on the piano, which was rather spoiled by the continual wrong notes. But most of the ladies clapped enthusiastically. Isolated in the township of Nowhere, some of the older ladies had arrived with husbands eager to find or make their fortune, either on the land or in the mines. The women struggled with the desert winds and harsh climate, the lack of running water, and that utter loneliness that was the lot of pioneering life in the West for a woman. This was a wonderful treat for them.

"Now, let's have a chat about what we want to accomplish as the ladies of Nowhere. I have it in my mind to set up a church here in the hotel, away from the noisy saloon. And," Dora said with her usual enthusiasm now at fever pitch. "And, I would like to have a few ladies joining me in starting a school for the youngsters, and a ladies' quilting bee and sewing circle, all here in the hotel."

"I reckon that might be good," said Eliza grudgingly to Amy. "As long as she doesn't play the piano at every event, it might well be a good idea."

Amy watched the ladies talk enthusiastically about how they would achieve these ambitious aims. She was an astute girl and realised that this was the beginning of civilising the Western way of life in Nowhere. Unable to see where she would fit into this new ideal society that Dora painted for them, Amy just sat and watched and listened.

The sudden eruption of shouting and yelling in the front reception lobby made them all jump up, startled.

"Where's the usual man? Tell him we've come to get our old room back. He knows the room we like, and tell him we want the usual bottles of whiskey sent up!" The loud voice was followed by guffaws of laughter. "He knows we want the usual girls sent up as well!" shouted one man. The laughter grew louder, and it was obvious there were a couple of men, if not more, in the hotel lobby and they had been drinking.

"Tell him we want a redhead and a blonde this time!" The laughter grew even louder and Dora, who had sat frozen in her chair, jumped up and in a wild fury raced out of the room.

"Don't expect they want to join the tea party, do you?" Amy laughed at Eliza, who chuckled back at her, and both women rose to their feet. The other ladies jumped to their feet and clustered together in a corner of the room, wringing their hands, a couple of them beginning to cry. Amy cast them a look of disdain and marched across to the door, with Eliza following behind her. The boots Amy wore beat out a loud, determined tattoo as she walked across the marble flooring to the three men.

CHAPTER THIRTY-TWO

One man—a scruffy, thin, weasel of a man—had grabbed the arm of the young maid and was trying to kiss her. She was twisting and turning away from him and trying to hit him with clenched fists. His laughter at this show of strength by her was echoed by his two companions, who stood around him, egging him on.

"Let her go! Get out of my hotel. I don't want riff-raff such as you staying here!" Dora's voice cut across the laughter and all three men turned to look at her.

Seeing only a tiny middle-aged woman dressed in widow's weeds, they laughed in her face.

Amy stepped forward in front of Dora. "You heard her. Let the girl go. And leave the hotel."

This time, the men didn't laugh. All of them stared at Amy and Eliza, who had joined her. They gazed at both women, and Amy felt herself squirm at that intense, measuring look which stripped her naked.

One of them, a heavyweight broad-shouldered man, clad in ill-fitting clothes and with scars over his face and hands, stepped forward. "How's about this, boys? Seems like we each got a woman here, ready for the taking. I'll take the little spitfire—reckon she needs a real man to handle her." Lumbering across the hall, he reached out a hand to grab Amy.

His alcohol-fuelled breath reached her in a smelly wave, and she almost stepped back in horror at it. But Amy held her ground and just looked at him. Her voice was calm, hiding the churning mixture of fear and anger within.

"I think you'd better go now. We don't want any trouble here. There's no room available for you. So, leave now!" Her voice had become more insistent, but still the three men laughed at her words.

The younger man, as dirty as his two companions, had a squinty look, and his dark brows met across his face. The long, pointed nose beneath the brows seemed to quiver in anticipation as he eyed Amy up and down yet again. He pushed past the heavyset man, sending him flying to the side of the hall.

"This one's mine. I reckon she needs a slapping to shut her up!" Reaching Amy, his arm drew back, his hand open ready to slap her across the face.

There was no contact with Amy's face. A sudden eruption of movement came from Amy, and the man flew backwards and lay on the floor. His two companions looked down at him, and then at Amy, in bewilderment and shock. Amy smiled down at him. "You were asked politely to leave. Don't try it again."

Unwilling to accept what had happened to his friend, the heavyset man rushed Amy with a fist clenched. Amy stepped back and with another flying movement and whirling, she gave a flying kick. Crashing to the floor, he lay there, semi-conscious and rubbing his jaw.

"That's enough, gentlemen. I think it's time you all left."

By this time, Amy had pulled a gun from her skirt pocket and Eliza, beside her, got out a gun from the bag she was carrying.

But it was that voice from the staircase that surprised everyone standing in the hall. Harry Martin stood there, one hand on the banister, the other pointing a small derringer at the men.

Both men on the floor scrambled to their feet and, helping the dazed one, they reluctantly left the hotel. The three ladies, pointing guns at them from different directions, were too much for them to handle. As one, they gazed back at Amy with surprise and awe as they rushed out of the doorway. To make certain of their departure, Dora went behind the reception desk and retrieved a shotgun. She stood there before going over to the door and watching them make their way down to the saloon.

On turning back into the hotel lobby, she looked at Amy. "What did you do there, Amy?" Dora asked. She had put the shotgun back in its place beneath the counter of the desk. "I thought he was going to grab you, but the next minute he was on the floor. What did you do?"

Amy slipped the gun back into her pocket and couldn't stop smiling at the others. "You know we have the two Chinese boys living with us, Tom and Chan? They know of some ancient type of self-defence moves. We discovered they are not the usual type of Chinese men that have come over to work. Pa thinks they were Chinese nobility. They taught these moves to Ben and me. That was some of them. Pretty good, aren't they?" Amy said with a broad grin.

"Yes, they were so good that *I* would be interested in learning them," said Harry Martin. The lady swept down the last stairs to stand in front of Amy. "Let's talk about it."

CHAPTER THIRTY-THREE

"Dora will never make a lady out of you, will she, Amy?" Eliza laughed at her friend, who was brushing down her skirt. "I'd better check on Manuel. I've left him alone in the general store for long enough." The front door of the hotel closed behind her. Dora had rushed off to the ladies, calming them down and explaining that this sort of thing would never, ever happen again.

Amy looked at Harry Martin—or Harriet, as she should really be called—and waited. The tall woman looked Amy up and down, then strode over to a door and, flinging it open, looked inside. "This will do. I'd like to talk to you about those actions you've just performed on those two men." She gestured to the door and the room beyond. "Let's talk."

"Fine, I'll talk—but I'm not sure I can help you," Amy said as she followed the other woman into the room. They left the marble-tiled hall and the carpeted piano room and found themselves in an empty room. No furniture, no carpet, just a plain wooden floor and plastered walls. The window had glass, that was all. No curtains; no blinds. Nothing softened the darkening afternoon sky.

"I'll pay you," said Harry, as she stood facing Amy. "I'll pay you well for those tricks that you performed on those two men. Could you teach me?"

Amy was startled by this remark and didn't reply at first.

Harry spoke again to Amy, her voice becoming insistent. "Do you understand me? I want to know how you did that. I'm willing to pay you if you can teach me at least one trick. That one where you threw him on the floor when he came toward you would be invaluable to me. I am, well, let's just say it would be useful for me to know how to do that."

The woman facing Amy had several expressions flitting across her face during this speech. The main one, Amy thought, was her obvious need for secrecy. She didn't want to explain to Amy what she did for a living. If Amy didn't know the truth, she would just assume that she was another lady seeking to protect herself in the wild and lawless frontier lands of Arizona.

Amy took a moment, thinking, before replying. This woman had been paid to come out and kill Josh. Amy wondered how Harry was going to do the deed and wondered what she could do to prevent it. She had seen Harry with the gun in her hand, and Amy had watched carefully as that gun was placed in a pocket very close to where the woman's hand was at the moment. There was no way Amy could take her unawares. The calculating look in the woman's eyes was enough to make Amy realise that this woman hadn't survived as long as she had without being shrewd and deadly.

"Well, will you help me?" A small reticule hung from the woman's arm. She opened it and held out several coins towards Amy. "I don't carry paper money, only coins of silver and gold. Here, I'll give you these. It's important to me I learn that trick."

The coins were held out on a hand towards her, and Amy gazed down at them. The realisation of how much this woman actually wanted her to show the trick made Amy think. There might be another way that Amy could get Harry to pay for learning the skill. Her eyes took in the woman's stance, the readiness with which she could easily kill Amy. Those almost black reptile-like eyes of the woman showed her peculiar lack of compassion or empathy. Yes, Amy thought, she is a killer—but she is a killer who wants, at that moment, what I can give her.

"I'll teach you the trick, but it will take practice for you to perform it properly. I can show you how to do it and assure you that if you practise daily, you will come up to speed with it," said Amy.

Harry Martin smiled at Amy and licked her lips. The other woman's anticipation made Amy feel Harry was becoming more snake-like each moment. Harry held out the coins to Amy, but was surprised when the girl shook her head.

The afternoon was drawing in. Standing in the cold grey room, it seemed to be bleaker than ever as it was gradually losing the light of the sun. The two women faced each other. This time, Harry had a puzzled expression on her face as she looked at the young woman before her who was actually refusing the money she proffered.

"If you don't want money, what can I give you? I don't think you'll do it for love of me." The words were pleasant enough, but had a sting in them.

"No, I'm not doing it for love of you, but for the love I hold for a dear friend of mine." Amy watched the puzzled expression deepen as the woman stared at her, unblinking, those almost-black eyes waiting for further explanation. "Keep your money. I'll show you this trick—if you leave Nowhere without killing Josh Barnes."

It slid over the woman's face, a masklike expression, hiding all thoughts as she took time to ponder Amy's remark. Then a look of curiosity took over, and the first question she asked took Amy by surprise: "How did you know? What gave me away? I don't like anyone knowing who I am, or why I visit a place. So please, Amy—that's your name isn't it? Please, Amy, I'd like you to explain."

"You didn't give yourself away. Josh knows assassins are being sent to kill him. He intercepted a letter giving your name and date of arrival to Nowhere. This letter said *you* were his killer—you were the next one to arrive in Nowhere." Amy baldly stated the facts to the woman.

Harry Martin looked at Amy, nodded her head, and began pacing the small room. Amy watched her, her hand resting on her skirt and the comforting bulk of the Colt within her pocket. She was well aware of the evil skills of this woman and did not, could not, relax her guard for one moment.

"What did he do? This Josh, what was his crime?" Questions were shot out at Amy as the woman stopped to face her again.

"He doesn't know. I found him unconscious in the desert. The blow on his head caused him to lose his memory," Amy replied.

The pacing up and down the room began again. The words were flung at Amy as Harry continued walking. "I didn't like the way this deal was struck. Each victim I kill usually acts outside the law and deserves to die. Didn't get this feeling here. So, Amy, you teach me that trick tonight, and I'll leave tomorrow."

Taken aback, Amy could only stare at the woman before gathering her thoughts. "Why? Why agree to my demand so easily?"

"That is a valuable skill I could learn from you. It may well save my life on occasions, and certainly would give me the upper hand in a fight. And I have half my fee already. I won't be out of pocket, and I'll have learned a valuable skill."

Harry Martin waved to Amy as she climbed up into the wagon for the return journey to Duloe. Amy waved back. She knew Harry Martin was a cold-hearted killer, but Amy had a grudging respect for her. Those few hours spent with her yesterday afternoon showing Harry a little of what she needed to do the trick had been productive for both women. In return, Harry had left Duloe, leaving Josh unharmed—and she'd shown Amy the trick of how to carry a short-barrelled pistol up her sleeve.

Amy waved goodbye to Harry Martin as the wagon drew out from the livery stable on its journey back to Duloe.

CHAPTER THIRTY-FOUR

The men rode in silence. Their faces held a grim determination and a desire to find the bandits who held the young men and boys captive. Pete rode on a horse beside Josh. Eyeing the young boy, Josh was amazed at how Pete managed to keep up with them. His knowledge of the mine and the cabin in which he said the captives were kept was going to be invaluable to them. Pete knew this, and the sheer grit he showed in travelling onwards to help all the captives escape, but especially his brother, amazed the men.

Ezra had needed no urging when Josh had arrived at Broken Horseshoe Ranch. Josh told the group gathered around him about the events in the general store, and how Sheriff Lance Grey felt there was a good chance of following the tracks of the bandits that day.

Flora, on hearing this, rushed out onto the porch. "I should come! My family is there, they must be. You all think they took my family to the mine when I escaped from the wicked men. I tracked Josh and Amy here to the ranch. I'm the best tracker—I should go with you." Flora stood defiantly on the porch, ready to jump on a horse and join the posse.

"That's a lot of 'I am's," said Nancy, with a smile at the young girl.

"I'm the best tracker!" Flora protested again, her lips in a truculent pout and her brows knitting together in an angry frown.

It was Ezra who knelt down beside the little girl and took her hands in his: "Flora, you *are* the best tracker. We all know that. But you are a young girl, and the journey will be hard and too difficult for you."

The bottom lip pouted still more; the eyes flashed fiery defiance. Her tiny hands clenched in anger as she stared round again at those standing on the porch beside her.

It was Josh who walked up to the hitching rail outside the cabin with a fresh horse and looked at Flora. He'd heard the conversation as he walked from the stable. "The sheriff told Amy she couldn't go. She can't go. So why should you?" Josh said and mounted his horse. The words were abrupt, but Josh was eager to get started on the ride to the scarred cactus. He didn't want to be late joining the posse.

Flora thought for a moment. "Amy isn't going? Where is she?"

"Amy is staying at the general store tonight. It's far too dangerous for her to ride alone at the moment. Bandits are everywhere from that mine, and gangs of them are in hiding in the hills and canyons. The sheriff has got the posse together, and we're going to ride into the foothills of Devil's Mountain to find and free the captives. No women or girls are needed for that task. It's too difficult and dangerous for them," Josh said. He gave a wave to Nancy, Luke, and the others, and turned his horse away to ride to the rendezvous. Ezra, by this time, had mounted his horse and joined Josh after giving a special wave to his wife, Leah.

They were waiting at the scarred cactus when Sheriff Lance Grey rode up with his posse. Ezra and Josh got a wave from Lance, and they followed on behind the gang of riders. There was a grim determination on every face. Every one of them had been affected in some way by the capture of these boys. If it hadn't been a family member, it had been someone known to them. In a small community, this dramatic evil of kidnapping the boys was felt by every one of them. They all intended to rescue the boys, and if there was the unfortunate occurrence of the bandits being shot dead—well, not one of them would shed a tear.

The land grew increasingly rocky and steep as they continued upwards. The grass that grew sparsely in places—and was still evident in the land around the scarred cactus—was no more. Plants that grew in the rocky terrain were thin and stunted, fighting for survival not only because of their poor soil but because of the ever-present winds that blew through the canyons and gorges of Devil's Mountain.

The narrow track winding round the cliff edges went upwards. The canyons began to be deeper, harsher, and went even further into the mountain range itself. There seem to be no end to the steepness and severity of the narrow trail. Occasionally, there would be a sign that they were on the right path: a freshly broken branch, upturned stones scattered away from the track, and the very occasional hoofprint freshly made on the soft earth.

Josh hated going higher. He disliked the heights in the Devil's Mountain canyons. The rocky floors beneath the terrifying drops seemed to allow no hope for any fallen person. Littered with boulders and huge spiky rocks, any unexpected descent would be fatal. Walking along the path would have been a better option, he thought, but Lance Grey wanted to move speedily onwards and a slow, careful walk was not for him. Trusting that Star, a horse he had ridden ever since his arrival at Broken Horseshoe Ranch, would continue to be as surefooted as he'd known him to be in the past, he held tight to the reins, trying not to show his nervousness to the horse.

CHAPTER THIRTY-FIVE

As they wound round yet another cliff and traversed a rocky incline, Josh would never admit to anyone—and even found it difficult to admit to himself—that he kept his eyes tight closed. There was nothing he could do to help his horse along. He could only trust that the horse knew where to put his feet. Rounding another cliff face, they found the land opened out onto a plateau. Pete was gesturing to Lance urgently. Josh rode nearer to hear what the boy was saying.

"I remember this. We stopped here. There's a spring over behind those rocks. They let the horses drink there. I can show you," the boy said proudly, eager to play his part in this mad adventure. Following the others, Josh took care of his horse, getting down and stretching for a bit. He looked at Pete, at the thin, drawn face, so full of worry. Such a young boy should be laughing and playing with his brother and friends. No wonder he's worried, Josh thought—he has so much to lose. Pete knows the hell his brother was now going through, and Josh admired his resilience in returning with them.

Refreshed, they continued on with the journey. Pete, with a renewed confidence in his abilities after finding the water, issued instructions to them. He warned them against going too fast as the mine itself was further around the next rocky outcrop.

It was as well Pete was with them. He had been correct: the mine was, surprisingly enough, midway up the mountainside, not in the valley floor below. The level plateau in front of them held a cluster of huts, iron machinery scattered about, and smoke from a campfire. With a smile of quiet satisfaction on Lance Grey's face, the posse crouched behind rocks, staring down at the camp below them. He had found it. The camp they were looking for at long last had been found. The sheriff was making good on his promises. Now all he had to do was free the captives and kill the bad guys. Josh gave a small smile to himself as he thought this. Now they were facing the tough part of the trip, when they could either kill or be killed. He saw Pete and Lance beside each other, chatting away as they crouched down behind a rock. Curiosity got the better of Josh. He rose to his feet and walked across to them, well behind a couple of men who were still eyeing the camp and hidden from view.

Lance looked up at him as he went towards them. "Sit down, Josh. Pete has been telling us about the setup of the camp before us. He says the prisoners are all kept captive in that wooden hut. If Pete could let them out and lead them up here without being seen, whilst we cause a distraction, that should get the captives to the security and safety here behind these rocks. No one can rush us here, and it would give us a chance to regroup with the prisoners before heading off back to Nowhere."

Josh nodded, but he wasn't too sure. He could see quite a few flaws in the sheriff's plan.

But it was Pete who got both their attention with his next remark. "There's dynamite held in that hut over beside the rock face," said Pete, looking at the sheriff. "It's kept well away from the camp and the mine in case it explodes." He looked at Josh. "Maybe we could get some dynamite and throw it behind them at the campfire before rescuing the others?" The question the young boy posed made them all stop and look at him.

Even though it was nearly dark, Josh felt he could almost see the blush of embarrassment that rose up the boy's neck and face.

"That might well help us get the upper hand. They are secure down there and have their camp in a well-protected area. Charging in blindly would lead us to getting men killed. I can't take that chance. Pete's idea would certainly turn the situation to our benefit," Lance said. To the boy, he said: "That's a great idea, Pete. Josh, can you go with him?"

Josh agreed and placed a hand of reassurance on the boy's shoulder.

Taking a deep breath, Lance whispered to them: "Off you go, the two of you. We'll watch as best we can. If you run into any trouble, take cover behind those huge rocks near to the cliff face, and we'll open fire."

Josh began with a crouching run down the narrow path towards the encampment around the goldmine. When he reached the bottom of the path, he turned to Pete: "What should we do first? Get the dynamite, or the captives?" It seemed absurd to Josh to ask the advice of a young boy. However, Pete knew the camp far better than he did, knew the routine of the men, and could guide Josh to the right places.

"Get the dynamite. The men won't see us going in because the door is at the back. But the door to the hut where my brother is can be seen by the men from their campfire," Pete whispered back to him.

"The dynamite it is," whispered Josh, gesturing for the boy to lead the way.

Moonlight was faintly illuminating the area. The cloud cover was patchy and meant that they could take advantage when the cloud hid the moon from view, covering their progress in darkness. In seconds, they were outside the hut that stored dynamite. To Josh's surprise, it wasn't locked. Then he reasoned: why did it need to be? They were all on the same side and the captives were always kept guarded or locked away. This was going to be to their advantage. He pushed open the door.

CHAPTER THIRTY-SIX

The men hidden above the camp, sat and watched as Josh and Pete began their silent movements towards the dynamite store. Josh led the way, darting through the shadows from the campfire and keeping his face down as low as possible so that the white blur of it would not be seen in the increasing darkness.

Josh looked at the men lounging around the campfire. He could see there was drink, bottles were being passed round, one to the other. There were tin plates on the ground, and there had obviously been meat cooked over the fire. Some other food lay uneaten beside them. Pete had told him of the shortage of food that the captives had endured. The small meals they had been given had not been enough for growing boys. But they were expected to work a full day on the meagre rations. Josh's blood boiled. How dare these men sit laughing at their leisure when, inside the hut, young boys, and children lay exhausted, in pain, frightened, and starving?

Both Pete and Josh reached the hut and stood for a moment, their breath coming out in quick gasps as they fought to calm themselves after their mad dash across the open ground. They could have been seen at any moment by anyone who turned round. Josh felt the tension flood out of his shoulders, and he moved them slightly, trying to loosen himself up, ready to tackle the dynamite store.

There was no padlock. Josh was relieved to see that there was only a heavy bar across the door, easy enough to move. Quietly opening the door, Josh was fearful it might shriek and the hinges give them away. But Josh relaxed again as it opened silently, and they peered in. The light of the moon shone a path into the shed. Josh spotted some sticks of the dynamite on top of boxes. He looked at Pete.

The boy whispered to him, "I'll take a couple. What about you?"

Josh passed a couple of sticks to Pete and took some himself. He grinned at the boy as they both came out, leaving the door ajar. A dynamite stick thrown in the hut itself would be a destructive distraction!

The men in the posse had given both of them small boxes of matches to use. Pete took his two sticks of dynamite and flourished the box he had been given excitedly.

"Light them only when you have the captives clear and well on their way up the path," Josh cautioned the boy, noting his excitement. "I'll stay here and watch you free everybody. Then I'll start with the explosions around the camp so that they don't chase after you."

Pete grinned, and Josh saw his teeth flash in the faint moonlight as the boy crept away to the captives' hut. On their way to the dynamite store, Josh, had with relief, seen that the captives' shed had a wooden bar across it. He hoped Pete would manage to lift it.

One man stood up at the campfire. Josh crouched down even lower, as his eyes followed Pete's progress. The boy was lifting the bar, and Josh saw him pull the door back. Slipping inside, the boy reappeared and was ushering a group of people towards the cliff face path leading upwards to the sheriff and the posse.

The man at the campfire was stiff and was stomping his feet about, much to the laughter of his friends.

"Pete, hurry—get them all up that path before that man turns round and sees them all." The words on Josh's tongue seemed to hang in the air as his eyes swivelled between the fleeing captives and the man at the campfire.

The last prisoner appeared, and Pete followed behind, looking towards Josh. He gave a slight wave. It was the signal. They were all out, and all were on their way up the path. Pete had done well. He had released the captives.

Josh's turn had arrived. He lit one stick of dynamite and threw it far across the clearing, away from the cliff face and the captives. The explosion was loud in the confined space of the canyon, between the rocky walls and peaks of Devil's Mountain.

The men jumped up, shouting, and began running towards the scene of the explosion. Josh lit another stick of dynamite and threw this into the campfire. The campfire seemed to explode. Embers flew across the clearing and burning coals rained down on those men still clustered around it. He heard two more explosions closely following each other on the far side of the clearing. Josh smiled to himself. That was Pete's work. Before the sounds had died away, Josh sent another stick in yet another direction, but away from the path on which he could see the last of the captives were now halfway up.

Gunfire erupted from the posse. They had raced down the path, squeezing past the fleeing captives with their guns, ready to capture or kill the bandits.

Running towards the posse, keen to make sure he was out of their line of fire, Josh turned back for a brief moment. The dynamite stick lit, with the fuse burning low, flew into the open door of the dynamite store. Josh swore afterwards that he never ran so fast in his life as when he raced across the clearing to join Sheriff Grey and the posse.

"Take cover! Get down—the dynamite store is going to blow!" His voice must've carried to the posse because as he flung himself flat in the dirt he saw the others fling themselves down with their hands over their heads.

The explosion rocked the canyon. It seemed to go on forever, leaving them with their ears ringing and debris falling around them.

"Anyone hurt?" Lance shouted out to his men.

At their reassuring replies, he got to his feet and said in his usual laconic way: "Let's get this job done."

CHAPTER THIRTY-SEVEN

Sometime later, the ground was cleared of bodies, debris and the wounded. To Josh's amazement, none of the posse was badly injured. One had fallen off his horse and sustained bruises, much to the merriment of his companions. One had a bullet graze his arm, which bled everywhere but was of no great importance.

The gang had been surprised by their attack, and paid the price. That unexpected and intense gunfire from the posse had accounted for the death of the four of the bandits, and three others were injured.

"I want to get those prisoners back to the jail. We've also got to get those folk we've released back to Nowhere," Sherriff Grey said, as he stood looking around the scene of devastation.

"I've been talking to some men who were captured. They say there's no more gold—the vein has run out. They were going to move camp tomorrow over into the next valley, where they found an old mine previously used by the Mexicans and abandoned after an Indian massacre," Reuben said when he came up to join Josh and Lance. "Good thing we came today, otherwise young Pete couldn't have shown us where they'd locked the boys away."

"Are they fit enough to travel?" Lance asked Reuben. "I'd like to get them back to Nowhere whilst we sort out the mess here."

"They want to go back now, no matter what state they are in," said Josh.

There were horses and mules stabled in a lean-to under an overhanging cliff. Lance, Josh, and Reuben went over to them, and began sorting out those that they thought were placid enough to carry the boys back to Nowhere.

"Josh, could you and Reuben take them back for me? Take Ezra as well. There are plenty of bandits still wandering about in the mountains, and I'd like you to guard them. The others from the posse can remain with me whilst we sort this lot out in daylight. The moon is bright now the clouds have disappeared. Once you get out of the canyon, it's a straightforward journey back to Nowhere."

The surrounding scene was indeed a mess. Josh was exhausted, not so much physically but from the tension he'd endured as he led Pete into the camp for the rescue. It was a relief to him to know that he could get back to Nowhere straight away.

A few horses were taken from the bandits' lair, and led up the narrow path by Josh, Reuben, and Ezra. Despite the narrow ledge, Josh felt no fear of the dangerous heights plunging down beside him. He was too tired to care, and he plodded on, leading Star and another couple of horses behind him. Reuben and Ezra followed him, and they emerged out of the canyon with the horses on a narrow plateau, where they found the group together.

"Are they all dead? Did you kill the lot of them?" Pete's voice was eager and hopeful.

An explanation was given by Josh to the group gathered there as they helped them climb on the horses. Some of the smaller ones shared with a bigger child.

"Josh? Is that you?" The woman's voice came out of a dark shadow towards Josh. He recognised her immediately as Flora's mother. "My daughter, I told her to …?"

"She's safe. She reached Dry Creek Ranch, and she's been living with us ever since," Josh reassured the woman, putting a gentle arm around her thin shoulders.

Tears of joy and gratitude—at their escape and the news of her daughter—ran down her face, and she squeezed Josh's hand. But there was no time for any further talk. Reuben was anxious to get them back to Nowhere safely. Both he and Josh were armed and, knowing that there were a couple of able-bodied men in the group, had brought arms up for them.

"Too many gangs have taken to hiding in Devil's Mountain. There is a need now to be on our guard against anybody seeking to rob us," said Reuben.

The journey was slow. They didn't want to push the horses carrying the double load, and the boys, in their weakened state, were struggling to stay on. As they were nearing the scarred cactus, Ezra came up to Josh.

"I'll take Flora's family straight back to Broken Horseshoe Ranch. There is no need for them to go into Nowhere, and you don't need me now, do you?"

"Yes, Ezra, that's a good idea," Josh said, and he smiled when he saw the eager face of Flora's mother on the horse behind Ezra.

The sun was rising as they reached Nowhere, and the first thing Reuben did when they reached the livery stables was to bang on his metal triangle to alert the town.

By the end of the day, every child and young boy had been reunited with their family. Word had spread throughout the area like a wildfire that the captured children had been found and brought home.

CHAPTER THIRTY-EIGHT

Next day, Sheriff Lance Grey marched into the general store waving some posters about.

"Wanted posters for you, Manuel. If you can put some of them up, do so, otherwise keep them here and keep a lookout for these men. They're dangerous killers, wanted in many states. Now I've heard they are hiding up on Devil's Mountain."

He placed them on the counter. Manuel and Eliza spread them out to look at them. Josh and Amy, who had recently arrived from Broken Horseshoe Ranch, came over to look through them.

Lance continued speaking. "Everyone is back home now. We rescued all the captive boys and young men. Some are the worse for wear, and it will take a time before they're back to normal," said Lance.

"What about the prisoners you captured? Are they still in the jail?" Manuel asked Lance with a twitch in his lips, as he tried to hide a grin.

Everyone waited for the reply from Lance. The Nowhere jail was still without bars, and three prisoners had been taken captive last night and brought back to Nowhere.

"Sent them off on the wagon this morning to Duloe. Got rid of them that way." The sheriff's reply gave nothing away, but everyone wondered why the prisoners didn't escape out of the window. But Josh, looking at the stern, hard-faced Lance Grey in front of him, realised they probably thought it was not worth the effort.

"Now all we've got to look out for is these wretched killers. No doubt the bounty hunters will be coming for them," said Lance.

"Bounty hunters?" asked Eliza.

"Yes, some of them are just as bad as the killers they go after. Often, deserters from the army, and failed sheriff's and lawmen—usually drunks as well. Got no time for bounty hunters, rubbishy crowd." With his usual slight nod towards them, Lance Grey went out of the general store.

"Well, Lance didn't think much about bounty hunters, did he?" said Josh, looking after Lance as he marched up the main street of Nowhere.

"Perhaps he will change his mind. There may well be good bounty hunters." Amy said as she flicked through the wanted posters.

Amy didn't realise her words foretold the future. The dramatic events that occurred in Nowhere upon the arrival of a certain charismatic and deadly bounty hunter made Sheriff Lance Grey think again.

CHAPTER THIRTY-NINE

Pearly fingers of dawn crept over Devil's Mountain. They cast an eerie light over Main Street, Nowhere. Three horses ambled slowly up Main Street, their hooves raising dusty echoes. They came to a halt in front of the sheriff's office. Two riders got down, walked over to the third horse. They cut the ropes. The body dropped to the ground with a dull thud.

"So much blood! Who knew he'd bleed so much?"

The body was dragged up the steps to the boardwalk in front of the sheriff's door. Hands were placed neatly on his chest, with his wanted poster beneath them. A note was attached to the poster, a message to send the bounty prize money to the Duloe bank under the name of Mr A. Venger. The riders returned to their horses and rode back out of town, leading the riderless horse.

Sheriff Lance Grey opened his office door. Always early, he unlocked the door after he had put on his coffee to brew. Each morning he liked to get settled into the comfortable chair beside the potbellied stove, where his coffeepot sat eternally brewing his coffee, his lifeblood of the day. He found the body lying in front of his door. The sheriff looked down at it and shook his head in disbelief. Then he stooped and looked at the wanted poster.

He spoke his thoughts aloud: "Pleased to see you, Mr Bank Robber. Says here that you were one of the worst killers in these bank raids. Now here you are: laid out, neat and tidy for me. Just like a surprise parcel." Lance shook his head and looked again at the poster he held in his hand. Neatly laid out, the wanted man was very dead, and had been brought to his door for a purpose.

"I don't know who killed you, but that was one neat

shot right in your heart. I'd like to shake them by the hand. A vicious killer like you is best off dead."

Ignoring his freshly brewed coffee, Lance walked round the body and strode up to the livery stable. Lance could hear Reuben, the blacksmith, already at work. As he walked nearer, he saw the glow from the fire at the forge was building into a white-hot heat, ready for the metal to be moulded by the blacksmith. Reuben stood there, his burly arms in his vest already covered with sweat, and he looked up as the sheriff approached him.

"What can I do for you, Sheriff? Early in the morning for you to be paying calls on me. Thought yet about getting me to fit those bars in the jail?" Reuben laughed. This powerful man shook with laughter.

"Not at the price you want me to pay," scoffed the sheriff. The new sheriff's office prison cell was without bars. The sheriff wouldn't pay the price the blacksmith quoted for them, and the blacksmith refused to lower the price. But the amazing thing was, no prisoner ever attempted to escape, open window notwithstanding. Not when faced with Sheriff Lance Grey. The tall, thin figure of the sheriff was always dressed in black. His black shirt, tie, and trousers were worn beneath a long black coat, the black hat covering the flowing black locks. His droopy black moustache gave him a melancholy air, which speedily vanished when roused to anger and the black eyes flashed a warning.

"Got a body for you, Reuben. Someone just left it in front of the door at the sheriff's office. Never had wanted men delivered like this before." Reuben—the town gravedigger as well as the blacksmith—nodded and went to the back of the livery stables, where he emerged with a small handcart. He pushed it down the main street alongside the sheriff. The two men, still stunned at this strange turn of events, didn't speak. Grey helped Reuben get the body onto the cart.

After removing the wanted poster and the note, Lance took them into the office and put them on his desk. Surprised at the note, he looked at it yet again. That was some reward voucher to be paid into the bank. Strange, he thought, most bounty hunters loved to come into town waving, and boasting their prowess at catching a wanted man. This was unusual. But Sheriff Lance Grey wasn't turning his nose up at this way of delivering the bandits: he preferred the dead ones. They were much easier to deal with, especially as he hadn't got bars in his cell window yet. He thought about Reuben as he walked off up the street, pushing the cart with the body. Both of them were amicable enough over business dealings between them, but—and it was a big *but*—he and Reuben had nearly come to blows over the price quoted for the bars for the prison cell. It now had reached a stalemate. Reuben wouldn't make the bars, and Lance wouldn't pay the price.

There had been offers of shutters, wooden bars, wire netting. Many things had been offered by the concerned citizens of Nowhere, who disliked having a jail cell open to miscreants. But those that the sheriff had captured and placed in the cell feared the sheriff too much to escape. "You go through that window, you arrive at the cemetery in a box," he'd said.

Sheriff Lance Grey smiled as he poured out the hot cup of coffee. This would solve his problem, he thought. If only all the villains hiding out in Devil's Mountain would be delivered dead in front of his door, he would be a cheerful man. He raised his cup of steaming coffee to the man who shot this villain through the heart. A $350 voucher would be sent that morning to the bank in Duloe to pay for the bounty.

But he wondered, who had been the bounty hunter? Why did he want to hide behind a name only? His coffee was drunk to the very last drop, and he refilled his tin cup. Doubt there will be another body tomorrow morning, he thought. No, he couldn't be that lucky.

CHAPTER FORTY

"Not many customers this morning," Manuel, the owner of the general store, said. He walked to the door, opened it and looked up and down the main street, of Nowhere.

"Opening the door and looking out again and again won't bring any customers," scolded his wife, Eliza.

The excitement of the day before, when the posse had captured an evil gang and brought them into town, had gone. The villains had been kidnapping young men and boys. After yesterday, the morning in Nowhere was quiet.

"Seems like Reuben and Grey are busy up there," said Manuel, watching them with a cart. He poked his head back in the door and called out to Eliza. "I'm just going to see what's happening." He stepped off the porch in front of the general store and waddled his portly frame up to the sheriff's office.

"Eliza, as it is quiet in here, I'll go up to the hotel and saloon and collect the account books. You will manage in here, won't you?" Amy said. She rose to her feet from the small table at the back of the store where she worked on the accounts of the various businesses in Nowhere. Flicking back the long brown hair over her shoulder, she walked up the main street of Nowhere. She strode along, her small boots—made for men—sensible on the dusty road. Her serviceable, heavy cotton skirt swung from side to side, lead shot sewn into the hems, weighing them down against the vagaries of the desert winds. Her trusty sheath knife and a Colt revolver were always in each pocket. The sound of horses riding up behind her made her move to the side and onto the boardwalk in front of the hotel.

"Is this the only hotel?" The voice made Amy pause

and turn to look at the newcomers.

"Yes, the one and only hotel in Nowhere," Amy replied. Her gaze at the woman talking to her took in two women astride powerful horses. The woman speaking to her was of an enormous build, her shoulders powerful—and the huge arms, of considerable strength, held the reins of the horse lightly, despite their power. Amy tried not to show her appalled reaction at the woman's face. It was marred by a huge scar from forehead to chin. "It's been taken over by Dora, who is refurbishing it, and it is now spotless!" Amy added.

"If it's clean, that will be wonderful." The other rider spoke to Amy. A complete contrast to her companion, the dainty young woman sat astride her horse. Blonde curls framed her heart-shaped face, and she gave Amy a sweet smile. "We are so dusty from travelling—I look forward to a bath and a night spent between clean sheets!"

"Yes, travelling in this heat and dust is not pleasant," Amy agreed.

Like thistledown, the young woman jumped down from the great black stallion she was riding and hitched his reins before walking onto the boardwalk beside Amy. After gently patting her horse and murmuring in its ear, she spoke again: "Where is the livery stable? We must get our horses fed and watered first. But I'll see if there are rooms available for us."

Amy said, "I'm sure Dora will do her best to make you comfortable," and led the way inside the hotel.

Dora, hearing the front door of the hotel open, came out to the reception area. Her eyes widened at the tall, muscular woman who carried in several saddlebags and was followed by the most beautiful young woman she had ever seen.

Amy had entered before them and walked up to Dora. "They have just arrived in Nowhere and are looking for a room. I assured them that the hotel is now clean and comfortable since you've taken it over," Amy said. She added: "I've come for the account books. I'll take them with me, and you can check in these ladies."

Dora gave Amy a pat on the shoulder: "Yes, my dear, I have them ready piled up on my desk. Please take them."

Amy walked into the small room that served as Dora's office and general sitting room: a stove in the corner, two comfortable chairs, and a table that Dora proudly called her desk held various letters, papers, and the account books and invoices that Amy had come for. She stood for a while, listening to the conversation between the two strangers and Dora.

"A large double room you want, and a bath each," Dora said.

The larger of the ladies spoke again: "And plenty of fresh towels."

"How many nights do you want the room for?" asked Dora. She opened the guest book on the reception desk, ready for the newcomers to sign.

"I'm uncertain. There is a possibility that we may settle here in Nowhere. I'm looking for property, so it may be for a week or two. Would that be agreeable to you, Dora?" The soft voice matched the beautiful young woman. The tiny dimples when she smiled added to the charm of her face. Her heart-shaped face was graced by large violet eyes, fringed with dark lashes, and lips shaped in a perfect Cupid's bow. Escaping from beneath a stylish blue bonnet fringed with lace, matching the elegant riding habit with its tight waist and flared skirt, were ash-blonde curls.

Amy felt conscious of her clumpy feet in the men's boots, her sensible clothes, hair tied back into bunches, and a man's hat slung behind her head. Never had she felt so clumsy, so unfeminine. The girl at the desk had an exquisite riding habit. Despite the heavy trails she'd travelled—judging by the dust on their boots and their horses—she was still fresh, feminine, and dainty-looking.

Looking closer at the girl, Amy noticed that when she moved her arm, the sleeve of the exquisite, deep-blue, stylish costume had blood on it. Quite a lot of blood had soaked into the cuff. It was up into the area where the elegant buttons, in matching blue, echoed those on the jacket. The jacket hugged her trim figure, showing off her feminine curves. Fresh blood—and lots of it!

CHAPTER FORTY-ONE

The account books and invoices in her hands, Amy walked out into the lobby. She passed the newcomers and smiled at them. And took a closer look. Yes, that was definitely blood—and it had not been long on the sleeve. The blood was still fresh; it hadn't completely dried.

Slipping past the group chatting over at the reception desk, Amy made her way out and down Main Street to the general store. Puzzling over the bloodstains, she shook her head. The newcomers were unhurt, and it was no business of hers. She had just entered with the books still in her hand when she saw Ezra coming in the back door of the general store. His face was solemn, and he hurried towards her.

"Amy, you must come back to the ranch now. Your father has had a fall, and Nancy is struggling to cope with him and young David."

Wasting no time, Amy found herself on her horse alongside Ezra, bewildered at the strange and sudden turn of events as they rode towards Broken Horseshoe Ranch. In her saddlebags were some fruit for her father and a bottle of brandy, given to her by a worried Eliza. In another saddlebag were the account books for the hotel and the saloon. From what she had heard from Ezra, she felt certain that all her future time will be spent at the ranch. Having the books to do would keep her mind occupied, and also bring in some much-needed extra money.

Manuel and Josh were out delivering goods to the surrounding area. Eliza now had Clara to help in the store, so Amy could leave her friend, knowing that she wouldn't be left alone. Both women had rallied round

Amy, helping her get ready and insisting that she rode back on Bella. The buggy could remain in the stable for Josh when he returned from his deliveries.

"What happened, Ezra?" Amy said, after they had travelled a short distance from the town of Nowhere. In the hustle and bustle of getting ready for her home, she had not questioned Ezra properly. His first brief comments were that her father had a fall and was injured, and this was all she had registered. Nancy had sent for her, and Nancy was no alarmist. Newly married to Luke, Amy's father, in a marriage of convenience, she was loved and respected by her new stepdaughter. Nancy must need help, and this was an urgent cry for help from the woman.

Amy's thoughts and worries on the way back home did not prepare her for the reception she met when she arrived. Visions of her father, lying deathly pale on his bed with a hushed group of people wandering around him, did not survive the reality of what actually met her on her arrival.

Flora, the young Indian girl, was outside on the porch with her family. Amy rushed past the group gathered there, she was so anxious to see her father.

Luke was sitting at the table with a metal box in his hands with a smile of joy on his face. He hardly greeted Amy when she arrived and seemed surprised at his daughter's unexpected return, anxious about his health.

"Stop fussing, Amy—I just overbalanced and fell forward onto the ground. It was when I found this box. Kneeling down and leaning over it, I expect I just lost my balance." He was turning the box over and over in his hands. An ancient rusted clasp locked it securely. Amy could see that he was anxious to get it open but was frightened to disturb the artefact he held so reverently in his hands.

Amy looked at Nancy, who was standing beside Luke, and she whispered the words: "How is he really?"

Nancy took the girl to one side and put an arm round her. "It was scary for a while. He did overbalance in a way, but I think he passed out, and it was some time before he came round again. I don't know much about doctoring, Amy, but it worried me. That's why I sent Ezra to get you."

When Amy had rushed in, young David, who was crawling, had hastened towards her. Now she was standing with him, trying to pacify the youngster and greet him properly, and at the same time get the information she wanted about her father from Nancy.

Amy walked back to the doorway, where she could hear Flora and her family arguing. She turned back to Nancy: "Before I go out there, what is going on? Flora has just got her family back from their captivity. Why are they quarrelling?"

Nancy shook her head and stepped closer to the girl. She put an arm round Amy's shoulder, bringing her closer as she whispered in her ear: "Flora wants to stay here— she wants her family to settle on the ranch, just like Sam and his family are doing at Dry Creek Ranch. But her father wants to go to the reservation and join his tribe."

CHAPTER FORTY-TWO

Amy looked at Nancy. "But her father seems very ..."
Words failed Amy: she could hear the father's solemn
tones as he spoke with the voice of authority to his young
daughter. She didn't understand their Indian language,
but she could sense the importance of what he was saying
by the solemnity of his voice and his measured way of
speaking. He had decided on the course of action the
family was taking. But young Flora didn't want to go
with that plan.

Nancy reached over for the little Indian boy, David. As
a baby, Amy and Josh had found him beside his murdered
parents. Bringing him back to Broken Horseshoe Ranch,
Amy had taken sole care of him. Nancy took him from
Amy's arms. "David, come with me. I'll find you
something to eat while Amy talks to Flora," Nancy said,
heading towards the stove.

Amy took a deep breath before going out to the porch.
She glanced back at her father, who was still sitting at the
table, smiling at—and touching—the box in front of him.
She had seen the two Chinese boys out in the garden, and
Amy now realised why there were both busy at work out
there. They had only just waved at her as she arrived with
Ezra. Sensible, she thought. They were keeping out of the
way of all this dramatic fuss with Flora.

Amy went out onto the porch.

Flora's father raised a hand, gesturing for his daughter
to be quiet. He turned to greet the young woman with a
smile. He fully appreciated the efforts that had been made
to ensure the safety of his daughter and get his family's
release from their captivity: "We thank you for taking
care of my daughter. You made her into one of your

family. You have also made us welcome here."

As Amy began speaking, he raised a hand to silence her.

"I wish to follow my tribe. The reservation is not a good place for my family, but it is the place where our people are and, whilst in captivity, I realised I need to be with my people. I want to follow the customs and ways of my people. Do you understand, Amy?" His face was anxious as he stared at her, hoping to make her realise how important this was to him. And yet, how he wished not to seem ungrateful for the kindness and help they had given to him and his family.

Amy smiled at the man, respecting his traditions and culture. She answered him: "Yes, I understand. There is a place for your family at our ranch whenever you want. But I appreciate your wish to be with your extended family and friends and live in your traditional ways."

Flora rushed over to Amy and clung to her. "I don't want to go, Amy! I don't want *them* to go! I want us all to stay here together, for ever and ever.".

Flora's mother was making to rush over to her daughter, but the tall Indian who was the head of the family laid a hand on her arm gently, to check her from joining her daughter. He spoke again: "Flora does not wish to come with us. Miss Amy, she wishes to stay with you. She also wishes us to stay with you. She is but a child. But she has had a difficult time and I understand it was hard for her, thinking that we were all dead." He put his hand out towards his daughter and Flora rushed over to his side, clutching his hand and lifting it up towards her cheek.

Solemnly, he began speaking to her: "Your mother and I are leaving now to join the tribe and our family members on the reservation. Your brothers go with us." Here, he gestured to the two young boys standing beside the family. They were solemn-faced at this drama being enacted in front of them. Amy looked at them with pity and saw that they were still bruised and battered after their days working in the goldmine underground. They were thin and still bore the look of deprivation they had suffered in the mines.

As Amy looked at them, one of them spoke up: "My father is right. All that time whilst we were in darkness, all I could dream of was grass and sunshine and our tribe. We both wish to go back to the reservation. Amy, like my father, we thank you, and …" He gave a hand gesture to Amy, signifying his inability to thank her.

Amy smiled at them both. "I understand. We will sort you out some food and provisions for your journey. Flora, I think you must go with your family. Let me finish speaking. Please, Flora, go with your family—and I'm certain that you will settle down and enjoy life with them back on the reservation. We have loved having you here, and if it doesn't work out, and you are unhappy, you can always come back and join us again. How would that be?" Amy said.

Now with the thought of the little girl leaving, she realised how hard it would be to cope with her loss. Flora had been irritating sometimes, a nuisance at other times, but always she had been willing and kind with David and tried to be helpful. Yes, Amy thought, the little girl meant so much to her. She was going to miss her.

CHAPTER FORTY-THREE

Flora's mother now stepped forward. She knelt down before her daughter and stared deeply into her face. "My daughter, you have mourned our loss for so long, and you overcame it with this family here."

Flora interrupted her, saying, "Yes, Mother, but I want all of us to be together. All of us stay here on Broken Horseshoe Ranch."

Flora's mother spoke as if her daughter hadn't interrupted her. "If your father permits, I think you should stay here, Flora. Making our way to the reservation, we will endure a long, hazardous journey. We don't know what will be there when we arrive. We have heard rumours; it is not a good place. You are happy here and well cared for. Stay here, my daughter. If we settle well on the reservation, we will send for you. If it's bad, we will come back—if Luke agrees." She hugged her daughter to her and then stepped back to join her husband and two sons.

There was a silence for a moment, and then the Indian put his arm round his wife and said, "Wise words. Well, Flora, do you agree with that? Do you also agree, Amy?"

Amy nodded her head. "I think that is sensible. Flora is as brave as a lion but still a small girl and not up to such an arduous journey."

Luke came out of the doorway behind them and smiled at everyone happily, oblivious to the drama being acted out on the porch. "Ben, Ezra and I are going to open this box somehow," he said. Luke walked along the porch down towards the stable, Ben and Ezra following.

Amy caught her brother by the arm and whispered to him: "How is he really, Ben?" But she didn't need to really ask or wait for Ben's reply. The haggard look on Luke's face told her everything she needed to know. Her father had collapsed, and it had not been a good sign. His health was deteriorating—fast.

Ben looked every bit the young, frightened boy she remembered on their journey out to the ranch. He clutched her hand: "Amy, can you stay at the ranch more? We need you here. Pa needs you nearby. I don't think he has much longer, and I can't cope without you. Nancy is great, but ..." Amy could see the tears in her brother's eyes, and he swallowed hard, trying not to let his emotions run away with him.

Amy thought about the companionship of Eliza, and how interested she was in the comings and goings of the people in Nowhere. She would miss every moment of the interaction between the people she knew in the small township. Those thoughts had to be put to the back of her mind. Her duty was obvious: she was needed here on Broken Horseshoe Ranch. Amy had to stay with her father and brother. The account books gave her money and enabled her to work at home. She must be thankful for that blessing. But why did Amy feel as if she was being trapped into a life she didn't want?

Things had calmed down on the ranch. Flora and her family were seated out at the spring, talking over their plans for the future. The tiny girl was devastated that her family was leaving without her. She was torn between her love for them and the deep attachment she had for her new family group at Broken Horseshoe Ranch. The Indian family got their possessions together. They had arrived with very little but were leaving with additional items given to them by Nancy. They refused the offer of horses. Her hand clasping Amy's, Flora watched her family walk on out of her life yet again. The tears flowed, but the little girl soon went off to play with David at Amy's request.

Amy had watched them walk away with some relief. She felt her nerves being pulled taut with their drama added to that of her father and the ongoing care of young David. His grandmother over at Dry Creek Ranch would willingly take the boy, but Amy knew David relied on her. The baby she had found beside his dead parents had only known *her* love and care. His grandmother had never been fit after the difficulties she had undergone. Amy felt certain that she would find this boisterous young lad too much to handle and care for.

After they'd gone, she and Nancy tidied the ranch house and made Luke's bed ready for him. "That man is going to collapse from exhaustion. He's too wound up and too excited. It's not doing him any good at all," complained Nancy as she straightened up Luke's pillow.

Standing on the other side of the bed, Amy stood for a moment before speaking to Nancy with great care and deliberation. "Nancy, I think I'd better stay at the ranch full time. Josh can go into town alone. He's needed to help Manuel with the deliveries. Now they have Clara living in the store and working full time, I'm not really necessary to help in the store. But I can do these account books of the businesses in Nowhere at home, and help with David and Pa."

Nancy had gone to the window, opening the shutter to let in more fresh air. She whirled round at Amy's remarks, a delighted expression on her face, and she smiled at the girl. "That would be wonderful, Amy. David would love that, and I could help with your father more. Chan and Tom need to be out in the garden far more now that Chan has extended the growing area. It would make such a difference to me, and to all of us, if you were living here at the ranch full time."

Amy smiled back at the older woman, at her delight in her decision to stay at the ranch, but inwardly her heart sank. She knew she would miss the companionship of Eliza and the interesting developments that occurred in Nowhere township. But it was clear where her duty lay, and so Amy would put a brave face on it. She smiled at the older woman and hid her true feelings.

CHAPTER FORTY-FOUR

A cry of jubilation came from the barn, and Luke and the group emerged from it, smiling.

Nancy and Amy came out of the cabin onto the porch to see what was going on. As they did so, Josh could be seen riding up to the ranch. Puzzled at the early arrival of Josh, Amy wanted to go over and ask him about his early return. But seeing the excitement of the group exiting the barn meant Amy went to her father first.

"You opened the box—what was in it, Pa?" she asked him as he reached the porch. With a sideways glance, Amy saw Josh go to the stable to see to his horse. She'd find out why he had returned so early when he'd dealt with the care of the horse, and she had listened to her father's exciting news.

Reverently, Luke showed her the now open box; lying within it was a leather-bound journal. "I think the writing is the same as on the map I have. I reckon this journal was written by the same man: the Jesuit whose map led us here. Amy, do you realise what this means? I did the right thing in coming here. This was where he buried his journal. Perhaps this is where the Jesuit priest is buried himself? I did the right thing, Amy." Luke's excitement was too much for him, and Amy could see a slight staggering in his step as walked onto the porch and through the door.

Amy grabbed him by the arm and pulled him to the chair at the table. "Sit down, Pa," she said. "You're getting too stressed out with excitement."

Luke sat down with a thump. He clutched her hand and smiled up at her. "Ever since we came to this place, I wondered if I had made a wrong decision. Did I make a selfish choice to bring you both out here? Night after night, I have wondered if your lives would have been much better if we'd stayed in the house where you were born and brought up. What do you honestly think, Amy? Did I make a selfish decision?" His hand tightened its grasp on hers and she looked down at the anxious expression on his face.

Smiling down at her father, Amy shook his hand playfully. "Wrong decision, Pa! No, it was the best decision you could have ever made. I hated my life back east. You know I never fitted in with those catty, mean-spirited girls and their constant chatter about clothes and manners. The freedom living on this ranch gives to me is wonderful. As for Tom, he can write to his heart's content, and he also loves the outdoor life here. No, Pa, you made the right decision whether or not you found the Jesuit's journal."

But her last words drifted away and went unheard by Luke; the journal was in his hands. He'd opened the first page, and he was lost in the world of the Jesuit priest who had written those words so many years ago.

Amy looked up at Nancy, who smiled at the girl and shook her head. "That's him. We'll get nothing out of him until he's finished reading it," Nancy said, laughing.

Josh walked in and went straight over to the stove for a fresh cup of coffee. On his way, his shrewd glance took in Luke and summed up the man's health in a second. With the tin cup of steaming brew in his hand, he turned to Amy and lifted a quizzical eyebrow.

Amy told him of Flora and her family, and Luke showed him the box and the treasure he had found within it. Excitement in the man was all-consuming, and Amy worried afresh that this would be enough to set him off on another passing-out trauma.

Josh drank his coffee and turned to Amy: "Amy, I'm riding back to Nowhere. I heard this afternoon that Charles Roberts is going to Duloe for at least three nights on business. It's renovations with that boarding house he's turning into a saloon. He's sorting it all out and getting it ready to open for business. I'm going to take the opportunity while he's away to break into his office tonight. There's no way he'll travel back this evening, whereas he may well come back tomorrow or the next day. What do you think? Do you think I should do it, Amy?"

"Do it, Josh! Yes, I think it is a brilliant idea. I wish I could come with you. How I wish I could look at his account books. If there are any discrepancies in them, I reckon I'd be the one to find them," Amy said thoughtfully. "Should I come with you Josh?" she asked hopefully. She wondered if there was any chance of escaping the ranch for a few hours to take part in the burglary.

At that moment, David's voice could be heard shouting for her. He'd woken from his nap and was looking for her. Amy turned as the little boy crawled out of her bedroom towards her. She stooped and picked him up and looked at Josh. "No, I'd better stay here," Amy said with a sigh.

A few moments later, Amy stood beside Josh. He'd saddled Star and hitched the horse to the rail. David, held in Amy's arms, stretched out to pat the horse.

Josh put a hand on her shoulder: "I'm afraid you are needed here, Amy. I was talking to Chan, and he said they're getting a bumper crop. He and Tom work all day and every day to keep on top of the crops. Manuel can take everything they grow, and it's an enormous boost to the finances of the ranch. Meanwhile, they both said that Nancy is finding it difficult to cope in the house. She's taken over some of the cooking, and what with that and your father and David, it's just too much for her."

Amy was quiet for a moment, and then she looked at Josh. "Yes, I know—Nancy looks exhausted. Off you go then, Josh, and take care. I don't trust that Charles. Watch out for booby traps in his office. I think it's going to be quite important, what you find in his office," Amy said.

Little did Amy realise her words would come true in ways that neither she nor Josh could imagine. The importance of the breaking and entering exploit into Charles Roberts's office would have far-reaching results for both of them and change their lives irrevocably.

CHAPTER FORTY-FIVE

It felt strange. He was on his own. Josh turned round in the saddle and looked back at the Broken Horseshoe Ranch house. Amy stood on the porch, her hands on the rail. She raised a hand when she saw him turn round, and he gave her a wave. Even at the distance he was from the ranch house, he could see her unhappiness at being left behind. Josh turned back and set his face towards Nowhere.

"Come on, Star, let's get going. I've a long night ahead of me."

The journey was spent by Josh thinking about his plans for the night ahead. Earlier, he had discussed his proposed burglary venture to Charles Roberts's place of business with Manuel and Eliza. They had been in full agreement. Disliking the man, they could not think that Josh was in the wrong. They had seen the damage and distress Charles Roberts had caused in the lives of those he had swindled. To this day, there were many families trying to make a living out of the land he had sold to them. The lack of water on their land caused their dreams of a bountiful life and fruitful crops to perish.

There was a bed for Josh in the back of the general store; Eliza had made one up for him. He would stable Star and see that he was bedded down for the night after the strenuous ride from Broken Horseshoe Ranch. Eager to get started on his burglary, Josh had encouraged the horse to make good time. Manuel had left the back door of the general store unlocked, and a candle stub and matches were placed on a shelf for Josh.

Josh stood at the entrance to the offices of Charles Roberts, trying to calm his breathing. It was a simple building, thrown up with more speed than finesse. The front door facing Main Street had two windows on either side, and Josh knew that the front office of the wooden building had a doorway through to a back room. Charles now slept there after being thrown out of the hotel. No longer welcome in the hotel now that George Binns was dead and the hotel had been taken over by his wife, Dora, Charles had taken to sleeping in his office.

Struggling to open the door at the keyhole, the piece of wire he was using bent awkwardly, and then, with a click, the door opened. Surprised that he had managed it, Josh stood for a moment. Had it been opened already? Surprised at the speed at which he got in, he stood there for a moment, listening. But there was only silence. He flattened himself against the wall of the building and looked up and down the street. No one. Not a soul seemed to stir. He wasn't surprised. It was late. Most of the residents of Nowhere were early risers and went to bed when it grew dark, not wishing to light up a room.

The last revellers in the saloon bar had also been gone for some time. Staggering home, or perhaps lying somewhere to sleep it off, they had all disappeared. His breathing slowed, and his heart was no longer beating frantically. Pushing open the door slowly, Josh edged round it. He'd lit the candle stub and had it in his hand. Shielding it from the sudden draught of his movement, he edged his way inside Charles Roberts's office.

"Don't move!" The voice was unexpected. Josh gave a jump, and his candle shuddered but mercifully stayed alight. He raised it a little higher and found himself looking into the face of the most beautiful creature he'd ever seen. "Don't move," she said. "Otherwise, I'll have to shoot you."

The words were said in a soft voice, a well-spoken voice. But there was no mistaking the deadly meaning of them. "If I shoot you, we'll have to explain why we are both in Charles Roberts's office at this time of night. What brings you here?"

His breath had returned, and Josh found his voice. "I'm hoping to find information about Charles Roberts's dealings with a killer. A man determined to seek my death," he said. "What about you? Why are you rifling through his files?"

In the short time Josh had been staring at the young woman, he'd noticed that she had a filing cabinet open and the lock had been damaged. Several files lay scattered on a desk, and she had some papers in her hand. The other hand held a small derringer. The small oil lamp sitting on the desk illuminated the room, but only the limited area around the desk and filing cabinet.

"I'm looking for papers dealing with his acquisition of a ranch. I'm *certain* he falsified documents to get it fraudulently. If I can find the original documents, I can prove he's a liar." Her words were whispered, but behind them Josh could sense the bitterness and hatred for the man. Also, Josh could see that her hand with the gun never wavered, and he had no doubt at all that, if he moved, she would indeed shoot him. There was a glacial coldness about her eyes that meant he would never argue with her. Not while she was holding a gun, pointing straight at his chest.

For a moment, she stared at him intently, weighing him up. Seemingly coming to some decision, she lowered the gun. Then she spoke again: "I've looked through these files. There was nothing in them for me. Suggest you look through them for your business." She pushed them over the desk towards him, and she reached into the filing cabinet for more to look at herself.

A file opened, Josh began searching through it for any details of payments to a Mr Duke, and any details of payments made to local businessmen. As he did so, he glanced up at the girl, who was searching methodically through file after file. What was a beautiful girl—well-spoken and dressed in the latest fashion—doing robbing a business in Main Street, Nowhere?

Never had Josh seen such a beautiful woman—or was she a girl? It proved difficult in the subtle light of the oil lamp to work out her correct age. It didn't prove difficult at all to show the elegance and style of her costume, and the trim figure beneath it. As she moved nearer to the lamp with a paper to concentrate on the fine print, Josh saw the tendrils of fine blonde curls slide forward past her porcelain-white cheek and onto the costume collar with the pale blue lace. She glanced up at him, suddenly aware of his scrutiny, and Josh was taken aback. Never in his life had he seen eyes that colour before. They were a brilliant blue-violet, and in the lamplight the violet seemed to be startingly bright. Caught staring at the girl, Josh felt himself blush and began concentrating harder on the task at hand.

CHAPTER FORTY-SIX

Some time passed. All that could be heard was the rustling of papers and the final guttering of Josh's candle. He took out another candle stub from his pocket and lit it from the old one. Josh was conscious of the occasional glance from the girl as she worked through the files. The office was small, and the candle smoke and the burning oil lingered in the room, creating a warm and cosy atmosphere. Josh was unsure why that should be. Here, in a time and space apart, they searched silently.

Charles had a reputation for fraudulent dealings. Both intruders were determined to find evidence of these transactions. The room smelled of stale cigar smoke and whiskey. To Josh's fanciful thoughts, there was a powerful smell of greed itself. The atmosphere clung to the wooden walls and worn-out leather chairs.

"Some papers here have stuck together. One of them mentions a ranch and has details of it. At the top, a note addresses the possibility of bypassing the legalities. The bottom paper was stuck to the one above, and I think this lower one may be what you're looking for. Is it the Wild Horse Ranch details you're looking for?" Josh moved over to the young woman and handed her the paper with its note.

Holding it nearer to her oil lamp, she glanced down at it and then smiled. "This is exactly what I wanted. Thank you for finding it." Despite her beautiful face, her smile took on a cruel and vengeful look. "Thank you," she repeated. Her finger moved down the legalistic jargon. Her eyes were intent upon it: "I would have missed that, seeing as it was stuck to the other paper. You breaking in to join me was a stroke of luck for me. This is it! I've searched for this for many years. Now I have it, and I can prove what I have always suspected." She folded the paper up and slid it into a bag she was carrying. Then she straightened up and stuck out her hand. "Cassidy. I'm pleased to make your acquaintance, even if it is in the most unusual circumstances."

Josh stuck out his hand and shook the gloved hand resting in his: "Josh Barnes. I am delighted to have been of service, Miss Cassidy. I'm looking for information on a man named Duke."

She shook her head: "Just Cassidy. My name is Rose Cassidy, but everyone just calls me Cassidy."

Cassidy gave a laugh, more of a throaty chuckle. She glanced at him, then moved to a different filing cabinet drawer. "Let me repay your good deed, and I'll see if I can find exactly what you're looking for." As she opened the drawer, she turned and gave him a roguish sideways look. "I don't think we'll get this chance ever again. Let's make the most of it, Josh Barnes. There may well be further documents relating to the purchase of the Wild Horse Ranch. What exactly are you searching for?"

Josh tried to make it simple, but the explanation of his predicament was difficult to phrase. "Payments are being made by a man called Duke to Charles Roberts. These payments are for surveillance of myself in Nowhere. They also are connected with killers sent out to Nowhere to find me and ensure my death," Josh said in a grim voice.

Her hand stopped its search through files and folders. The face, heart-shaped, with its brilliant violet eyes, turned and looked at him: "What did you do to this man? What deed was so evil that it requires killers to be set upon you?"

Josh shrugged his shoulders and held out his hands in a gesture of ignorance. "I don't know. Maybe I deserved it. Perhaps I should be killed for some terrible action of mine. I just don't know!" Josh slammed his hand down on the desk in an impotent fury. "I was found in the desert, unconscious, with nothing on me but the names of Broken Horseshoe Ranch and Josh Barnes on a piece of paper in my pocket. There was never any Josh Barnes living at the ranch. Everyone thought I was Josh Barnes. That's now my name. Then I discovered people were being sent to kill me. The only thing I know is that this man Duke wants me dead."

Cassidy sat down on one of the leather armchairs. For a long moment she stared at him, her eyes looking him up and down, as she seemed to calculate the truth of this statement. "Now you're seeking this man, Duke, and you know Charles Roberts is in his pay. That's why you're here looking through his papers."

Never taking her eyes off him, Cassidy tapped her elegant fingers on the arm of the leather chair. Josh was aware of that calculating gaze, and also beginning to realise that Cassidy should not be underestimated. He remembered that derringer pistol—it had appeared in seconds. For a wild moment, he wondered if he'd got everything wrong. Sure, she was looking for those documents concerning an illegal transaction over the Wild Horse Ranch. However, she *could* be on the payroll of Charles or Duke. Could she be the next assassin sent to kill him? Had he been a fool in accepting her story and leaving himself open to certain death?

CHAPTER FORTY-SEVEN

The air in the room seemed electric. The breath in Josh seemed to vanish, and he struggled not to gasp. Her scrutinising violet eyes made him feel vulnerable, fearing instant death if he failed to meet her expectations. A long moment stretched between them. Josh felt the palms of his hands become sweaty, and the blood pounded in his head; he felt hypnotised by the young woman before him.

The moment that had frightened Josh and made him feel near to death was no longer present. This was no woman to be feared, sitting in front of him. No, the petite blonde with a heart-shaped face and those violet eyes that danced with laughter at him could never have threatened him. He was imagining things. How stupid of him.

Cassidy's voice brought him back to the present and out of his strange thoughts. "Were you going to tidy up once you had finished searching?" she asked him.

Josh looked around at Charles's business premises. He had to give the man credit. His office had been well ordered, spotless, and showed his attention to detail. Now papers were strewn about, and alphabetically labelled card files were open and scattered on one side of the room. Those they had not searched through were piled up on the desk, ready for their attention.

"No, I hadn't planned on tidying up. Looking about me, it's just as well. I wouldn't know where anything went. Why do you ask? Did you intend to leave no trace after you'd gone?" Josh asked her.

Cassidy looked around the room at the mess they'd both made and shrugged her shoulders. "No. I'd rather he knew someone was looking through his stuff. There are several files still to go through. I thought I'd have a brandy while I carried on searching. Do you fancy one?" Jumping up out of the well-worn leather chair, she walked across to the small table that held decanters and glasses. Taking two glasses, she opened one decanter, sniffed it, and put the stopper back on it. "Some sort of sherry. Must be for the elderly ladies he likes to bamboozle and rob of their savings. Aha! This is a fine quality brandy." She put the stopper down and poured two generous servings of the fragrant liquor into the glasses. Handing one to Josh, she clinked their glasses together: "Here's to a successful burglary."

Josh grinned at her and took a sip of the brandy. "This is excellent stuff. I don't know how I know, having no memory, but I reckon this is the finest I've ever tasted."

"Let's finish up here. I don't want to be missed from the hotel. Dora dislikes Charles Roberts as much as I do, but I don't want her to be involved in my escapade." The words were thrown over her shoulder as she reached for more files and started flipping through the papers.

Silence descended yet again. But Josh, looking out the window, was aware of the darkness receding. They had to hurry. Charles would not be back yet, at least not by wagon. There was, however, the possibility that he would ride back. Unlikely—but it wasn't worth taking a chance.

There was nothing in any of the files Josh had looked through. He threw the last of them down on the floor in disgust. It had been a mistake coming here. Nothing about Lord and his transactions with Charles could be found.

"This concerns you," Cassidy whispered. She looked over a paper once, and then again, before handing over to Josh. Another swallow of the brandy, and the empty glass was placed on the table as she watched him read the paper.

"It's a promise of payment from him. He's paying Charles monthly for information about my activities. As I do very little, he's paying out for nothing," muttered Josh.

"Look at the small print over the page," she said, pointing at it. Josh turned the page and found the bank details: the sum of money that was paid monthly and the bank it was paid from. It was the bank in Duloe.

"No name! There is *still* no name. I now know for certain that Charles is being paid to watch me. How can I find out who is paying that money out of their bank account?"

Cassidy smiled and then spoke: "I think one of the poorly paid clerks at the bank may well provide you with information. You can either bribe the man or threaten him. Either way, I think you may find out the identity of the man who wants you dead."

Resuming their search, both continued looking through the files. Cassidy found a box in the bottom drawer of the filing cabinet. She lifted it out and placed it on the table. It was a wooden box with a padlock. Using the letter opener, she swiftly broke the padlock. Opening it, she flung the wooden lid backwards.

Josh, by this time, had come to her side to look at the interior of the chest. They both gave whistles and gasps at the interior of the wooden box. A few small canvas bundles, which they reckoned would contain gold, were piled up one upon the other.

"Gold!" Josh breathed out in a gasp of astonishment.

"And money, and jewellery," Cassidy stated and began poking an elegant finger through piles of ill-gotten gains. Her body became frozen. Standing beside her, Josh could feel the tightness of her body and the tension of this young woman. She poked her finger into the mass of jewellery and drew out a ring. It was ornate, made of a fine gold, and fashioned almost crudely with initials. A craftsman-made ring, rather than a product of a fine jeweller. Cassidy put it into the palm of her hand and stared down at it. Then her hand closed over it tightly and she swore under her breath. The words were so soft and low Josh couldn't make them all out. He knew they were swear words, and that they had been forced from the girl by the overwhelming emotions she was visibly labouring under.

CHAPTER FORTY-EIGHT

"You know this ring?" Josh had to ask. What did finding this ring mean to Cassidy? She was obviously in the grip of intense emotions at the sight of it. More than anything, he wanted to help her—but unless he knew what the sight of this ring meant to her, there was no possibility of him helping her in any way whatsoever.

"This ring was my father's. I suspected Charles was involved in the fraudulent acquisition of my father's ranch. I know that now; I have the papers to prove it. What I didn't know, but finding this ring proves, is his involvement with the gang that murdered my parents." The words were delivered in a flat, emotionless voice from Cassidy as she stared fixedly at the ring. "My father was wearing this ring when he was thrown off his ranch, and they were murdered on their way to the next town, supposedly by bandits. If Charles Roberts has this ring in his possession, it proves he was in cahoots with that gang."

"Will you tell the sheriff about his involvement with the gang?" Josh asked her. He felt helpless against this appalling crime that had been visited upon her and her family.

"What use would he be against a man like Charles Roberts? How could I explain finding this?" She waved the ring about. "No—I'd like to kill Charles Roberts. At this moment, I would love to put a bullet through his head." The determination in her voice made Josh thankful that Charles Roberts wasn't standing there in his own office. He knew in that moment that, despite her delicate demeanour, Cassidy would shoot her parents' murderer.

Instead of speaking to her, or trying to calm her down,

Josh went over to the small table and poured out another glass of brandy for the girl. "Here, you've had a shock, finding that ring. Take a sip of brandy." He handed her the glass and gently took her arm and guided her back into the big leather chair. She sat back in it, one hand clutching the ring; with the other, her fingers tightened round the brandy glass. At that moment, Josh knew he would do anything, anything in the world to protect and shield Cassidy from the evil surrounding her. He knew he had never felt like this for anyone else. The thought of Amy fleetingly crossed his mind. But Amy was always in control. Amy was sturdy and had learned to be tough and strong in the Arizona desert lands. Coming to Broken Horseshoe Ranch, Amy had relished throwing off her feminine trappings, as she called them, that she had grown up with back east.

Cassidy sipped again at the brandy. The ring, she clung to. Then, she opened the tiny reticule she always carried and brought out a handkerchief, lace-edged with purple and embroidered with violets. The aroma of violets themselves wafted towards Josh. She carefully wrapped the ring in the middle of it, folding it over and over again to make sure it was safe before replacing it into the reticule. Cassidy tightened the reticule strings and hung it back on her wrist. A deep breath from her was followed by her draining the last of the brandy. She held the glass out to Josh: "Thank you for the brandy. And thank you for not badgering me with questions and comments."

Josh took the glass from her and replaced it on the table beside the decanters. He turned back towards her and laughed. "And if I had asked you questions, and badgered you with comments, what then?"

"I'd probably have shot you," Cassidy laughed. Josh laughed back, but the slight tingle of doubt swept across his mind in a flash. Did she really mean that? Was it really a joke?

She stood up. The costume she was wearing swished as she smoothed down the skirts and straightened the jacket, patting it down. The tiny buttons down her jacket's bodice were mimicked on its sleeves. Josh noticed a bloodstain on one sleeve but thought nothing of it. Cassidy looked at the box again and poked through it but seemed to find nothing of interest in there. "Do you want any of this gold?" she asked Josh. The question hung in the air. Josh knew his answer was important to the girl, but he didn't know why. He looked down into the box and turned over the coins and the small bags of gold.

"No, I want none of his stolen goods. It should go to those that he robbed, not to give him a fine home, expensive clothes, and food. Others, such as the homesteaders, are starving because of his evil manipulation of those adverts encouraging them to buy worthless land. No, Cassidy, I don't want it."

Her hand was taken out of the chest and the lid was pushed down, and she replaced the box in the bottom filing cabinet drawer where she'd found it. All the papers had been looked through, and no more information could be found for either of them.

It was Cassidy who decided first she was leaving, that she had accomplished all that she sought to do. She turned to walk out. Josh followed her and closed the door carefully behind them. Without a word, she was gone— soundless as she slipped along the boardwalk to the back of the hotel. For a moment Josh wondered if he should have offered to accompany her. Somehow, he had realised she wanted to be on her own. Finding her father's ring like that had shaken and distressed her. Josh didn't realise how important the ring was to Cassidy. He didn't realise how far-reaching the consequences of finding it would be for all of them in Nowhere. Taking that ring had been bad enough. But Charles Roberts's big mistake had been keeping it. Cassidy finding it in his place of business had signed his death warrant.

CHAPTER FORTY-NINE

When Josh had returned to the general store, Cassidy had slipped away into the darkness. Josh looked after her. For a moment he stood, trying to come to terms with the impact that Cassidy had made on his life in just a few brief moments. Then he shook his head, as if clearing it from a dream, and turned his steps towards the general store.

It took Josh an age before he could fall asleep. The mattress and blanket laid out for him at the back of the general store by Eliza was comfortable enough, but his mind was whirling. All that occupied his thoughts were Cassidy's violet eyes. With her heart-shaped face and her petite body, clad in the elegant costume she wore, she was a delight for any man's eyes. Even Josh chuckled at the old-fashioned thoughts running through his head as he imagined saving her from dragons. He had become familiar with the capable Amy, with her down-to-earth approach to life and the hazardous situations they often found themselves in.

But: he thought again of Cassidy, and wondered why he felt so conflicted about her. There had been a moment when he felt the pretty, naïve young woman seated in the big armchair before him had vanished. There was no movement in her body. Her hands remained clasped loosely in front of her. She had not moved a muscle, but an intensity had begun to emanate from her. Those eyes—that had been sparkling with laughter—changed: soft violet eyes had glittered into hard stones of amethyst. Yes, that was it, Josh thought. A new, calculating look appeared within them. This promised trouble for him, if her summing up of him had not been favourable. Josh almost shuddered at the thought. How could he think that of such a beautiful young woman? Then Josh thought back to his instinctive actions when struggling with Amy in dangerous predicaments. He'd followed his instinct so many times, as had Amy, and they had both been proved right. Josh realised he was captivated by Cassidy but would be careful about moving forward in his acquaintance with her. Somehow, he felt there was far more to Cassidy—and that he would be grateful, in the future, for his instinctive awareness of how possibly dangerous she could be.

Meanwhile, Cassidy had, on reaching the darkness behind Charles Roberts's place of business, stood quietly watching Josh. She saw him look after her, the candle stub guttering its last flickers, before he walked away.

The figure materialised behind her: "Well?"

Cassidy turned and spoke to Martha, who had been waiting for her in the darkness. "I found the original lease, and his notes. I also found my father's ring." The words were simply stated, but the emotion behind them could be felt by the older woman, who reached out and put an arm round the young woman beside her.

"What now?" Martha asked, looking down at her mistress in name, but in truth a friend—a person for whom she would lay down her life.

"Now we go back in and take some of the gold that we discovered. Josh didn't want to be accused of stealing gold if he was caught for burglary," said Cassidy.

"And you?" The question was posed bluntly, but with a chuckle in the voice.

"How well you know me, Martha!" Cassidy walked back towards the door, which was still ajar, and into Charles's place of business. She took a match from her reticule and, striking it on the wooden door frame, lit the small oil lamp again.

"Martha, have a quick look around and see if I've missed any more papers concerning the ranch. I'll take some of those bags of gold for myself. The gold coins—some of them I'll put in Manuel and Eliza's store. They can help the homesteaders with their bills. It's probably all their money, anyway. I think Josh has the right of it, and I will leave most of it here in the box."

The large woman walked lightly, despite her immense size, and worked efficiently as she checked through papers and documents. "Nothing. But there's a lot of documents here that lead me to believe he has been delving into some shady deals. I think he's got himself involved with some very dangerous people," Martha said. She smiled at her young mistress, who was cramming the gold and coins into her reticule. "Here, there's a canvas bag over here for money, lying empty. Put it all in the bag, and let's get out of here. Someone in this one-horse town might not sleep through the night. I'd hate to be caught here with all this mess."

Whilst Martha waited impatiently at the door, Cassidy placed the coins in another canvas bag she had found. Cassidy trusted Eliza and Manuel would use the money to help the homesteaders feed and provide for themselves for some time ahead. Martha was going to drop the bag off as she walked around to the store the following morning, with a note explaining what they were to be used for.

When they reached the safety of their bedroom in the hotel, Martha stood facing Cassidy, her arms crossed in front of her. "What now, Cassidy? You found the documents you were looking for, and you have your father's ring back."

***

Next morning, seated at the mirror on the chest of drawers in the bedroom, Cassidy put down her comb and patted her hair, putting the very last curl into place. She cast an appraising look over her outfit. Today, her riding habit was of a dark green, cut in an almost mannish style, yet the jacket contoured perfectly to her curvaceous figure, creating a truly feminine look. She stood up, bending backwards to peer in the tiny mirror to check that the skirt hung correctly and that the costume lay flat along her shoulders and back. Then she turned her attention to her reticule, making certain the required necessities were in it.

Cassidy's reticule was larger than the average woman wore. It had to be, because it carried so much more. Her derringer lay on the dresser itself, cleaned thoroughly and ready to slip into the tiny pocket sewn into the sleeve of her costume. Martha was wonderful at needlework and had perfected hidden pockets in all of Cassidy's costumes. There was the derringer in her sleeve and a knife in her skirt, and a pocket for a small length of chain to be hidden in the hem of each garment. Surprisingly enough, that length of chain not only weighted the skirt down during journeys and walks through Western desert countryside, but it had become extremely useful in many other ways. Cassidy never hesitated to use it from binding up a recalcitrant outlaw's hands, or even strangling him. Cassidy's face showed a wicked smile as she recalled tightening the chain around someone's neck. She had no qualms about it, no regrets, and certainly no pity for the man. *He* had shown no pity when he'd mutilated and killed the children and parents of a ranching family. No,

Cassidy killed—but only those who deserved it, and it was always carried out on men wanted by the law.

CHAPTER FIFTY

It didn't seem longer than a few minutes before Manuel shook Josh by the shoulder.

"Josh, wake up. The sheriff is getting a posse ready. I've to man the sheriff's office. I've got to be his deputy again. But you're wanted in the posse. Take my horse, it's fresh. Star had the journey to Nowhere from Broken Horseshoe Ranch." With that remark, the swarthy, overweight proprietor of the general store waddled off full of self-importance. His voice could be heard muttering to himself again and again. "Deputy Sheriff. That's me, Deputy Sheriff of the town of Nowhere."

Josh yawned, stretched, and knuckled the sleep out of his eyes. He rolled up the mattress and blanket, ready to be put away.

Eliza walked up to him, carrying a steaming tin mug of coffee. "Drink this, Josh. You wouldn't have had much sleep. You'll need the coffee to get you going."

Gratefully, Josh took the tin mug and began drinking, despite its scalding heat. "What's happened? Manuel didn't tell me much."

"There's some trouble out at the Grangers' place. That's why the sheriff is getting a posse together. Your horse is saddled and ready to ride, Josh. Manuel did that already. So, drink that coffee and have a bite to eat quickly. The sheriff is still getting the others ready to ride to the Grangers' place."

Swallowing a few hasty mouthfuls and gulping it down with the remains of his coffee, Josh questioned Eliza again. "What exactly happened to the Grangers? Are they dead? They are a wonderful couple. I'd hate to think anything bad has happened to them."

Eliza's face clouded over. "Ramon, their foreman, was out rounding up some stray cattle when he saw some riders heading towards the ranch. Then he heard gunfire and shouting. Before he could return to the ranch, the same group rode away on fresh horses and carrying further saddlebags." Eliza shook her head. The Grangers were a couple well liked by everyone, and she feared the worst had happened to them. She continued telling Josh the little she knew.

"All we know is that Ramon was nearer to Nowhere than the ranch. So, he rode directly to Nowhere to alert the sheriff and get the posse to go out to see what had happened. It's obviously some wanted gang who are seeking to hide out on Devil's Mountain. It's time they were got rid of for good!" Eliza said, angry at this new incursion of wanted men into the mountains around Nowhere.

Handing Eliza her tin mug with his grateful thanks, Josh picked up his jacket and hat, put on his weapon, and raced out of the general store to the horse that was waiting for him. No sooner had he gone round to the front of the general store than he saw Sheriff Lance Grey. He was riding down the main street of Nowhere with a large group of men behind him. There had been no need to encourage men to join the posse. The Grangers were well liked in Nowhere town. They were among the very few ranchers who had arrived with money, yet were always willing to give to a good cause, and their ranch house was always open to anybody passing by. Mr Granger, a genial host, pressed coffee, beer, wine, and spirits on anyone who dropped in, whilst his wife was renowned for the wonderful cakes she baked. Her love for baking turned into an obsession, leading her to sell her goods at the general store. Manuel and Josh always brought back a few cakes during their weekly deliveries. The trouble was that very few of her cakes reached the customers who came into the general store: Josh and Amy, and Manuel and Eliza, always took a cake for themselves and the family at Broken Horseshoe Ranch!

"They are *too* good to waste on the customers," Manuel always said, and made certain that he and Eliza got the coffee cake that Mrs Granger excelled in making.

How Josh hoped that this amiable couple had been left unharmed. It was with a grim face he joined the group of men riding out towards the Grangers' place. Josh wondered what they would find when they reached the ranch.

Josh rode up to the head of the posse to hear Ramon explaining to the sheriff what exactly had happened.

"They didn't see me. I was riding out away from the ranch, looking for a couple of stray cows. There were five of them, riding toward the ranch, shooting their guns in the air and yelling. There was no doubt at all of what they were about to do." Ramon took a deep breath and gulped before continuing. His face was set in deep lines of horror and anguish. "But I couldn't help, as I was only one man. I knew my only way to get help for them was to ride for Nowhere and the sheriff."

Every man riding in that posse, who heard Ramon's story, carried the same expression on their face: anger, and a determination that—if possible—the Grangers and Ramon's wife would be saved. If, as everyone feared, they were to be found dead, there would be no mercy given when the posse caught up with the gang.

Silence fell over the group of horsemen as they rode as fast as was safe to the Grangers' ranch. Guns were checked out and rifles made ready for ease of a quick shot if necessary.

"I reckon they'll head up to Devil's Mountain," said Grey, turning to Ramon. "There's a pass up away from the river, isn't there? That leads them round the back of Nowhere."

The Mexican thought for a moment, and agreed with the sheriff: "It's where I've heard a couple of other gangs are hiding out. They've found it a convenient place—and it's difficult for any lawmen to reach them."

"We'll see what's happened at the Grangers' place. But if, as we think, they head up to those canyons up in Devil's Mountain, that's where we'll go next. And we'll get them and make them pay," said the sheriff.

Murmurs of assent from all those riding alongside him greeted these remarks. The rest of that frantic journey towards the Grangers' ranch passed in silence.

CHAPTER FIFTY-ONE

The track to the Grangers' wound around a narrow canyon before opening out onto some flat level land sloping down to the Avon river. Starting from Devil's Mountain, it meandered through rocky canyons and gorges before reaching this flat land and descending to the lowlands and desert. The Grangers had bought their ranch because of its proximity to the river. They had money and enjoyed a pleasant lifestyle on their property. Mr Granger was well known for being a hospitable host. Whenever Josh and Manuel delivered to him, they had always to have a coffee or a glass of something. Mrs Granger, however, outdid her husband with hospitality, by producing the most delicious cakes Josh had ever tasted.

Josh thought of the friendly, cheerful couple and hoped they had somehow survived. Ramon's wife had always been pleasant and smiled at them on every visit, and again Josh couldn't bear the thought of what had happened to her. A quick glance sideways to the man riding alongside him showed that the swarthy Mexican had his face set hard and was obviously trying to prepare himself for the worst possible outcome.

Sheriff Grey drew his horse up and raised a hand to slow the posse down: "Around those cliffs, we see the land going down to the ranch. I think we'll go slower now, and be prepared for any ambush from the bandits. I doubt they'll do it, and I reckon they'll be far away by now, but it's best to be careful." The nods of agreement were followed by guns being loosened in holsters and some rifles laid out across knees, ready for action.

Silence greeted them as they finally rode beneath the

wrought-iron sign proclaiming the Grangers' ranch. Josh looked up at it and thought of the many happy times he had ridden under it to the ranch. Then he thought of the other times, when—well fed, and mellowed by alcohol—he and Manuel had ridden out again. How he hoped that somehow the Grangers had survived.

"The horses have gone. All our good horses have gone—and they've left their rubbishy ones behind," Ramon said as he jumped off his horse and raced towards the farmhouse.

Josh and Lance were close behind him, guns at the ready. Heedless of the sheriff's pronouncement to take his time and go slowly in case of ambush, the Mexican raced through the doorway, shouting Rosita's name at the top of his voice.

Josh followed him, Lance behind him, and the three stood looking around. The farmhouse was wrecked. The bandits had searched for jewellery, gold, and money—and, when they hadn't found any, they had ruthlessly destroyed everything. Going into the kitchen, Josh could see that provisions had been stolen and, again, a mess had been made.

"There's nobody here. Where are they?" Lance said quietly in Josh's ear. Ramon followed them into the kitchen and yelled again for his wife.

There was a loud creaking noise, and a large cupboard in the kitchen swung out towards the three men. All three crouched down, guns at the ready, facing the opening as it grew wider.

A voice cried out: "Ramon, is that you? You're alive!" And out tumbled Rosita, who flung herself into her husband's arms.

Following her, and edging round the cupboard door,

was Mr Granger. He emerged, his face lighting up with delight as he saw Josh and the sheriff. He turned back and reached out a hand: "Come on, my dear. We have been saved. The sheriff has arrived."

The members of the posse felt relief when the Grangers and their housekeeper tumbled out of their hiding place. But the relief was short-lived: Mrs Granger burst into tears at the sight of the house she had once been so proud of.

"We heard them talking," Mr Granger said as they all congregated in the kitchen. The housekeeper and Mrs Granger struggled to find something for them to drink and eat.

"There's a spy hole, so we could look out at what was going on. Two of the men stood talking just beside our hiding place," Mr Granger continued. His face had taken on a wrathful expression, replacing the relieved look from earlier. "'Can't find them,' they said. One man said it didn't matter. Charles had told them he wanted no murders, just wanted us chased off the property."

The sheriff locked eyes with Mr Granger and spoke quietly, his face set in hard lines. "You are sure about this? There's no mistaking what was said?"

Mrs Granger turned to the sheriff: "Yes, there's no mistaking that name. When the other man asked why we were to be chased off our property, he said Charles does that time and again, and then buys the place cheap."

Her voice fell into the growing silence as the enormity of what had happened sank into those men standing around the kitchen. The appalling state of the property after the five bandits had arrived, and the sheer greed of the man who had ordered it, dismayed each one of them.

"At least we're alive," said Mr Granger. He looked at

his wife, at her tear-streaked face and shaking hands, and he walked over beside her and put an arm around her shoulders. "But it's worked. We're moving away, aren't we, my dear?" he said in a flat voice, looking down at her.

"Yes, I love it here. I love the people in Nowhere. But most of all, I love my garden." Her voice dropped to a whisper, and they struggled to hear her. "But I can't stay here after this. He's won. Charles has got his way. We have to move." As she uttered the last words, she put a hand to her mouth and, sobbing, rushed out of the room.

CHAPTER FIFTY-TWO

The men shuffled their feet and cleared their throats, not one of them knowing what to say to Mr Granger.

"Do you want to ride back to Nowhere with us? We can escort you to safety. Dora in the hotel will make you both welcome," the sheriff said and looked at the dejected ranch owner, still standing in the centre of the kitchen. He was staring after his wife, who had rushed off crying.

Mr Granger gave a deep sigh, then, casting a last look around the place he had loved for some years and happily called home, shook his head: "We've to go, so it's best we go now. Can we pack a few things?"

***

Dora was delighted. At last, all her dreams and ambitions for the hotel had come to fruition. Of course, she was sympathetic towards the Grangers and their misfortune at their ranch. But to play hostess for them after their dramatic experience, and to have two other ladies staying at her hotel, was wonderful.

"Please ask me for anything you need. I lost my home when my husband gambled it away, so I understand a little of what you're going through," Dora said. She opened her newly refurbished double room for them and gave Mrs Granger a consoling pat on the arm as she ushered her in. "Would you care for some refreshment brought up to your room? It's not something I do usually, but I'm pleased to make you comfortable. I don't expect that you would wish to talk to anybody at the moment."

Mrs Granger walked over to the bed and sat down on it. Tears streamed down her face as she sat there staring into space, her hands clasped in her lap.

Mr Granger took one look at his wife and shook his

head, unable to think of what to say to ease his wife's suffering. "Thank you, Dora. Perhaps, if possible, could you please bring up a pot of coffee for my wife? I'll have something stronger—whiskey if you have it." He went over to join his wife on the bed and put his arm around her.

Dora backed quietly out of the room. Downstairs, she walked into the lobby to find Sheriff Lance Grey and Josh talking to the beautiful new resident, Cassidy, and her maid, Martha. They looked enquiringly at her as she walked towards the kitchen.

"I'm having some coffee and some whiskey sent up for them. Poor Mrs Granger, she's in such a state. I gather she wants to go back east again. Such a pity. She spent so much time and effort making that ranch house look beautiful, especially her garden."

There was much shaking of heads. Everyone knew of Mrs Granger's garden. In a land where water was scarce, and in many ways far more valuable than gold, to have a garden that actually grew flowers was a rare occurrence. Water was used for crops, to keep livestock alive and in good condition, and to make certain that families existed in those arid lands.

"What's happening to the ranch, then?" Cassidy asked the sheriff. "Are they going to sell it now, after this raid?" Those violet eyes rested on the sheriff with an intensity and calculation that only Josh recognised. To the others it was a polite enquiry, meaningless, just a remark in a casual conversation.

"Oh yes," Lance said. "On the way back here to Nowhere, Mr Granger was adamant. He is selling that ranch to the first person who offers him a reasonable price. After we heard that Charles Roberts may well have instigated this attack, I only hope *he* doesn't get his hands on it." He shook his head. Then added, "If only we could get some evidence to prove that man is a fraud. We all know he is, but there's nothing we can do about it until I have the evidence in my hand."

Dora had returned to join them, having given her instructions to the maid in the kitchen. "Not everyone waits to get the right piece of evidence, Sheriff!" Her remark fell into the silence. No one spoke. But everyone knew that in the West not every sheriff relied on evidence and fact to eliminate the wrongdoer.

Ignoring that remark, the sheriff began to make a move. "Well, Josh, time we left these ladies." The sheriff clapped Josh on the back and the two of them left the hotel.

Dora looked at Cassidy. The beautiful young woman stood in the centre of the lobby, her eyes fixed on a picture hanging on the wall. But Dora knew she wasn't even looking at it properly. Deep in thought, Cassidy's index finger rested lightly on her lips, as if about to chew her nail. She didn't. Obviously coming to a decision, she put the hand down and turned round giving Dora a smile. A conspiratorial smile. Then she moved closer and spoke confidentially to the older woman. Agreement was reached between them, and both relished the plans they had made and the need for silence. Dora realised Cassidy was a beautiful young woman—but Cassidy was no fool, and Dora was only too pleased to be on the right side of Cassidy.

Dora watched Cassidy go upstairs to pack for her journey the following morning. Although it was early to go to bed, the young woman had stated she would remain in her bedroom all that evening until early morning.

Beautiful, charming, and with an intriguing heart-shaped face, Cassidy had initially been nothing more to Dora. Just a pretty young woman. But Dora, after that conversation and the plans Cassidy had proposed, now knew otherwise: Cassidy was a young woman with an agenda. She had set her heart on achieving her goal, and Dora realised that nothing and no one would stop her. Dora was, somehow ,a little bit frightened of the young woman, but couldn't say why. As she walked on into the kitchen, she could only be thankful that Cassidy saw her as a friend and ally.

CHAPTER FIFTY-THREE

Josh was exhausted. Leaving the sheriff at his office, he walked down Main Street towards the general store. The afternoon was now late. He knew he should get back to Broken Horseshoe Ranch. Amy would expect him. But after his night of burglary, followed by the mad chase by the posse to the Grangers' place, and the return to Nowhere, Josh felt too tired to face another journey on horseback. He pushed open the door to the general store.

"Come on in, Josh. You must be so weary. Go and wash up. I've got a meal ready for you. You aren't thinking of riding back to the ranch tonight, are you? There's no moon and I reckon you are too tired to face the journey." Eliza had walked up to him. She took one look at him and saw the lines of tiredness and dirt engraved on his face. "Come on, Josh." Laughing, she grabbed him by the arm and hauled him into the back of the store, where she pushed him towards the water jug.

"Best do as she says, Josh," Manuel said, waving his fork in the air. Smiling affectionately at his wife, his teasing made Josh laugh. In seconds, he'd seated himself at the table, washed up, and was ready to eat.

Next morning, Josh woke on the mattress in the back kitchen of the general store. He couldn't remember lying down on it. There hadn't been a time when he'd consciously thought he would go to sleep. As he rubbed his eyes, stretched his aching limbs and turned over preparatory to getting up, he realised all he remembered was sitting down to that meal. In his fatigue, he must've eaten it, but he didn't even remember a mouthful. He stood up, rolled the mattress, and was just stretching once more, trying to remove the kinks from his back and neck from the lumpy mattress when Eliza bustled in. In no time at all, coffee was brewing, and she was producing breakfast for herself, Manuel, and Josh.

The general store was busy. Exceptionally busy. The news about the Grangers and yet more gangs in the area had brought out the gossips. Those that were frightened at the thought of even more violence in their small township came in to chat about it. Eliza was exasperated, but she smiled and served those who wanted serving. She had to be polite and welcome paying customers, even if they weren't buying much.

Ezra arrived with produce from Broken Horseshoe Ranch. He and Josh unloaded and discussed ranch matters in the stable yard. "Ezra, I've been wondering what's been happening at the ranch house. How is Luke?" Josh said as he looked into the face of the elderly man beside him. The weather-beaten face with the craggy suntanned features was like a mask. Never did Ezra show any emotion on that face, so it was difficult to judge what was happening to him, and to the others at the ranch, without persistent questioning.

Lifting one of the latest boxes of vegetables from the ranch, he looked at Josh and gave a small grunt. "It's not good. Luke had a funny turn yesterday. He just disappears into himself. That's what Miss Amy calls it. He doesn't seem to know he's had it, which is good, I suppose. Nancy and Amy are really worried."

"I wish I could help," Josh said, looking with concern at the old man.

Ezra patted Josh's shoulder: "Nothing you can do, Josh. Enough people cluttering up the place."

"Thing is, Ezra, I broke into Charles's place." Josh looked around as he said that, just in case there was somebody listening.

Luckily, Ezra was quick to understand: "Was it last night? Was it successful?"

Josh gave a big grin and smiled at Ezra. "Tell Amy it was very successful. I got some information, important information. But to act on this, I have to go to Duloe. I was thinking I'd go today, that's if I'm not needed at the ranch. If I am, I'll postpone this trip," Josh said.

Walking into the general store, Ezra had the list of provisions that were needed by the ranch in his hand. He stopped and looked at the younger man beside him. "There's nothing you can do there, Josh. Nothing I can do either. I think it is best you follow this lead. There are plenty enough bodies on the ranch to help Miss Amy. It's just she gets exhausted and very fed up being confined to the ranch. I reckon she misses those long trips out with you looking for the gold."

Josh remembered those trips with affection—although some of them had been far from pleasant, if not downright dangerous. Yet his thoughts were not on those past trips, but on future ones facing him.

They both reached the general store and were standing talking to Manuel when the door of the store was flung open, the bell barely having time to give its usual chime. Standing there, with all eyes fixed on him, was Sheriff Lance Grey. His irritation was apparent as he waved a sheet of paper above his head.

"Again! It's happened again! Have any of you seen this man in the town recently?" He waved a wanted poster, walking around displaying it in front of each customer, finally reaching Manuel and Eliza.

Manuel looked at the poster and then at the sheriff: *What's happened again*? Seeing Lance Grey's angry expression, Manuel decided not to proceed with his remark.

It was Eliza who took the poster from Lance and looked at it. For a moment, she was silent. The whole general store seemed to hold its breath, as each person stared intently at Eliza, who held the poster in her hand. She nodded her head. "Yes, he was in here yesterday. He was with another man. They bought some provisions and then were going to the saloon before riding back to their camp. That's all I know. This is a wanted poster." Holding the poster nearer to her, Eliza looked at the smaller print. Her mouth opened, and her free hand went up to her face in a look of horror as she gazed at Lance. "He was a killer! A bank robber. It says here that he killed a man when robbing a bank last month. And I served him with his goods." Handing the poster back to the sheriff, Eliza moved back, searching for the chair, and promptly sat down with a thump. Now both hands went up to her face as she looked wide-eyed at Sheriff Grey.

"What's happened to him? Has he killed someone else?" Manuel asked Grey as he walked over towards his wife, putting an arm around her shoulder. "Are you going to search for him? Are you getting a posse together?" Manuel's shoulders went back, and he puffed out his chest as he looked around the room at the customers standing there. All were avidly watching the scene being played out before them. "Do you want me to be acting Deputy Sheriff again?"

"No." Lance waved the poster at him and shook his head. Lance looked round at the worried bystanders, alarmed at this news of a killer wandering about Main Street yesterday.

"Should we go home? And lock ourselves in? Is this

killer still on the loose in our town?" A large, matronly lady clutched her canvas bag of provisions to her chest as if keeping them safe from any marauding bank robber. Her worried gaze was mirrored by the others in the general store.

The sheriff spoke to them: "There's no need for panic. That bank robber arrived dead, with his arms folded across his chest, in front of my door this morning. This poster was on his chest." A mixture of expressions flitted across his face.

Josh watched the man whom he was beginning to know well. He recognised the pleased expression of the lawman, knowing that another killer was no longer at large to kill again. There was also the puzzled expression at the arrival of a second wanted man—literally on his doorstep.

Josh spoke to him: "Was he shot the same way?"

All Josh got in reply was a nod of the head, and the door was flung open again as Grey stormed out. Josh could see that he was puzzled at this bounty hunter's way of producing the dead bodies. But Josh found it amusing, and also was delighted that another killer was dead rather than walking around Nowhere as he was yesterday.

CHAPTER FIFTY-FOUR

"Ezra, tell them I'll be out at the ranch in a couple of days' time. I should have everything sorted by then. At least I hope so." With that remark, Josh rushed off to find Manuel and Eliza to tell them his latest plan.

Later, Josh ran up Main Street. He could see Slim with the wagon, and it looked as if he was about to set off. "Hey, Slim! Have you any room left?" Josh shouted as the man looked about to climb up, ready for the start of his journey.

To Josh's great relief, Slim heard him and paused, and then came towards the back of the wagon to help Josh up. Normally, Slim had a box which he produced with a flourish for the ladies to climb up and down. There was no box for gentlemen—and certainly not the likes of Josh. Slim pulled back the canvas for Josh to climb aboard and grinned at him with his toothless smile. "I'll get your money at the end of the journey. Lucky for you, I was running late."

Clambering in, Josh found he was not alone on this trip. There were two older women with baskets, both sitting uncomfortably on the bench, ready for the journey. A tall, thin man, whom Josh had seen wandering about the area around the saloon, sat beside the women. On the opposite side were Cassidy and her maid, Martha.

Murmurs of greeting came from each one of them, and Josh acknowledged this with a smile and a good morning as he slumped down, ready for the long, tedious journey ahead. He looked at Cassidy and her maid sitting beside her. Why was she going to Duloe? Was it anything to do with the information they both found in the burglary? Or had she decided to leave Nowhere and move on? For a moment, Josh was worried by the thought that Cassidy leaving Nowhere should upset him so much. He tried to put that thought to the back of his mind. It was none of his business. Josh knew he had no right to think about Cassidy and her plans. After all, they were mere acquaintances.

The journey was long, tedious, and uneventful. There was very little chat between travellers. Most sat, sunk in misery, with the endless jolting of the wagon as it made its way over the rough trails to the town. Both Cassidy and her maid, Martha, seemed to be exhausted, and Josh noticed they slept most of the way. Josh was relieved to see and hear the growing town of Duloe draw nearer to them.

The mines that had been discovered on the outskirts of the town had led to a mushrooming of the town itself. Josh recalled how men would flock to areas to seek their fortune during the gold rush, resulting in the rapid development of goods and services. This was what was happening now in Duloe. Josh also remembered the tales he had heard about the deserted townships and empty buildings when the gold ran out.

The journey was over. As Josh got down after the ladies, he was allowed the additional treat of a box put down by Slim. Josh had the money ready to pay Slim and told the wagon driver, "I may well be back for a bed tonight. I don't know yet. You leave tomorrow morning, and I may well return with you to Nowhere."

Walking away from the livery stables to go into the town itself, Josh hadn't heard Cassidy move closer to him. But he knew she was there. The scent of violets drifted towards him, and he turned around to face her.

"I wonder what brought you into Duloe town, Josh."

The dancing violet eyes and roguish smile on her face made Josh smile in return.

"I'm here on business, Miss Cassidy, and I'm going to find out what information I can about Duke from the bank," Josh replied in answer to her question. He turned towards the maid and smiled at her: "Good morning, Martha." His good manners in acknowledging the nurse brought a sudden smile to the older woman's face. Josh realised that—because of her ungainly build and disfigured face, and her servile position to Cassidy—few people noticed her or acknowledged her. His sincere remark towards the woman had brought forth that charming smile from her, and a nod of approval from Cassidy. Josh was amazed to think that his greeting to the woman should elicit such a response.

As he walked alongside both ladies, carefully maintaining his position on the outside of the boardwalk, he replied to Cassidy: "Yes, but I hope not run into our mutual friend, Charles. You are also here on business?" He wondered what had brought her to Duloe, knowing it was none of his business but hoping she wasn't planning on leaving Nowhere. That would be unthinkable.

"I'm here to see a lawyer about various matters of business. I've got a recommendation to see one from Dora, so I'm acting upon it, and then I shall return to Duloe tomorrow," she replied.

Remembering how Dora, on his last trip to Duloe, had asked Josh to come with her to the lawyer, Josh turned to Cassidy. "I know you ladies are perfectly capable of discussing your business with a lawyer. But last time I came to Duloe, Dora asked me to accompany her to the lawyer because it is expected to have a man present at these meetings. If I can be of any help to you, I'm quite willing to accompany you," Josh said, and looked at Cassidy, wondering if he shouldn't have broached the subject.

This morning Cassidy had started the journey in her costume, derived from the riding-habit style in the same colour as her eyes. The pale violet of the wool fabric was echoed in her fine leather gloves and the bonnet she wore. This bonnet was larger than usual and Josh realised it was to protect her from the dust that swirled around the wagon when Slim moved it along at speed. The journey, with its dust, had left her relatively unscathed. After brushing the dust off, both she and Martha looked fresh and able to tackle any number of lawyers or businessmen.

An unspoken conversation passed between Martha and Cassidy as both gazed at each other. Martha gave a slight nod of her head and, at that, Cassidy turned back to Josh with a smile: "Thank you. I'd appreciate your company to the lawyer's office. He is a pompous little man, Dora says, and is always eager to tell her what to do in her business affairs. I hate being the 'silly little woman'. But if you could back me up on my decisions, I'm sure that would carry some weight with him and stop his ceaseless prattling at me." They walked on for a moment. "Dora also told me you knew where the lawyers' offices were, and that you went with her the last time you were in Duloe."

They had moved away from the bustling livery stable, out of the way of the horses that were coming and going. Standing at a street corner, they watched for a moment the people rushing around, the men riding in on horseback, and the occasional buggy trotting up the busy street. Josh was amazed at how he had lived in a town or city like this. Somehow, despite the blank spaces in his memory, he knew certain things. He was certain that his had been a life led in amongst the crowded streets of a heavily populated city or town before the attack.

"After the small town of Nowhere, I find that this noise and stench seems overpowering," Josh said, as they both skirted the large amount of horse dung to cross the road to the other side of the busy street. It not been without danger, Josh thought. They had to dodge between a large man riding an enormous horse, and a fast-moving buggy and a heavily laden wagon.

"The lawyer is just in the next building, and up those stairs. Do you have papers for him?" Not knowing why Cassidy was visiting the lawyer, Josh was curious to find out. No doubt all would be revealed, he thought, when he sat beside her, lending his masculine authority to whatever transaction she had in mind. His curiosity was growing.

CHAPTER FIFTY-FIVE

Cassidy paused at the entrance to the lawyer's office. The leather satchel she held under her arm, she passed over to Josh. "My papers are in there. It will look better if you have them in your hands." Tilting her head to one side, she looked quizzically at Josh. "What remarkable restraint you have, Josh Barnes. I know you are desperate to find out what this is all about, and I think I'd better tell you before we go in front of the lawyer." She opened the satchel and without taking out the papers, she pointed to them.

Josh looked down at the papers as she spoke. "This one is signed by Mr Granger and witnessed by Dora and Sheriff Grey. In it, Mr Granger signs the deeds of his ranch to me." As Josh began to speak, Cassidy raised her hand for his silence. Then, she pointed down to the next document: "This is my money order for the bank to release into Mr Granger's account the agreed price."

Those roguish eyes of hers looked up at him as she finally let him speak. Josh spluttered out the words: "You are going to buy the Grangers' place? That is wonderful. But Charles wanted it. It could be dangerous for you to thwart his ambition." Josh's elation at the thought of this wonderful creature living in Nowhere was dampened down by his fear of the Charles's reaction.

"We are all keeping silent about it. Mr Granger is going to keep Charles dangling for some time. Without ever refusing or accepting his offer, it will give us time for the property transaction." Cassidy closed the satchel and began to walk into the lawyer's place of business.

Josh stepped forward and held out his arm towards her: "I think it best we go in is an obvious couple. That way, there will be no questions asked, and it will look as if I have the authority to oversee your affairs."

Cassidy paused and looked up at Josh. Those violet eyes danced with mischief: "I'd like to see you try to manage my affairs!"

Josh raised both hands in surrender. "I'm sensible enough not to even try," he replied and laughed with her. But an uneasy feeling grew within him. What it was he didn't know, but he knew that any man who tried to order Cassidy around would not like the consequences!

Pushing open the door, Josh, and Cassidy walked into the well-appointed offices of the lawyer. A worried young man approached them, took their names and darted off down a corridor. They could hear him knocking on the door of an office and then poking his head round it and giving their names. He returned and told them they would not be kept waiting for long. Taking a seat beside Cassidy, and noting the expensive carpet and drapes, Josh felt pleased that he was smartly dressed for once.

He'd have to thank Manuel, Eliza, and Clara for his present appearance. Their combined efforts had made him into a gentleman presentable enough to be seen escorting the beautiful Cassidy on his arm. He grimaced slightly to himself. The three of them, hearing of his proposed journey with Cassidy to Duloe, had jumped into action. Clara had boiled water to fill the metal bathtub in the stable yard. Unceremoniously, Josh had been sent out to bathe himself and scrape the dirt from travelling with the posse, and from lying on the general store floor all night. Then, Eliza, who fancied herself a gentleman's barber, had attacked his hair and beard. Now clean-shaven, freshly bathed and with his hair cut, he had entered the general store wrapped in a huge towel and into the bedroom where Manuel was waiting for him. The general store owner had put on a considerable amount of weight since buying the store. In his closet hung several items of clothing from the much slimmer days of Manuel. Now sitting in that fashionably furnished lawyer's office, Josh was thankful for his friend's ministrations. His hair was indeed shorter, and he had only a few nicks on his chin and at the back of the neck. Now the bleeding had stopped, they were no longer noticeable. Manuel's trousers fitted him lengthwise but were slightly baggy in the seat. Josh couldn't complain. They were so much better than what he had taken off. And he really liked the suede jacket with the fringes that Manuel had proudly pushed him into. He smoothed the fringes on the suede jacket, feeling how much smarter it was than his old worn wool one.

"I see you got smartened up for your journey to Duloe," murmured Cassidy beside him. "I approve." She gave him a warm smile, which made his pulse quicken—and despite all his efforts, he felt certain there was a slight blush in his cheeks. She gave her charming, throaty chuckle. "I think you will get better service in the bank looking like that."

Before Josh could answer her, the door down the hall opened and a rotund man stuck his head out and yelled Josh's name. Both Dora and Cassidy had been correct. Without his presence, Josh was certain that Cassidy would not have been given so much respect. Her name had not been mentioned, although it had been given to the young man. The lawyer seated behind the huge expanse of his desk had trouble fitting his paunch behind it whilst overseeing the documents Cassidy had brought with her.

He looked up and spoke directly to Josh, ignoring

Cassidy. "These are all in order. I gather from this other letter from Mr Granger that you wish this transaction to be kept secret for at least a month. Is that correct?" His pompous voice floated over the desk towards them.

"Yes, that is correct. There are other business transactions that Mr Granger and I wish to pursue. Secrecy would help us bring them to a satisfactory conclusion," Cassidy said. Josh sat beside her, smiling. He was getting sick of that smile, but he felt he ought to have a pleasant expression on his face. But at these remarks, however, his smile slipped. What secret transactions? What were Cassidy and Mr Granger up to? Why did they have to remain a secret?

CHAPTER FIFTY-SIX

They both blinked a little as they emerged from the lawyer's office and stood on the sidewalk. Martha had been waiting for them. She stepped forward. "Shall I go to the boarding house and book a room for us?" As Cassidy smiled her agreement, Martha looked at Josh: "I can book a room for you as well. Shall I?"

Josh was in a quandary. He didn't know how much it would cost, and he had only limited finances. His work for Manuel and Eliza contributed to the upkeep and running of Broken Horseshoe Ranch. Both he and Amy took a small amount of money as personal wages. But it wasn't much. Should he accept this room in the boarding house? Or would he be better off going back to sleep in the livery stable? He thought of the prickly hay mattress. It was the thought of the smell of the stable clinging to him and his clothes on the journey back in the confined space of the wagon with the fragrant Cassidy that decided him. "Thank you, Martha. I'd appreciate that."

He held his arm out for Cassidy and they both walked through the door and into the entrance hall of the bank. It was clean, and a young man rushed to greet them: "Welcome. How can I help you?" The words, learned by heart, were chanted out by him.

With a look at Cassidy, who gave him a slight nod, Josh spoke to the young man. "We are here for business concerning property transactions."

The solemn young man ushered them into a small back room. "Mr Jonas, this couple wishes to discuss property transactions with you."

Following him, Josh saw a large desk. It shone like glass and the vast expanse held expensive writing equipment. The small man seated behind it was dwarfed by its magnificence. He got to his feet and rushed round to shake their hands: "Welcome, welcome. Do sit down and tell me how I might be of service to you both."

Cassidy gave Josh a nudge and passed him the bag with the documents in. "Oh yes," Josh stammered and pulled out the papers from the bag. "I have here some signed papers by Mr Granger, who is selling his ranch to Miss Rose Cassidy. It has been witnessed, and seen by the lawyer, and we'd like you to transfer the monies." Josh was quite pleased with the concise way he explained the situation. He looked sideways at Cassidy, who gave him a slight nod of approval.

Mr Jonas looked through the papers and cleared his throat. He looked through them yet again. Taking his small spectacles from a case, he placed them over his nose. He looked straight at Josh and smiled. "Excellent, excellent. These are all in order. I gather you want them placed in my safe for security?"

"Yes—please," said Josh.

There was silence between them and, with mounting concern, Josh saw the banker look through the papers yet again. "These papers and this property are deeded to Miss Cassidy. You, sir—in what capacity are *you* here?" A suspicious look was growing on Mr Jonas's face.

Cassidy's tiny hand reached out and gripped Josh's arm. It was a sign for him to keep silent, he surmised. "Oh yes, you must be wondering, Mr Jonas, why Josh is here with me." She gave a tiny, girlish giggle, which made Josh turn and stare at her. It was so unlike Cassidy's usual throaty chuckles. "We didn't tell you, did we? How rude of us! Why, Mr Jonas, this is my fiancé, Josh Barnes. We're doing it all in my name at the moment, but as soon as we get married, of course, you understand the legal position as it applies to marriage partners."

Josh's startled squawk quickly turned into a cough. Pressure of Cassidy's fingers on his arm intensified, and he felt it prudent to just smile at her remarks. It was a weak smile.

When they got outside, Josh turned to look at Cassidy.

"It seemed a good idea. Don't *you* think it was?" she said, smiling at him. "I know quite a few gentlemen who would like to be engaged to me." Again, Cassidy gave that throaty chuckle.

Josh looked down at the heart-shaped face, those roguish violet eyes twinkling up at him, and—against his better judgement—he too laughed. "Cassidy, you astonish me at times."

"Only at times? I must be slipping. I would much prefer to astonish you *all* the time, Josh Barnes!"

The meal in the boarding house that evening was plain, wholesome, and filling. The gaunt landlady, Mrs Kipps, kept the place clean—and it was a plain, wholesome establishment, like her food. But she was no conversationalist. She wasn't unfriendly, but just did not like to speak to any of them other than the words necessary for running the boarding house.

The meal over, they trooped into a small parlour that was especially set aside for guests. "I was wondering, Josh, if you are needed back in Nowhere immediately?" Cassidy said, settling herself down in one of the hardback chairs placed around the room.

Josh, who had followed both women into the parlour, had taken his seat in an upright chair beside the stove. A tall man, who had been seated at another table in the dining room, had not joined them. He gave them a brisk good night before retreating to his bedroom.

"I'm not expected back for a day or two. Why do you ask, Cassidy?" Josh said, puzzled by the question. He watched Cassidy as she cast a questioning look towards Martha. Her maid seemed to understand exactly what was asked of her. With no words being spoken, Josh saw her nod in agreement before rising to her feet and leaving the room. Cassidy watched her maid leave and then turned back to Josh to answer his question: "I was hoping you might accompany Martha and me to the Grangers' ranch tomorrow. We could stay there for the night and return to Nowhere the next day."

Josh was dumbfounded at this invitation to change his plans—and could only wonder at the reason for it. What was Cassidy up to now?

CHAPTER FIFTY-SEVEN

"You want to see the Grangers' place? Haven't you seen it before? Did you buy it sight unseen from Mr Granger?" Josh was surprised at this, somehow feeling that Cassidy must have visited it before arriving in Nowhere.

Cassidy looked at him, her eyes dancing with mischief. "Yes, I bought it without looking at it. But I was so determined to stop Charles from buying it. We all know he drove the Grangers from the ranch so that he could buy it at a cheap price. Well, Josh, when I suggested to Mr Granger that I buy it from him, he was delighted."

His eyes widening in surprise, Josh found it difficult not to let his jaw drop in astonishment. But he began laughing as well: "I can just imagine that Mr Granger would be thrilled to stop Charles from getting his hands on his ranch. It's a wonderful place. I'm sure you'll be delighted to live there. When do you hope to move in?"

Cassidy rose to her feet and walked over to look at the fireplace. The glow of the wood's flames seemed to cast her golden curls in a dancing light, causing them to shimmer as she moved her head, almost as if they were alive. Her gaze became solemn, and she seemed to weigh up what to say next to Josh. He sat back on his hard wooden chair and stared at the girl in front of him. Petite, light as thistledown on her feet, she moved with a grace that he'd never seen before in any woman. Josh instinctively knew that going with Cassidy to the ranch was perhaps going to be the most dangerous thing he'd ever done in his life.

Martha would be with them. There would be no impropriety, but that was not what Josh was afraid of.

Both their reputations would be intact, but Josh wondered if his heart would be completely whole after that length of time spent with this captivating creature.

"I thought I would hire a buggy to take us to the ranch. You accompanying us would be an added protection—and I would relish your company. Martha is loyal and trustworthy and my greatest friend. But, Josh, she has no conversation! Surely you wouldn't condemn me to all that time without accompanying cheerful chatter."

What could he do? Josh felt himself sinking into the depth of those violet eyes and told himself he was a fool to agree to this trip. "Very well, Cassidy, but I would like to get more information about Charles and the man they call Duke before we leave Duloe," Josh replied.

"Martha has gone out to see what she can find out about Duke and Charles," said Cassidy, with a triumphant grin. "I knew you would want that information before leaving the town."

"But what can Martha find out? Surely, she ..." Words failed Josh. All he could do was stare at Cassidy, who was smiling at him. She resumed her seat. "Martha shouldn't be long now. I'm certain she'll find out more than you and I could ever hope to. Wait, and you will see."

The next few minutes passed with Cassidy bombarding Josh with questions about the ranch that she had just bought. He was surprised by the intelligence of the questions she posed. It showed that she had a knowledge of ranching, of crops, and of life in general on an isolated homestead. After a while, she sat back and stared into the fire again. Josh had already replenished the dwindling flames that had fallen into embers, and the new fresh wood was now crackling merrily.

Finally, the door opened and Martha came in. She had returned straight from the street without removing her outer coat. The dark duster coat seemed to envelop the woman, and the hood, which she now pushed back, must've hidden her face from view. She took a deep breath before sitting down on the chair beside Cassidy.

"Come on, Martha, sit down. You went to the livery stables and ordered the buggy for tomorrow?" Martha nodded assent. Cassidy continued speaking: "Tell us if you found anything out about Charles. I promised Josh that you would have some information for him. If you haven't any information, it's doubtful he will accompany us tomorrow," teased Cassidy. She laughed at the look of outrage that spread over Josh's face.

"Stop that nonsense, miss. Don't you go teasing the young man. He doesn't know you and what you're about. But you're in the right of it. I have information." Martha swallowed hard, as if thirsty after her search for information.

Before she could speak, the door opened and the gaunt owner stood there, looking around the room and counting the numbers within it. "I bring a tea tray for guests each evening. Just before I lock up and retire for the night."

Josh wanted no more expense upon his limited purse strings and shook his head. Cassidy, however, looked at the lady in question standing at the door, and gave her a winning smile. "That would be lovely, thank you. We'll all have tea." When the woman had left the room, Cassidy shook her head: "I think Mrs Kipps has read some manual on how to be a boarding house keeper. I'm not sure that any other boarding house would do this rigmarole at night. But I know you are thirsty, Martha, and it won't hurt me to have a drink of tea. Or you, Josh."

They waited in silence. Not one of them felt like discussing anything about Charles whilst Mrs Kipps could enter the room at any moment and catch the tail end of their conversation. Josh realised that the tea tray must've been ready and only needed the addition of the boiling water because, in no time at all, Mrs Kipps appeared. She planted the tea tray down on the table in the centre of the room after moving the aspidistra from it. Then she wished them a good night. Instructions on stacking the cutlery and crockery on the tray, to be left there for her to collect on the morning, were given in detail.

Cassidy rose to her feet and, in no time at all, they were sitting down with their cups of tea. Josh had had no option but to accept it. Normally a drink he disliked intensely, being a hardened coffee drinker, that night, for some reason, he enjoyed it. They were all thirsty, Martha more so than the others. She and Josh had two cups each. When they were all finished and the cutlery and crockery neatly stacked as their landlady had instructed, they all sat back and relaxed into conversation. Well, as much as anyone could relax on those hard chairs, Josh thought.

Martha began her story of what had happened on her excursion in the town: "I asked Slim in the livery stables for the buggy for the morning. He went off to attend to a customer who had just ridden in. I took the opportunity to chat to old Abe. I remember Mr Josh saying he got some information from him before. So, I thought it was worth a try. I found a little more from him. I heard that a letter with instructions for Charles had been in the postbag that morning." Martha took another long drink of tea and swallowed it gratefully.

"Thank you, Martha. I don't quite know what it means

or how it helps. At least we now know that Charles is still getting instructions from Duke." The others nodded after this remark from Josh.

"Then I went into the saloon." Martha laughed at Josh's shocked expression. "Don't worry, Mr Josh—I only sit at the back in the shadows. I'm in no danger. Lordy, who'd want to have me in the brothel above?" She gave a raucous laugh, and Cassidy chuckled along with her as Josh smiled.

But he was shocked. "Why did you go in there? What …"

Still laughing at him, not in a nasty way, but chuckling over his shocked face, Martha continued speaking: "I often sit at the back and pick up gossip and chatter. It often flows freely after a few drinks. It's surprising what I can hear just sitting at the back in a corner."

Josh struggled to contain his impatience. He leant forward and waited to hear what this astonishing woman would say next. "It was a quiet night. Only a few customers and a couple of the girls came to sit at the back of the saloon. They come there to get a breath of fresh air, and to get away from those few men that have no money and no intention of paying them. We got chatting," Martha said.

A peal of laughter erupted from Cassidy. "If you are long enough in our company, Josh, that expression of Martha's, 'we got chatting', will be a signal to you. That means she has indeed got some tasty morsel of information for us." Cassidy leant forward, clasping hands in earnest entreaty. "Come on, Martha, let us have the news and gossip."

CHAPTER FIFTY-EIGHT

"The man, Duke, isn't liked by any of them. Thinks he's above them all and is rude and insulting. Pays well but is not overgenerous. I gather from the girls that if they approach him, he swears at them. Some of them are quite content to be in his pay. From what I gather, they give him information about various people he has an eye on—and the one person he is constantly checking up on is our friend Charles. From what these girls say, Charles is not popular with Duke. He suspects Charles of deceiving him and skimming off profits."

There was silence for a moment as both Cassidy and Josh thought about the information Martha had collected. It was Cassidy who spoke first: "I should think that Duke is correct. Charles would steal from anybody, even if it was a foolish mistake."

Josh was impatient and turned to Martha: "What else did you hear, Martha? Was any of this gossip of any help to me?" Josh was furious at himself. He was almost pleading for information from this woman. But it was so important to him; it meant so much to him. After all, it was a matter of life and death. *His* life and death.

But Martha had no information at all about Josh. He wasn't mentioned, and she didn't like to introduce his name into the conversation. Josh was disappointed.

***

The early morning ride was one Josh would always remember. The air was fresh without the heat of the day's temperature. He and Cassidy rode along in a companionable silence, with the odd remark passing between them. He marvelled at how the petite young woman sat astride her horse and rode it with an expertise that he would not have expected from her. There was no lack of horsemanship, despite the beautiful costume she wore that morning. He realised he had seen her only a few times, and each time it seemed she wore a different outfit. Josh was used to Amy having the same well-washed outfits, alternating for cleanliness.

"This is all the Grangers' property now? Isn't it" Cassidy called to him and waved an expansive arm around her.

"Yes. We'll be at the ranch house in another hour. As we get nearer the river, you can see the soil becomes more fertile and the grass lusher," Josh said.

"Mr Granger told me he was going to speak to Ramon and his wife and ask them to go back to their duties at the ranch again," Cassidy said.

"Does he think they *will* go back? I think Ramon will go back, but I'm not sure his wife would after the attack," replied Josh. "Will they know you are the new owner? Is he going to tell them?"

Cassidy smiled at Josh. "Mr Granger agreed that he would like to keep it a secret for now. We both want to leave Charles in the dark about what's happening. Ramon will say that the Grangers are willing to go back. I have a letter from Mr Granger to give to Ramon telling of the new arrangements and swearing them both to secrecy."

They rode on, sometimes in silence. Josh was thinking about this new arrangement. He hoped for Cassidy's sake that Ramon and his wife *would* stay at the ranch. Ramon had been an excellent man to run the ranch, as the Grangers knew nothing about it and had left everything to him. He felt certain that Cassidy could do the same. And knowing Ramon as he did, he felt certain that the man would relish continuing to be in charge of the ranch.

"You'll need to help us, Josh," Cassidy said, swinging her horse nearer to Josh to discuss this new topic on her mind. "Martha and I have been having such fun." She chuckled and Martha, who was driving the buggy quite close to them after hearing this, gave her hearty guffaw.

Martha called across to them: "Yes, Josh, let's have your ideas. Can't be worse than some of ours!" Again, Martha guffawed and glanced at Josh with that cheerful smile of hers, which only occasionally broke through the older woman's usually dour expression.

In the short time Martha and he had become acquainted, Josh found her to be intelligent and caring for those she trusted. Not knowing the background to that appalling scar on her face, Josh could only marvel at the woman continuing to cope with life as well as she had done. Cassidy relied on her utterly, and she loved Cassidy back as if she were her own child. Suspicious of Josh first, she had become to accept him gradually. Now, after the trip to Duloe, and their mutual aim to destroy Charles Roberts, she had accepted Josh wholeheartedly.

"There it is! The Grangers'—but not for long. Cassidy, you really must decide on a new name for the ranch. We've had a lot of fun between us, thinking about names. Now, you have so many to choose from. Have you decided yet?" Josh said, pointing out the wrought-iron sign, an archway at the entrance to the ranch house itself. The Grangers' name, spelled out in large black letters, would have to go. The last few miles had been spent with lots of laughter at the weird and wonderful—and plain ridiculous—names they had planned for the new ranch owner. Cassidy had been the worst, concocting the strangest names she could think of.

Cassidy rode under the archway and looked up at it:

"That will have to go. But it could stay for the time being—all the better to fool Charles."

Josh watched Cassidy as she rode under the archway and into her new property. Her eyes were glowing, and her face had the eager look of a child receiving a Christmas present. He had seen Cassidy with a bitter look, a mischievous look, and flirting look, but never had he seen her look around with such joy on her face. He glanced across at Martha, who smiled back at him.

As she got off the buggy and Josh dismounted beside her, Martha touched Josh on the arm. "I think she has come home. I hope it will be a home for both of us." Her grip tightened on Josh's arm. She looked him straight in the face, the scar becoming even more pronounced in the brilliant sunshine of midday. "And Josh, my friend, I hope you will also make it *your* home." The stare coming from Martha was direct and intense. Josh was dumbfounded and didn't know what to say or do. The intensity of that gaze from Martha, along with the grip on his arm, left him speechless. The large woman turned away and began walking up the steps of the porch to join Cassidy, who she stood in the doorway of her new home.

Josh, still stunned by Martha's remark, stood with the reins of his horse still in his hand. He looked up at the two women standing on the porch in the sunlight. It shone on both of them as if a spotlight were dancing around them. They stood as if on a theatre stage, and both were gazing around. Martha had a smile of satisfaction and had placed an arm round Cassidy's shoulders. A protective arm it was, but also showed that deep love of the older woman for the younger woman.

Spellbound, Josh couldn't look away from Cassidy as the sunlight made her curls glint with gold lights. Those violet eyes of hers were wide and open as they gazed about with interest. The costume she wore was slightly dusty, but nothing could detract from its stylish elegance. Today she had worn not the usual violet or blue but a deep wine colour. The tiny buttons she so loved paraded down cuffs and her bodice, emphasising the tiny waist and the slender proportions of her body. But Josh knew that Cassidy's looks were deceptive. He also knew she was a deceitful young woman. Where had the money come from to buy this ranch? Where had she learned to shoot and ride as she did? Yet she proclaimed herself to be from an eastern city.

CHAPTER FIFTY-NINE

Ramon began shouting at them as he ran to the ranch house. "They've gone! Mr Granger's special horses are missing. They escaped through a fence and are running up to the foothills of Devil's Mountain. The earth shook, and they ran off scared. They were away from the ranch in the canyon, so they were not stolen like the other horses."

"Special horses?" queried Josh as both he and Cassidy ran towards the worried man.

"Yes—he was going to breed the special horses to send back east. They cost him a lot of money. There are only two of them, and another pony with them. There is no one spare around to chase after them. The men are out in the far corner of the ranch." Ramon stood, anxiously twisting his hands as he stared off in the distance to where the horses had gone.

"We'll go, won't we, Josh?" Cassidy said, looking at Josh.

Their horses had been taken away to the stable by Ramon earlier. At these words, Ramon looked at them both and asked, "Are you sure? You've ridden from Duloe already today. Will you ride again?"

The solemn face of the moustachioed Ramon brightened a little, and he looked hopefully at them.

"I can do it. What about you, Josh?" That elfin face with the enormous violet eyes met Josh's gaze. He knew he had to agree—otherwise, he would be forever damned in her eyes, as a weakling.

"Yes, Ramon, you get horses ready for us, and we'll ride after them," Josh said. He didn't enjoy spending more time in the saddle, but he was willing to do it, if necessary, to retrieve the horses.

Back on the horses they had been given, Josh and Cassidy rode towards the rocky terrain in front of them. The horses ahead of them had had a good start on their escape to freedom. It was quite a task they were undertaking in following them.

"What was Ramon talking about? The earth shaking itself, especially in the foothills and mountains?" Cassidy asked Josh. "Did you ever have any earthshaking at Broken Horseshoe Ranch?"

Thinking carefully back to any conversations he had heard since his stay at Broken Horseshoe Ranch, he recalled Ezra, in particular, talking about them. The old man and his wife, Leah, had lived for many years at the ranch, having built their cabin behind the ranch when it was the property of the original owner. Remaining there through several owners, they had now become almost part of the family since the Tanner family had arrived.

"No, we heard about them. Ezra and Leah have spoken often about rushing out of any building and then onto the open ground and lying flat. They had a bad one about ten years ago. Leah said some of her china fell off the shelves and smashed. Even now she has her best china placed securely in case of another shake," Josh said.

"I hope we don't get any ground shakes. They sound frightening," Cassidy said with a shudder. She continued speaking. "Ramon said the horses don't go far. They were not wild horses originally. Mr Granger rode and petted them daily. And there is the chance they will be pleased to see us and come back with us willingly," Cassidy said.

"I hope he's right," said Josh as they rode on together.

Ramon had loaded them up with all that he thought necessary to entice the horses back with their favourite treats and to help lead them back to the ranch.

There were tracks every so often in the dust and dirt, and to Josh's eyes they seemed to meander around more in circles than racing off. Both riders paused for a moment to look ahead. There was one route the horses could have taken along a dry riverbed—or straight ahead into the narrow opening of a canyon.

Cassidy bent over the side of her horse, looking down at the dirt: "This way, Josh. I see hoofprints going into the canyon. With any luck they are trapped in there, and they will be easy to capture."

Only a short distance through a narrow pathway, between towering rocks on either side, they felt the atmosphere change. There was an eerie silence. The birds flying about had gone silent and disappeared. Josh felt that even the insects had hidden away.

Ahead of them, the canyon opened out into an area of flat grassland with a small stream meandering through the middle of it. They were nearing the end of the narrow canyon walls.

Josh knew they had to reach that area of open grassland. Why, he never knew. Some sort of presentiment urged him to race their horses to reach it. "Hurry, Cassidy! Quickly! Ride to the centre of the canyon, into the open land!" Josh shouted as he half turned to Cassidy, checking that she was close behind him. He rode, pushing the horse, urging it away from the towering rocks on each side of the towering canyon walls and into the grassy open area. He didn't look round again. He didn't need to. Cassidy was racing behind him. He could hear her urging her horse along, and the hoofbeats of her horse kept pace behind him.

That short distance away from the rocky walls and

into the green oasis of land seemed endless. Josh knew they had to reach it. Ever afterwards, he couldn't explain how he'd known that danger was imminent. But that presentiment of disaster had been correct. The earth convulsed. Both of them jumped from their horses, trying to calm the frightened beasts. Beside the stream, some scrubby trees fought for survival in this harsh land, and both Josh and Cassidy tied their horses to the trees. They moved closer together, standing on the flattest piece of land they could find.

That initial tremor passed. But the noise of falling rocks that had been dislodged by the tremor continued. They both knelt down and drank from the stream. Sitting back on the grass, they looked around the canyon, wondering if there were more tremors to follow.

A few minutes passed before it began again. This time Cassidy flung herself closer to Josh, and they clung to each other as the shaking ground seemed to fling them from side to side. One side of the canyon had loose rock and shale, which flowed as if turned into liquid. Down and down it fell, sliding and crashing onto the floor below. A horrendous scraping noise came from the rocks grinding together. Then, the shaking stopped.

Apart from the occasional rock, previously dislodged yet only falling after a time, there was silence within the canyon. Then, from around a far corner of the canyon, came the horses they had been seeking. They tossed their heads and came to a stop beside the other two horses from their stable. Josh got up and went to his horse. He took down the sack of the horses' favourite treats that Ramon had given to him. Josh poured out some on the ground before them. When they came to eat, he found Cassidy at his side, with the halters ready to take the horses and tie them beside their stablemates at the trees.

"They were frightened. I expect they've come to us for help and company," said Cassidy. "Do think it's finished, Josh?"

Before Josh could speak, the earth beneath them resumed shuddering and shaking. Cassidy clung to him, and he put a protective arm around her, holding her close. Over her head, he could see the narrow entrance through which they had just entered the canyon. Another violent shaking caused the towering cliffs above the narrow entrance to move. Josh watched in horror as the rock walls split, and large chunks and pieces slid to the ground with a tremendous roar, crashing into millions of pieces and sealing off the entrance. The noise seemed to carry on forever around them. But there was no more shaking from the earth beneath them. The earth had gone quiet. But, around them, rocks still tumbled to the ground, dislodged by the initial shakes as they fell, dislodging rocks beneath them. Finally, there was silence.

Cassidy and Josh clung to each other as the surrounding silence seemed deafening after the cessation of the overwhelming noise of the earthquake.

"We're trapped, aren't we?" Cassidy's voice was flat, without emotion, as she stared back towards their pathway into the canyon. Rocks filled the narrow gap well above head height. No way could they be shifted easily—if at all.

"Yes, there are huge boulders fallen into the passageway," Josh said. He was pleased that the girl beside him showed no tendency to break out into hysterics or cry copious tears over their predicament. He found himself at a loss and could only stare helplessly at the enormous volume of rocks and boulders blocking their escape from the canyon.

"We have water. That's one blessing. Have we any food with us?" Josh said, looking hopefully at the girl.

Still looking back at the blocked entrance to the canyon, Cassidy shook herself and turned towards Josh. "Ramon's wife pushed a bundle into my hands as we left. I'm hoping it is food," Cassidy said and got up to go to her horse. Shaking the dust and debris from her skirt, she then straightened her hair and looked down at Josh, who was still on the grassy floor of the canyon. "Are you going to lie there all day?"

Josh got up slowly and smiled at her. "Thank goodness you haven't gone into hysterics." He also walked towards the horses, patting each one in turn and murmuring to them. Their eyes had rolled during the earthquake, and they had stamped and whinnied an alarm, but otherwise had stayed calm. He was so thankful. As he stood there beside the horses, he noticed the stream.

To Josh's eyes, it seemed to flow faster and was overreaching the banks. He took in a deep breath and thought back to those journeys he had taken with Amy. What was it Ezra had warned about? Flash floods could be caused by many things. Looking towards the end of the canyon, which curved round a large outcropping of rock, he could see the water in the stream gradually rising.

CHAPTER SIXTY

Grabbing his horse and the other three horses, Josh turned to Cassidy: "Take hold of your horse and run! We must get to higher ground." To his relief and astonishment, Cassidy looked at him for a moment and then grabbed her horse and followed him as he raced to the higher ground. A rock outcropping caught his eye, untouched by the earthquake. He prayed it would be a place of safety for them.

The terrain had been rough and scattered with rocks and pebbles even before the earthquake. Now it had become a nightmare to travel across. Fearful of injuring the horses, they moved as quickly as they could, but it seemed to take forever trying to reach the rock ledge.

"What is it, Josh? Why are we running?" Cassidy gasped out the questions. Like Josh, she was hurrying as fast as she dared, weaving her way through the scattered rocks and debris from the earthquake.

"Not far now, we'll get to that higher ground, then I'll explain," Josh said as he urged the horses on.

The silence that had fallen in the canyon after the earthquake was now broken by an increasing roaring noise. The noise seemed to come from behind the bend in the canyon. Josh swallowed hard. That noise was familiar to him. He'd heard it before, and he had hoped he'd never hear it again.

Breathless, he reached the last steep climb to the top of the rocky outcrop. Climbing up onto it and guiding the horses, he paused and looked down towards Cassidy. Tiny as she was, she had kept up with him, but was now struggling to reach the top. He tied his horses to a tree and then rushed to help Cassidy climb up the last few feet.

"Here, I'll help you." He climbed down part way and, taking her arm, hoisted her upwards, the horse following on behind her. With the effort from both of them, she reached the top and, gasping for breath, sat there looking at Josh.

"I think you'd better explain, Josh Barnes! Why have you hoisted me up here? And why the mad hurry?"

Josh didn't answer. He gently took her shoulders and twisted her around as he pointed towards the end of the canyon.

Round the corner of the rocky canyon walls leading to the far end of the canyon—which they couldn't see—came the increasing noise towards them. It had been a slight rumbling sound at first. Then it became a roaring noise. Now it was a thundering roar that seemed to engulf the whole canyon in wave after wave of tremendous noise.

"Water! It's water making that noise! Is it going to flood the canyon?" Cassidy's voice became shrill with fear and alarm. "Oh, Josh! *That's* why you pushed us up here. That's why you made us hurry to this higher ground."

For a long moment they watched the wall of water as it grew bigger, spreading across the canyon floor. Rocks tumbled one over another, crashing into each other and grating on the ground beneath them, making such a noise that Cassidy put her hands over her ears. The water grew ever closer to them, and now they could make out entire trees whirling over and over again as a wall of water carried them along.

Josh watched, horrified not only by the tumultuous maelstrom of water that swept down the canyon towards them and was now beginning to sweep around the rock they sat on, but also by the water reaching the blocked entrance. What would happen then, he wondered? That wall of water, if blocked by the rocky fall in the narrow entrance to the canyon, would return and flood the canyon even further if it couldn't get out.

The water swirled about their rocky outcrop. Cassidy looked in shock at the sight that met her eyes. She edged closer to Josh and looked round at the canyon walls that hemmed them into their strange, watery prison. Taking a deep breath, she turned to face him. "Are you and Amy going to be married?" The unexpected question made Josh jump, and he gulped for a moment.

"No, Amy and I are not going to be married. We're just friends," he blurted out and looked at her in surprise at this unexpected question.

"From what Eliza says, it's a foregone conclusion that you both will marry." Cassidy persisted in her questions. "Does *Amy* think you're going to marry her?"

Taking a deep breath, Josh answered: "Amy and I are not courting. I know nothing of my past life. There may have been a sweetheart or even a wife. I don't remember. Amy and I could not entertain our friendship developing into something more because of that."

Cassidy twisted a lock of golden hair around her finger. The heart-shaped face grew thoughtful, and she sat there, thinking this over. Josh felt his breath catching in his throat as he looked at the girl sitting beside him. Her bonnet hung behind her head, and the sun brought out golden lights in her hair. Her brows were drawn together in a frown as she looked, unseeing, over the disaster scene. Despite the now torn and dusty clothes she was wearing and the smears of dirt on her face, she was still a beautiful woman.

"You never asked me, Josh, but I imagine you've wondered where my money is coming from. I have plenty." As Josh reddened and tried to deny his thoughts on the matter, she laughed and waved a hand in dismissal. "My money has been earned legally. That's all I'm saying. I don't care about your past, Josh. All I care about is the present. Josh, I don't even care about the future, and looking about us I doubt we're going to have one!"

Josh was about to deny this bald statement, but he realised that would be useless. Cassidy was correct. They would be very fortunate indeed to escape from their present predicament. Instead, he looked at her, waiting for her to continue speaking.

"If I don't care about your past, could you ignore my past and just accept me in the present, as I am now?"

The question seemed to Josh to mean so much to Cassidy. He wasn't sure of what it meant to him. But he looked around. He was no fool, and he realised the predicament they were in. "Yes, Cassidy, I can accept you and your past. And I think it is best we live for the moment. That might be all we have in this present predicament we are both in."

A slow smile crept over her face, and her rosebud mouth tilted at the corners, as her little white became visible in a broadening grin. "That's all I needed to know," she whispered and gave a throaty chuckle. Her arms went round his neck and her face drew closer to his. Violets, her perfume signature, were all around him, and he bent his head to hers. It was a gentle kiss between them. "For now, the present moment is all that matters."

The churning water rushing down the canyon carried rocks and trees and would mean certain death if they fell into it. Its level was rising, and their rocky outcrop lay only a few feet now above the maelstrom that rushed past. Josh helped Cassidy up, and they stood with the horses and began edging themselves further back to the rock face.

"I'd rather be crushed by rock falls and go into that …" Cassidy gestured at the water.

"I think I'd prefer to stay alive and get out of this canyon," Josh said. His attention wandered away from her, despite Cassidy nestling into his arms for comfort and reassurance. He was watching the level of the water as it reached the entrance to the canyon.

"Look, it's above the level of the rocks blocking the canyon entrance. Now it's flowing over the top of them," Josh said, pointing to the swirling waters that had now risen above the canyon's blockage of boulders.

The noise took them and the horses unawares. They all jumped in alarm. Startled, Josh put his arm around Cassidy, holding her close as they gazed around, wondering what was happening now. "Is it another quake?" Cassidy whispered. "What now, Josh? What's happening now?"

CHAPTER SIXTY-ONE

"No, it's not an earthquake. The ground isn't moving. The noise is coming from over by the entrance of the canyon." Josh grabbed Cassidy's arm. "Look, Cassidy! The waters are piling up against those rocks. I think they're moving."

Both stared as the grinding, crashing noise came from the rocks. Josh was correct. The boulders were being pushed by the water's pressure. The noise continued for some time.

"I think," Josh began speaking, and then he grabbed Cassidy tighter. "No, it's happening. The water is clearing the rocks away. Look, they are moving away and the water is going down!"

Neither of them wanted to breathe. They were frightened that the miracle happening before their eyes would stop. But no—the water, with its immense strength and power, was moving the rocks through the canyon's entrance. The water itself was losing height. Josh looked to the far end of the canyon, and he saw that the water was no longer as powerful and had dwindled to a mere trickle.

The crashing and grinding of the rocks faded away. The water beneath them dropped down and dried up.

"It's gone! The water has gone. And the rocks have gone, Josh. What do you think it means? Is it possible that ...?" That heart-shaped face of hers was alight with joy and hope as she looked up at him. Her lips parted, and she broke into excited laughter. Josh lifted her up and whirled her around. The excitement he felt had to be put into action.

"The water is gone. We no longer have to fear we'll

drown. And Cassidy, we may stand a chance of getting out of the canyon! Shall we try?" His eyes sparkled with laughter and joy and hope.

Water lay in deep puddles. Rocks tumbled up by the churning water had to be clambered round. Leading the horses was undertaken with great difficulty.

"I think we are almost there," Josh said. He looked back at Cassidy, whose face was white with fatigue. She followed him and encouraged her horse as it trudged along behind her.

"I think it's around the next bend we go, and then we're out in the open," Josh told Cassidy.

It was getting darker, but it was still only late afternoon. The earthquake and the following flood had seemed to last for hours. And Josh felt it was incredible that they had passed through such an experience in only an unbelievably short length of time.

The canyon was behind them, and they rode on in silence now. Exhaustion, mingled with relief, was taking its toll on both of them.

"It's Ramon! Look, Cassidy, they are coming to meet us!" Josh's voice could be heard by the others from the ranch, who were riding up towards them. The shouts of relief echoed across the flat land as Ramon, Martha, and another hand who had stayed on the ranch galloped up to meet them.

Martha began shouting at Cassidy, her joy mixing with the fear she had endured when the earthquakes began in earnest. As they rode back to the Grangers' place, a thrilling excitement filled the air, and Josh, gazing at Cassidy, sensed the promise of fresh starts in their future.

That night, after a hearty meal made for them by Rosita, they sat in front of the fire in the large room that the Grangers had made comfortable. Josh found it hard to believe that the couple who made such friendly and generous hosts would never return to this ranch. He looked across at Cassidy, who sat with a glass of whiskey in her hand, staring into the fire.

Martha sat in a chair beside her, her fingers busy with some needlework. The firelight and the candlelight were kind to the woman, and the scarred face was partly in shadow. Her meaty hands seemed impossibly large to be coping with such delicate, fine stitches, but the needle flew in and out, catching the firelight in tiny sparks of light.

Ramon and Rosita had been told by Martha and Cassidy to join them. But Josh was aware how ill at ease they felt, never having joined the Grangers.

"What was here when the Grangers arrived?" Cassidy asked Ramon. "There were other people living here before them. What was it like? I don't expect they grew flowers." She smiled, thinking of Mrs Granger's passion for them.

Ramon smiled at Cassidy. "No, no flowers then. It was a family. They had goats, pigs, chickens, and grew enough crops to keep us all throughout the year. But the family grew older, and the three young ones went off to live and work in the cities. The couple grew older, and it became too much for them. That's why they sold up to the Grangers."

"The Grangers built all this after they arrived?" Cassidy waved a hand as she looked around the large room leading out to the veranda, with its ornate trellis work and vines. She paused, as if thinking for a moment, and then continued questioning the man.

"Ramon, you know this ranch, its soil, and what will

grow? Can I rely on you to decide what's best to make it successful?" Cassidy said. She looked at the Mexican and then continued speaking: "I know nothing of how a place like this should work. But I love it here, and I intend to make a go of it. In the future, I'll leave everything to you, but you and Rosita must tell no one who owns this ranch. Not yet."

The husband and wife looked at each other. Silent communications passed between them, and Rosita gave a nod and smiled at Cassidy. Ramon, obviously getting agreement from his wife, also smiled at the young woman. "It will remain a secret. There will be no surprise at me running the ranch. Although Mr Granger wandered about as if in charge, we both knew that I managed the daily routine of the ranch."

Josh been sitting silently throughout this conversation. He was impressed at how Cassidy had handled this situation. "Just one thing. When it is no longer a secret, and the Grangers move away, what are you going to call the ranch, Cassidy? Have you thought of a name for it?"

CHAPTER SIXTY-TWO

Amy had been up most of the night with David. He had been sick. It had taken time to calm him down and finally get him back to sleep. She had changed his clothes and the bedding and, finally, the mess from the bedroom floor. Now he slept peacefully at last.

Tiptoeing out onto the front porch, she sat in the rocking chair, gazing across to Devil's Mountain. Dawn was breaking now, and she could see the sunlight creeping over the peaks, the sun's rays shining over the land beneath those craggy rocks. Amy was tired and depressed. How she longed for one of those days when she and her companion, Josh, had ventured from the ranch into the hills in search of the Jesuit gold. Day after day they had travelled, alone but for the wildlife that roamed the mountains. Seeking neither to kill nor hunt them, they had witnessed many elusive animals not otherwise seen. Freedom. That's what it was. The animals had been free and so had she and Josh.

Now she had responsibilities. Her father was growing weaker by the day, and the dizzy spells and blackouts were becoming more frequent. David was growing up into a lively toddler and, as Leah had said, she needed eyes in the back of her head to watch him. Leah's remark had been correct, Amy thought, thinking back to the woman's sayings. But Leah was growing older now, stiffer in the joints, and the normal backbreaking work she had once done with ease around the ranch was becoming too much for her. Only Nancy and Ezra remained the same. Without them and their help and support, life would have become unbearable.

There was movement within the cabin. But Amy,

huddled in a blanket, stayed in the rocking chair, too tired to move. Then the door opened, and Nancy appeared with a cup of steaming coffee for her. "I heard you up with David during the night. Is he all right now?" she said, handing Amy the tin cup. "I thought you'd welcome this."

"Thank you, Nancy," Amy said, and hurriedly wiped the tears away from her face, hoping the older woman wouldn't see them.

Nancy just nodded and went back into the cabin, re-emerging with her own cup of coffee. She sat on a chair beside Amy and cast a quick glance at the girl. Nancy saw the sad look on the tear-stained face, and the tired eyes, and she sighed. There was little she could do. Life on the ranch seemed so dull and boring to the girl after the interest, conversation, and general liveliness that working in the mercantile store had given to her days.

Silence stretched out between them. Long moments when they drank their coffee and watched the sunlight stretch over the land, burning up the cool of the night and promising the searing heat of midday to come. Then the ground shook, and there was the noise of crockery and pans crashing to the floor inside the cabin.

"Earthquake!" yelled Nancy. "We must get everyone out of the cabin!" So saying, she ran back inside the cabin. "Get David—I'll get your father."

Amy rushed into the cabin and shouted at the top of her voice, "Ben! Ben, wake up! Chan, Tom, everyone— get outside. It's an earthquake!"

It was only seconds, but to Amy it had seemed like hours before everyone was outside, standing looking at each other. David was whimpering but still sleepy and drifted off in Amy's arms. Everyone stood, white-faced and gazing around in bewilderment and fear. After the initial shaking, nothing happened. If it hadn't been for the upturned coffee mugs on the porch and the rocking chair on its side, it could have never happened.

Silence fell, and even the animals went quiet, as if waiting. Then, the ground beneath their feet seemed to convulse and shudder. Wide-eyed and white-faced, they clung to each other, and stood waiting for the tremor to pass.

"Ezra, you have had many of these since you lived here?" Luke asked the older man as they stood waiting.

Shaking his head, the old man persuaded his wife to sit down. "Few, had a bad one about fifteen years ago. The mountains shifted around some, and there were holes and cracks in the earth we had to watch out for. Some buildings in Nowhere itself fell down. That were a bad one. Mostly, we get a few shakes and shudders now and again. Mind you, this feels like a bad one. Best stay out here in the open for a bit until we see what's happening."

Ben and Chan both dashed into the house to grab chairs and blankets, which they brought out for the older ones to sit on, especially Luke and Leah. Later, Nancy and Amy went to get food and drink while the others stayed outside.

"What's happened to my dig site?" Luke said and made as if he was going to walk off towards it. "I ought to see what's happening there," he fretted. Luke seemed more worried about his dig site than his family and ranch.

"Don't worry about it. Your dig will survive somehow. You know where it is. We can always dig it out again if it gets covered over," Amy said with patience—but it was a patience she was far from feeling. Her father seemed to only think about discovering even more artefacts in the soil.

The day passed with uneasy moments as the ongoing tremors gradually diminished throughout the day. But when night fell, the earth had been silent for some hours. They felt it was safe to go back into the cabin to sleep.

It was morning. And early. The light coming through the shutters in the cupboard bedroom in which Amy still slept was faint and still grey. Why had she woken up? What had made her wake so early? Usually, she slept until young David woke her. His childish excitement at a new day often crashed into her exhausted sleep.

Amy's uneasiness grew. Slipping silently out of the tiny room, she stood in the centre of the cabin, listening. No sound. No one else was up. Or were they? A slight breeze must have caught the cabin door because it swung ajar. It was always locked at night, and ever since the cabin had been built the bar of wood was always placed across the door. The safety habit was one that was automatically kept nightly.

"It's open," whispered Amy. She looked round the room carefully this time, checking to see what was out of place. Had someone entered last night and …

With a jolt of consternation, Amy noticed that the stick her father had used, and which he hated, no longer leant against his chair. She looked round the back of the door at the wooden pegs. Her father's hat had gone. So had his coat.

CHAPTER SIXTY-THREE

Amy slipped back into her room and hastily flung on her clothes, pulling her boots on as quickly as she could. Her gun, she automatically reached for, placing it into her pocket. Amy, the girl from out east, had certainly adjusted to life out West. Frantically worried about her father she may have been, but Amy was not such a fool as to rush out without being dressed properly—and armed.

"You've gone out to that wretched Jesuit man's dig, haven't you, Pa? I know that's where you've gone. And you've walked there, all that way on your own!" Amy rushed to the stable. Her horse, Bella, looked surprised to see her. Leading Bella out of the stable, Amy leapt on the back of her and guided her horse straight towards the rocks. The rocky ledge could be seen easily in the increasingly bright morning light. They had found the Jesuit's journal, cross and relics hidden beneath them.

The earthquake had left little sign of its passing. There was no damage done that Amy could see. However, as she looked towards the mountains, Amy could see where rocks had split from the cliff face and tumbled onto the ground beneath the lofty peaks.

The ledge, and the rocks upon it which had sheltered the last remains of the Jesuit priest, looked no different to Amy as she rode nearer. There had maybe been a few rocks dislodged, but that was all.

"Pa! Pa!" At first Amy called his name. Then she screamed it. Before she even jumped off Bella's back, Amy knew. Her father lay with his hand outstretched as he clutched something. His other arm held an object tight to his breast, and as Amy gently turned him over to check him, she saw he was smiling. Clutched to his chest were the last pages of the journal. A wooden box, crushed by rocks, had been brought to the surface by the movements of the earthquake, and it lay in pieces. Her father had found the last bit of the man's journal and a small pouch. The pouch held a few nuggets of gold.

The tears wouldn't come. She sat back on her heels and stared at her father. Last night she had known the earthquake tremors had worried him. All he could think of was what destruction was happening to the Jesuit's last resting place. Now, Amy saw it had become her father's last resting place as well. He had searched for the Jesuit for many years. He had pursued his dream out West, cutting all ties with the life the family had known back east after her mother died. As he died, he knew he had been successful. He had found his dream of Jesuit gold.

Slowly, Amy rose to her feet. The noise behind her made her turn. Ben and Chan were riding towards her. As she looked at her brother's face, she knew he realised her father had died. Hurtling off his horse, he rushed towards her, and together they stood looking down at the man who had brought them out West in pursuit of his dream.

Ben had been a young boy when they'd arrived at Broken Horseshoe Ranch. He had matured—not in years but in strength and experience. Now he stood beside his sister, no longer her small brother. He was now the same height. They both stood silent, looking down at their father, who had brought them out West. Single-minded in his quest, he had led them here, certain that he was on the right path. Nothing had stood in his way. Not even a frontier life full of difficulties could deflect him from his dream.

Ben bent down and picked up the last pages of the journal. Then, he stooped again to retrieve the tiny pouch of gold nuggets from his father's hand.

"Pa found it, then. He finally got what he wanted most in the world," Ben said, his arm around his sister's shoulders. Together, they stood looking down at the man who had a dream. And in searching for that dream had brought them here to the vast emptiness of the ranch that lay at the foothills of Devil's Mountain.

CHAPTER SIXTY-FOUR

Nowhere township felt the effects of the earthquake that morning. Buildings shook and people ran out into Main Street. The shuddering of the earth passed, and still folk stood, chatted, and gazed around, wondering if there would be any more shakes and tremors. A few hours passed and there were no further tremors. It was becoming hot. The sun was turning Main Street into a dusty hot oven. People began drifting back into their homes and places of business. With a shrug of the shoulders and hopeful glances around at the quiet, still earth, they tried to carry on with their normal everyday affairs.

***

Early that morning, Rosita made them a breakfast before they left for Nowhere. Martha was going to take the buggy, leaving it with Reuben, who would see it returned to Duloe. Cassidy and Josh rode alongside the buggy. The morning air was still cool, but the hot coffee, bacon, beans, and fried potatoes kept the worst of the cold away from them. Josh was full. He had been so hungry that morning, he felt certain he'd made a pig of himself at breakfast. He knew it was a reaction after the ordeal he and Cassidy had endured the day before.

Ramon and Rosita had joined them that evening in front of the open log fire in the cabin of the Grangers'. Usually, they retired to their own small cabin behind the main ranch house. But that night Cassidy had insisted they join them for a general chat about her plans for the future. Ramon had at first been wary of the young woman. But her fragile beauty and soft-spoken words were deceptive.

The grizzled old Mexican thought he had seen everything. But that was before he met Cassidy. Realising that this young woman was intelligent enough to stand back and let him run the ranch as he saw fit, he had relaxed. His plans for the general welfare of his animals and the productivity of the land had been ignored by Mr Granger. The ranch owner seemed only to enjoy playing the genial host and indulging his wife's love of flowers. Enthusiastically, Ramon laid out the plans he had thought over and spoken of to Mr Granger so many times.

"Ramon is delighted that you have taken over the ranch," Josh said. His words broke the silence as they rode out of the ranch under the wrought-iron archway that proclaimed it the Grangers' place.

"Yes, he seems a good man, and I'll do well to let him have his head and run the ranch," was her reply.

Martha called to them both from the buggy. "What you going to call the ranch, Cassidy? Will we have another big sign like that one?" She gestured back to the flamboyant sign, so out of keeping in frontier country.

"No big sign! A wooden board with the ranch name on it. But I can't think of what name I *should* call it. Until we let it be known that it *is* my ranch, we can think up names." Cassidy's lips curved in merriment. "It should be fun thinking up a suitable name." Her eyes danced as she looked teasingly at Martha.

The journey passed, and they rode into Nowhere. "We'll drop you off at the general store, Josh. I have a list of provisions that Rosita wants Manuel to deliver. The usual delivery that the Grangers had is no longer necessary. And I'll have to explain that to Manuel."

Pushing open the familiar door of the general store, Josh walked into a scene of chaos. He stopped, unable to make sense of what greeted his eyes. Martha and Cassidy came in behind him.

It was Martha who took over the situation. "What's happened to him?" She strode forward, her immense bulk looming over Eliza and Clara, who were kneeling by Manuel.

"He tripped over a basket and fell heavily," Eliza said, looking up at Martha. "I think it's his ankle." She pointed to Manuel's foot, which was turned awkwardly at a strange angle.

Martha knelt down and looked at the white-faced Manuel. Then she gently touched the man's boot. Josh, looking over her shoulder, could see the swelling above the boot and imagined that it was worse further down, nearer his foot.

"A knife!" The command was barked out by Martha. Josh reached over the counter to the knife that was always kept handy there. In no time at all, under Martha's direction, Manuel's boot was cut open and the swelling around his ankle could be seen. "It's a bad break. Is there any doctor in Nowhere?"

"The sheriff sometimes helps, but it's only him and an old lady who lives on a ranch outside town." Eliza said, wringing her hands.

"I have some knowledge, but only a little. I'll do my best," Martha said as she rose to her feet. Then she glared at both Manuel and Eliza. "But don't blame me if it goes wrong! Is that understood?"

At Manuel and Eliza's mumbled agreement, Martha swung into action.

Clara was to occupy herself with baby Isabel. Eliza went to get Manuel sorted with Martha. Cassidy and Josh were to man the general store and serve any customers who came in.

"This will be a new experience for me." Cassidy laughed as she took off her bonnet and placed it and her gloves behind the counter. "I've never done this before." She gazed around the store as if seeing it for the first time. Her throaty chuckle escaped her, and Josh felt his heart warm to her, at her willingness to help these people and enjoy it.

"You find this fun? Don't you? You try to enjoy everything that happens to you. Don't you, Cassidy?" Josh said.

"Why not? We have to live through enough sadness and despair. The only way to get through it is to enjoy the other things in life." Her sudden descent into an overwhelming sadness stunned Josh. He could see that there was more to Cassidy than he ever imagined. This beautiful creature, whose enchanting smile could light up a room, had depths and a complexity to her he had never imagined.

"Josh, I don't know how I'm going to manage. Without Manuel, life will be so difficult running the general store." Eliza's voice came from behind Josh; he turned to face her. The woman was distraught, panicking at the thought of coping with the store herself. "What am I going to do?"

Before Josh could answer, the noise from Main Street caught their attention. They rushed to the door, flinging it open as the voices and clamour grew louder.

One man running past the store shouted at Josh and Eliza: "It's the Dawson gang! Two of the brothers are still alive. They've got another gang now. Slim saw them on their way up to the Devil's Mountain!"

CHAPTER SIXTY-FIVE

There was a lull in the late afternoon. The exciting news about the Dawson gang had fizzled out. No one could be sure that Slim really had seen the two Dawson brothers, so the gossip finally wound down.

Josh found himself alone in the general store. Eliza was sitting with Manuel, who had finally drifted off to sleep. His shouts of annoyance, and even his whining at his predicament, had finally subsided. Josh wondered if it had been the liberal helpings of whiskey that both Eliza and Martha had given to Manuel that made him sleep. As Martha left the general store, her eyes lifted to heaven as she passed Josh. She walked out of the store, almost slamming the door in her annoyance. Josh felt certain that Manuel should be thankful that Martha left before she gave him a piece of her mind at his constant complaining.

Clara was tinkering with some hardware stuff, straightening it into neatness again after the three miners had arrived, searching carelessly through it for the exact equipment they needed. Clara had tutted when they left but was delighted at selling so much equipment and felt certain that Manuel would be happier after hearing of the sale. Yes, Josh also felt Manuel would be happier at the thought of more money coming in. That would please him.

Josh lifted a brush from the back of the store and swept the dust and dirt that had made its way in with the many footsteps that morning. He swept the dirt out through the door and swept the boardwalk clean in front of the store, looking up towards the hotel. Cassidy was on his mind. He'd spent all that time with her. They had been through a near-death experience in the canyon and yet, and yet … Sweeping the last pieces of mud and dirt off into the road before coming in, Josh shook his head. The overwhelming feelings he felt so strongly for Cassidy he couldn't ignore any longer but, he knew nothing about her—even now. Cassidy was a puzzle, and one he knew it would be dangerous to become involved with.

Josh put the brush away. Manuel had made it clear that it wasn't only women's work to keep the general store clean and tidy. Everyone had to lend a hand so that the store got an excellent reputation for cleanliness, and people would return. Josh straightened some vegetables, sorting through them in case any had gone bad during their previous hours of trading. As he did so, he came across some from Broken Horseshoe Ranch. He knew without looking that they would be in good condition. Tom only produced the best goods for the general store. He prided himself on the quality of the fruit and vegetables he sent to Manuel and Eliza. Josh stood looking down at the fruit. What was happening out at the ranch? How was Amy coping? He knew she *would* cope. But he also knew that she would be in pieces behind her masked front. It didn't seem right to Josh that he was here and not helping them out of the ranch. Ezra, however, had told him to stay and help Eliza.

"Josh, Manuel is asleep at last. Isabel is as well," said Eliza, joining him in the general store.

"You should take the chance to rest," said Josh.

Eliza shook her head that these words. "No, I'd rather get out here and check everything. But I see I needn't have bothered worrying. Both you and Clara have been busy, and everything is just as it should be."

They both stood, thinking about the events of the

morning. Then, Eliza seemed to shake herself back into the present and asked, "Were you caught in the earthquake, Josh?"

Josh looked down at the little woman and could see the worry in her eyes. Also, he saw the need for some distraction, something else to think about, to take her mind off the worrying about Manuel and the store.

"Yes, Eliza. Cassidy and I were chasing after some horses that had got lost and we followed them into a canyon. Then the earthquake struck." Eliza's lips parted in horror at this tale. She sank down on the chair and gazed open-mouthed at Josh.

Delighted to have a listener hanging on every word, and seeing Clara join Eliza, Josh told the story of his and Cassidy's canyon adventure. Much of it was missing. Josh only gave a brief and edited version. At his story, though, both women clutched each other's hands and gasped in horror at how near death both he and Cassidy had been.

"What was she doing out at the ranch, Josh?" From Eliza came the inevitable question.

Cassidy had known questions would be asked about her visit to the ranch and had told Josh what to say.

"Cassidy was told Mr Granger might have news about her uncle. The Grangers lived in the same town as he did, and after her parents' death, she was looking for him." Josh's reply had been rehearsed with Cassidy.

"That poor girl. She's all alone in the world?" Eliza gasped in horror. Her family was widespread and many, and she could not think of life without them. "No wonder she is out looking for her uncle. Did Mr Granger help her?"

"No, he's staying at the hotel with his wife. They

escaped when the Dawson gang attacked their ranch. Cassidy will chat with him now. She's also staying at the hotel," said Josh.

Clara spoke out. "One of those miners told me that the Dawson gang and another gang are being helped to hide out in Devil's Mountain. Someone, in Nowhere, is laying supplies at secret canyons in the foothills for these gangs. In return, they give him some of their loot. That's why the gangs are here. It's no accident at all. Someone is helping them!"

CHAPTER SIXTY-SIX

The general store was lit by a small oil lamp at the back. Its feeble light reaching over the store was enough for Josh to work by. After supper, he began work on getting the deliveries organised for the morning. Zach was going to help on delivery day. As Josh already knew the route and the customers from his weekly trips with Manuel, delivering presented no problem to him. But Manuel had always prepared the sacks and crates for delivery in the evening, ready for an early morning start.

"Josh, what are you doing? You should rest after your experiences yesterday in the earthquake." Eliza's voice came from the darkness, and she walked up to the young man and placed a hand on his arm. "Aren't you tired?"

Josh smiled down at the Mexican woman, the lines of worry deepening after Manuel's accident. "I *am* tired, Eliza. But I won't sleep, knowing that these deliveries have to be sorted out ready for the morning. When I lie down to sleep, knowing that the deliveries are organised will make me doze off sooner."

Eliza was about to speak, and Josh knew she was going to offer to help him. "Go to bed, Eliza. You'll have enough to do tomorrow with Isabel and Manuel. You know he's going to be difficult to keep still, so you need every bit of sleep you can get to cope with him."

"If you're sure, Josh?"

"Yes, Eliza, go to bed. I can manage." Again, Eliza's hand went out to pat his arm. This time, she squeezed it and then trotted off to the back of the general store, to the bedroom she shared with Manuel and Isabel.

Left alone in the store, Josh felt the tiredness sweep over him. How he would have loved to lie down and sleep. No, it would be chaos in the morning if he did. Manuel would fuss about, and Josh knew it would make him get in a muddle. This way, he could do it slowly and carefully and make sure everything was done correctly.

Needing an item from the front of the store, just behind the window, Josh walked across to reach the basket. As he paused, he glanced outside. Earlier, he had noticed how quiet Main Street was. There was laughter and loud voices coming from the saloon, but the rest of Main Street was shrouded in darkness. The light from the sheriff's office could be seen. Lance lit it as a deterrent for the drunks coming out of the saloon. Knowing that the sheriff was awake, they tried to behave themselves.

Josh was moving away when he saw a figure flit up Main Street. There was no mistaking the bulk of that figure. Following closely behind, he saw another, slighter, person. He knew those two! There was no mistaking them. It was Martha and Cassidy.

In seconds, Josh had unlocked the front door of the general store and slipped quietly outside onto the boardwalk. Staying on the opposite side of the road from them, he kept apace, silently shadowing them.

Then they waited. Outside the saloon, both figures stood silently—waiting. So, Josh also waited and watched them. Should he go and speak to them? Ask them what they were doing? No—Josh remained where he was.

The door from the saloon burst open, and two miners came out laughing and joking. They staggered, arms around each other, towards the livery stable. Josh reckoned they would sleep the night in the hay. He knew it wouldn't matter to them where they slept: they were obviously drunk.

Both women had stiffened when the saloon doors

opened. As the light flooded out and lit up the faces of the two men, Cassidy and Martha flattened themselves back into the shadows.

"You are waiting for someone," Josh murmured to himself. "Who are you waiting for? And what are you going to do to them when they come out?"

Josh didn't have much longer to wait. The saloon doors crashed open and two men came out, laughing and joking with each other. They stood for a moment, illuminated by the light from the open doors. He recognised them. Sheriff Lance Grey had their pictures up on his wanted men's gallery. They were the two younger Dawson brothers—the remaining Dawson brothers, now the two eldest ones had been killed.

Why had they come to Nowhere? Josh wondered, recalling that the two eldest Dawson brothers had been found outside the sheriff's office, each with a bullet through their head. He had been so busy watching them, he'd taken his eyes off Cassidy and Martha. Their sudden movements made him stiffen and reach for his gun.

What were they doing? To his horror, Josh watched as both Martha and Cassidy walked up to the two men. Silently, Josh slipped across Main Street and, in a pool of darkness, began approaching the four figures silhouetted against the saloon's lights. He took out his gun and readied it for action.

What on earth? Josh was flummoxed. What the hell should he do? If he moved, he would startle Cassidy and Martha and perhaps give the men the upper hand. If he made to join the ladies, would that even up the score?

The heavy cloud that had been present all day parted, and moonlight streamed down on the scene in front of him.

"Hey, look at the big fat one! She's got a huge scar on her face. That's *your* trademark, isn't it, Harry?" one brother said, staring at Martha. "But you never leave them alive, do you?"

Josh drew in his breath so quickly and so hard it hurt his chest. This must be the man who had given Martha that horrific scar.

"Maybe I didn't leave you dead last time, but I'll make sure this time!" A knife was suddenly flourished in his hand, and he waved it in front of her, playing with his victim as he thought.

"You both killed my parents, didn't you? At Wild Horse Ranch six months ago," Cassidy said in a quiet voice. "Who told you to go there? And who's helping you hide out in Devil's Mountain now?"

"Ask a lot of questions for a tiny thing, don't you? You and me should have some fun before I send you to join your parents. Yes, we killed 'em. And were paid well for it!" He gave a sneering laugh. "Generous man, our boss is. Always pays us well."

"Who is he, then?" Cassidy persisted in her questioning. "Who *is* your boss? The generous man who pays you well?"

Both men shuffled their feet. Then one looked at the other. In the moonlight, Josh could see him shrug his shoulders. "You might as well know. You're not going to live long enough to do anything about it."

CHAPTER SIXTY-SEVEN

"Charles Roberts is our boss. He's settled us in a nice camp up in the mountains. Mind you, he demands a hefty share of our profits."

From where he stood, Josh could see both women relax slightly. That was what they wanted to know, Josh realised. Cassidy wanted the name of who was behind the death of her parents. Cassidy looked at Martha and then asked the men, "Did you kill that Mexican family at River Crossing? And the family at the Double Z ranch? You killed everyone, didn't you—men, women, and children?" Then, as if the words were torn out of her very soul, she demanded, "Why? Why kill them all? What had they ever done to you?"

The two men began laughing. "Look here, little miss, they'd done nothing to us. But we enjoy killing! After we've had some fun with you two, we'll kill you!" The taller one slapped the other one on the back, and then said, "That's enough talking."

"Yes, it is. Quite enough talking." Martha's voice was harsh, and both men stopped laughing and looked at her.

Two gunshots rang out simultaneously in the night's stillness. It was as if the shots had been fired so closely together they seemed like one. The men fell: dead. Each had been shot in the middle of their forehead.

Josh couldn't move for a moment. The women were safe, and he realised *they* had fired the shots. While he stood motionless, the women had swung into action. Both men were turned over, their hands folded onto their chests, and out of Martha's pockets two wanted posters were produced. One was placed under the hands of each man.

"That was for my parents and all the others you murdered." Cassidy's voice, although softly spoken, reached Josh's ears.

"That was for the many women you scarred and abused!" Martha's voice followed Cassidy's.

Both women turned and ran down Main Street, disappearing between a couple of buildings into a back alley.

Seconds. It had only taken seconds. Josh had stood motionless throughout. Voices from the saloon came after the shot, and men tumbled out through the swing doors onto the boardwalk. Excited chatter broke out as they looked down at the slain men. Josh backed away from the scene and disappeared into the night, running back to the general store.

He didn't reach it.

Cassidy and Martha came back out of the alley. Josh remembered it was no longer a through-route. Building works had begun and timber had been piled up, closing it. They met each other, and Cassidy cried out. "Josh, what are *you* doing here?" The faint moonlight played on each of their faces and she could see the shocked expression on his. "You saw?" It was more of a statement than a question.

Martha's indrawn breath, and the realisation of what Josh had seen, made Cassidy reach out her hand to stop Martha as the older woman reached for her gun.

"Josh won't tell, will you?" The entreaty in her voice was matched by her assurance that she could rely on him.

Josh knew that both Cassidy and Martha could rely on him. There was no way he would give their secret away. Those men deserved it, deserved a far worse death than a bullet to the brain. It was a merciful release for them after the heinous crimes they had committed.

Before he could speak, the earth shuddered and shook beneath them. The surrounding buildings started to sway, and Josh shouted at both women, "Out to the middle of Main Street, out into the open!"

Martha ran out across the boardwalk. Cassidy and Josh made to follow her, but another, more violent tremor threw them off their balance. They crashed into each other and back into the alley. Flinging himself across Cassidy, Josh huddled over her, his hands over both their heads, seeking to save them from the falling timber that was crashing about them. The tremor seemed to go on and on. Then, it stopped. The ground itself stopped moving, but the timber buildings around them carried on shifting as the wooden beams crashed before settling into place.

"Cassidy, are you hurt?" Josh tried to move but realised they were trapped.

"Cassidy, Cassidy!" Josh's urgent whispers, in the confined space in which he found himself, became frantic.

CHAPTER SIXTY-EIGHT

"I'm unhurt, but I can't move my leg. Something is on top of it," replied Cassidy.

Josh adjusted his body, then immediately stopped as he heard the wooden beams above him groan and shift.

"Can you move at all?" whispered Josh. Gingerly, he began moving his arms and legs. He found he was unhurt. They seemed to have been trapped under a beam that lay on top of some other rubble. Moving one hand, he found that by shifting a piece of broken wood aside a feeble light could be seen.

Cassidy's whisper came back to him. "Yes, Josh, I'm managing to move everything. I'm unhurt. But we seem to be trapped, and if we move …" Her voice tailed away in a whisper.

"We'll get out somehow, Cassidy. We got out of that canyon, didn't we?"

There was silence for a moment. Neither of them dared to move. They could hear voices, and that small light was widening. The debris surrounding them was being shifted, bit by bit.

"Cassidy! Cassidy!" Martha's voice could be heard shouting through the rubble at them.

"I'm here, Martha! I'm unhurt. Josh is with me, but we're trapped," Cassidy called out to her companion.

The reply came back, encouraging them. "We're moving everything. But we're going slowly. We don't want it to collapse onto you. Hold on there, we're coming." This time, it was Reuben's voice they heard.

Josh could visualise the huge blacksmith working side by side with the enormous build of Martha. With those two working to free them, Josh felt confident that they would both escape their wooden prison in no time at all.

"You saw, Josh, didn't you? You saw what Martha and I did?" Cassidy's whispered in Josh's ear. They had somehow moved closer together, and his arm was now around her. Still, he kept that protective shield of his body over hers.

For a moment, there was silence between them. All that could be heard were the shouts, and the noise of the steady movement of rubble and wooden beams being carefully taken away.

Josh took a moment to consider his words. "I saw you and Martha, and I heard what you did. It has been you and Martha leaving the dead bandits in front of the sheriff's office. Why, Cassidy? Why do you face those villains and put yourself in such danger?" Josh could hear his own voice and its pleading tone and felt annoyed with himself.

Cassidy moved closer to him, and her words were whispered, and her breath tickled his ears as she unburdened herself to him.

"When my parents were killed and Martha was left for dead, something died within me, Josh. I knew then if I didn't stop those villains from inflicting on others the pain I had suffered, and my family had suffered, I wouldn't sleep peacefully in my bed again. With each one I kill, I know that innocent people will not suffer at their hands again." Josh felt the body of the young woman move closer beside him. She gave a shuddering sigh as the words seemed to be pulled out of her. He found himself at a loss. Somehow, the callousness of her killing the men had stunned him. But he understood it now. And she was legally within her rights.

"Josh, will you keep my secret? Or are you going to

tell the sheriff and the others what Martha and I were doing?"

"I'll keep your secret but I ..." Josh found it difficult to breathe. He became aware that the confined space in which they were sheltering was slowly filling with smoke. He cast a glance behind him and saw in the far reaches of the tangled wreckage of the buildings a faint glow. The smoke was increasing, and he distinctly heard the sound of crackling flames.

"Reuben, Reuben—hurry! There is smoke and fire getting closer to us. You'll have to hurry to get us out of here. Hurry, Reuben!"

CHAPTER SIXTY-NINE

Josh pulled his jacket over his mouth and held it over Cassidy's face. The two of them huddled together, and his lips gently kissed hers. She put a hand up to stroke his stubbled chin, and he could hear her give a little chuckle. "I wondered when you were going to kiss me. But I never expected it to be in a place like this. Or when we were facing imminent death together." Josh felt himself smiling. Despite the dangers they faced, Cassidy chuckled.

The huge beam above them was suddenly flung clear. Other pieces of wood surrounding them were pulled away, and hands reached for both of them. They were pulled out, blinking into the light of candles and oil lamps. Josh was clasped in a hearty hug by Reuben, who demanded to know if he was hurt. Josh was pleased to say he wasn't. That hug would have made any injury suffered ten times worse. He could hear Martha crying and scolding Cassidy as she, too, was hugged. When he finally opened his eyes properly against the glare of the light Reuben held, he saw people running everywhere. No one paid any attention to them, and Martha took Cassidy's arm and said to Josh and Reuben, "We were never here. Keep our secret, please." With that, she hurried Cassidy away towards the hotel, which still stood unscathed.

***

Morning light showed the devastation the earthquake had caused. Everyone agreed it would have been far worse if it hadn't been for Sheriff Grey. Bucket chains with water had been formed by him, and all fires had been put out speedily. Fires were the biggest fear after an earthquake in a frontier town. Most buildings were made of wood and canvas. There were a few casualties, mostly broken limbs. The earthquake itself had not been fierce but had been indiscriminate. Some buildings stood unscathed, intact but for a few crockery breakages. The general store was one. It had survived, but the sheriff's office and a building beside it had suffered worst of all. The alleyway where Cassidy and Josh had been trapped had seen the worst incident. The livery stable had suffered from fire, as the forge itself had been toppled to the ground. All horses had been led away to safety. Luckily, the hotel had suffered little damage, being soundly built with foundations of stone, keeping it fireproof.

Cassidy was taken off to the hotel to be cosseted by Martha. Josh had been pounced upon by Eliza and soon joined Manuel, becoming yet another invalid in the general store. Josh felt so much better after bathing in the tin tub out in the stable yard. The smoke had got into his clothes and his hair. Once free of the lingering smell of smoke, he realised how fortunate he'd been. His arm was bruised and had a huge gash, but that was all he had suffered, despite the heavy beams falling upon him. The angle it had fallen at had somehow protected them both. Josh got to thinking about Cassidy. What had happened that night? It seemed like a bad dream—or was it a nightmare?

There was no doubt about it. Those bodies, mostly from the Dawson brothers' gang, had arrived dead in front of the sheriff's office. Now Josh knew who was doing it. To think that the beautiful, ladylike Cassidy could orchestrate their deaths and dispose of their bodies.

"Thank you, Eliza, my arm is no problem for me. I can manage the deliveries with Zach's help. Manuel needn't worry—it will all be carried out exactly like he normally does it," Josh said. He took the steaming hot coffee from Eliza's hand and reassured her about the day's deliveries.

The provisions were all loaded, and Josh stood beside the wagon, waiting for Zach to join him. His thoughts returned to the sight he witnessed last night. Now he knew where Cassidy's wealth came from: the bounty paid to her for the deaths of such notorious outlaws was considerable. Surely, once she had avenged her parents' death, she would not continue with her bounty-hunting activities. Or would she?

Automatically, Josh joined with Zach in delivering all the goods he had packed last evening. In return, they took vegetables and fruit, jams, chutneys, and even baked goods to sell in the general store. Each item was noted down for Eliza to check off and recompense the giver of the items. It was a system that worked well and benefited both the rancher and homesteader, eager to make some more money. Manuel, in turn, had a varied and interesting display in the general store, with this daily fresh produce.

All day, Josh thought again and again about his relationship with Cassidy. Amy had been straightforward—direct in all her dealings, honest and trustworthy. Josh knew Cassidy was deceitful and a killer. She was a woman who, despite her stunning beauty, he should be wary of. If he knew what was good for him, Josh reckoned he should avoid her.

But could he? Cassidy's bounty-hunting activities would not stop with the death of the Dawson brothers. She was on a mission to get rid of *all* the bandits who were hiding out on Devil's Mountain. There was no way Josh could steer her away from this dangerous path. But could he stand back and let her and Martha go it alone?

Or would he be lured by her violet eyes into joining her on her crusade to defeat the bandits on Devil's Mountain?

On his return to the general store, Josh began unloading the boxes into the store.

The bell chimed as the door opened and Sherrif Lance walked in with Charles. Rushing up to the counter, Charles spoke hurriedly. "I've been burgled! Someone came in and trashed my office. Did any of you see strangers up around my place yesterday? I don't know whether it happened before the earthquake or after. But I travelled back with Slim this morning from Duloe and found the mess."

Both Eliza and Josh shook their heads, neither daring to speak. It was Manuel who spoke out. "Robbed? Did they steal much? Was it valuable?" His questions seemed to alarm Charles. In fact, he seemed to back away from the counter and Manuel's questions.

Charles was disturbed and angry at his office being ransacked, but Josh knew also that he was frightened of whoever had done it—and what they were looking for.

"I think someone may have been sent from a villain living in Duloe. Did any of you see a stranger at my door?"

There were shaking heads and murmurs of "don't know" as his gaze swept even the customers standing in the general store. He gave a cry of disgust, turned to the sheriff and cried out, "Fat lot of good you are. Call yourself a sheriff! Even the bandits are delivered to your doorstep! And you haven't even got bars in the windows of your cell!" He stormed out, everyone watching him go.

Sheriff Grey stood for a moment in the middle of the general store, staring round at everyone. Such was the charismatic presence of the man that everyone paused what they were doing and ceased talking.

"This sounds like a far-fetched tale to me." He stroked the long black moustache, of which he was inordinately proud, and then spoke again. "There have been reports now reaching my office of ghosts. Malevolent spirits have been seen wandering around homesteads, camps, and up in the mountains. One is a Jesuit priest, who is looking for his gold, the other a Frenchman who cannot find the goldmine he had worked the previous year. Don't know if I believe any of this nonsense, but thought I'd tell you all to be on the lookout." Sheriff Lance Grey dashed out of the general store before questions could be put to him. An enormous hubbub of questions arose as everyone discussed this latest development in Nowhere.

Will Charles Roberts find out who burgled him? Will Josh join Cassidy on her bounty-hunting trips? What will the ghosts of the Jesuit priest and the mad Frenchman do to the people of Nowhere and Devils Mountain? Find out in the next tale from Devil's Mountain!

About The Author

Janey Clarke writes charming, witty, cosy mysteries. From septuagenarian shenanigans in Cornwall to the intrigue of Regency-era whodunits and now to her newest venture into the rugged drama of the Wild West. When not plotting her next twist or researching historical details, she can be found exploring the stunning Jurassic Coast in Dorset with her loyal spaniel by her side. With a passion for tea, old books, and well-timed humour, Janey Clarke creates stories she hopes will whisk readers away to delightful worlds where solving a mystery is always the order of the day. And always solved by a feisty heroine!

Visit Janey at www.janeyclarke.com to learn more about her books.

www.blossomspringpublishing.com

www.ingramcontent.com/pod-product-compliance
Lightning Source LLC
Chambersburg PA
CBHW050725180626
46814CB00002B/615